No Sleep for the Dead

Adrian Magson

Jim
To a fan!
Adrian Magson

CREME DE LA CRIME

First published in Great Britain in 2006 by Crème de la Crime
Crème de la Crime Ltd
PO Box 523
Chesterfield
S40 9AT

Typesetting by Yvette Warren
Cover design by Yvette Warren
Front cover illustration by Peter Roman

ISBN 0-9551589-1-5

A CIP catalogue reference for this book is available from the
British Library

www.cremedelacrime.com

Printed and bound in Great Britain
by Biddles Ltd, King s Lynn Norfolk

Adrian Magson is a novelist and freelance writer, and lives with his wife Ann in Oxfordshire.

www.adrianmagson.com

Acknowledgements

As ever, my grateful thanks to Lynne and everyone at Crème de la Crime for their continued belief and commitment. Thanks also to Christie, ace spotter of errors, typos and moments of involuntary stupidity, for her wise suggestions.

For Ann, who makes it all so much fun.

Germany – 1989

Like nature's sugar icing, a thin layer of snow soon began to dust the runner's body.

Two hundred metres away, beyond the strip of barren land marking the border between the two Germanys, a watchtower loomed against the sky, a sinister symbol of repression that would, like the Berlin Wall three hundred kilometres to the north-east, soon be a ghostly landmark in history. On the tower, a guard in a heavy coat scanned the scene through binoculars. Below him, a patrol vehicle's engine gave a raucous clatter. A guard-dog yelped eagerly, its cries echoed by others in the distance, each a soulful, lonely message, drifting on the wind across the fields.

Minutes before, the runner had been a living, breathing being, hugging the ground among the thin brush growing in a tangle along the low ridge. He had inched with agonising care past warning markers and stones, checking for tell-tale ripples in the soil indicating a mine, or the hair-thin glint of trip-wires. Ahead lay a field, his route to the West. A US army tower in the distance was a reflection of its East German counterpart. The thick windows showed no sign of movement.

He flexed his shoulders, dislodging a layer of ice crystals formed while lying motionless in the night. In the nearby tower, the guard yawned towards the coming dawn, impatient for his shift to end.

The runner wormed free of the thin cover, sucking in deep, energising breaths. Then he was up and stumbling at a stomach-burning crouch, one hand reaching to touch the frozen earth. Twenty metres, thirty, forty... he was in full view if the guard should turn and look west. Not that he would, if all went to plan...

He ran faster, responding to the tantalising pull of safety. Suddenly, over the sound of his exertions, a shout. His stomach tightened. He ran harder, dancing sideways as a searchlight sliced through the thinning gloom. He tripped and fell, then pushed off again, coat flapping like broken wings. The searchlight caught him a glancing blow, moved away then darted back, bathing him in its glare. His shadow, thrown ahead by the light, raced on alone, unstoppable, toward the west.

Another shout, followed by two flat reports snapping out across the cold morning air. The runner staggered, splay-footed, then pitched forward and lay still.

And the new dawn began edging the horizon.

On the western side of the border, clear of the searchlight's reach, stood three men. Two wore leather jackets and boots, with woollen hats pulled down over their ears. One of the men was zipping up a long, slim bag, which he threw over his shoulder.

The third man wore a long, dark coat and a burgundy-coloured cashmere scarf. Middle-aged, of medium height and build, with thinning, sandy hair, his glasses were speckled with moisture. He nodded to the others.

"Call it in," he said quietly, his voice tinged with what sounded like relief.

The man with the bag walked over to a mud-spattered Range Rover nearby. Placing the bag on the rear seat, he picked up a radio handset and began to speak.

"Twenty minutes," he announced minutes later, rejoining the others. He clapped his hands, the sound echoing out across the field.

The man in the long coat checked the emerging outline of some woods half a mile away, and a farmhouse, huddled low as if clinging to the earth. He thought he'd seen movement earlier, but knew that couldn't be. Nerves, that was all.

"When they stop playing with that bloody searchlight," he muttered, "go fetch him. Don't leave anything behind." Then he turned to the Range Rover and climbed in. Picking up a flask, he unscrewed the top. The interior of the car instantly filled with the smell of coffee. As he poured his drink, the searchlight dipped and went out, and his two companions looked at each other, before stepping out warily across the uneven field.

Change was coming, the man was thinking idly as he watched them. Change of a magnitude that would repaint this sorry corner of Europe forever. And God help those who hadn't seen it coming.

The two men returned with the body, putting it down near the car. Twenty minutes later, a dark green Opel estate appeared from beyond a belt of trees, bouncing along the track from the main road. It was the only sign of movement, the headlights pushing back the gloom and highlighting the skeletal trees, withered grass and sagging fence posts marking the boundary of the farm's land. The vehicle had a long radio aerial bolted to the tailgate, and contained two people.

The man got out to meet them, flicking away the remnants of his coffee.

2

London – 2006

"So, why are we doing this again?" Riley Gavin glanced at the lean figure of Frank Palmer as they walked down an alleyway and emerged on to a street lined with shops, small businesses and the occasional office block. They were in Harrow, north London. Traffic was light, with a scattering of pedestrians and window-shoppers, but that would change towards lunchtime. Then the pavements would be bustling with pale-faced office workers, making eager forays for food in the early summer sun.

"I'm serving papers on a scumbag," replied Palmer dispassionately, skirting a gaggle of black bin bags outside a pizza restaurant. "If I do it right, I can send somebody an invoice, which means I get paid, which means I can eat." He looked sideways at Riley. "You're not getting the jitters, are you? Only you said -"

"Palmer, I wouldn't be here if I was getting the jitters. Even though I do have work of my own to do. What I meant was, why do you need me to act as a decoy? Why not walk straight up to this… McGilligan or Gulligan or whatever his name is, and serve the papers? I thought you private eyes did it all the time."

"His name's Gillivray, and if it was that simple, I'd have already done it." He dragged her out of the path of a delivery truck as they crossed the road towards a tall, brick-built office block set back off the street. "Doug Gillivray is as slippery as an oil-driller's boot. I swear he's got in-built radar. Here we are." He paused in the entrance and peered through the glass front, scanning the list of occupants on the inside wall. They seemed to be mostly insurance companies, shipping agents or accounting firms, along with a bank of somewhere he'd never heard of, a solicitor or two and a handful of companies with initials which probably meant something only to their financial advisers and clients.

"Stairwell Management," he said, spotting the name on the panel for the sixth floor, "is a misnomer, because managing is what they do least. Gillivray's not listed as such, but he's a director, and he usually gets in at ten-thirty every morning." He checked his watch. "Five minutes ago. He stays for an hour, probably to write a few cheques and make sure they're not all surfing the internet, then ducks out again, coming back in the late afternoon. So far I haven't found out where he goes or what he does in between."

"So what has he done to have you on his case?"

"Robbed people blind, mostly. He sells things that don't exist – usually services that disappear after the first call. Property management is his current favourite. He'll charge a fee to oversee a building, undercutting everyone else. He gets the contract, makes a few obvious moves to show willing, then does a bunk with whatever he can pick up. For an operation that sounds pretty crude, he's very smooth."

"OK. So you want me to go into Stairwell and punt for any security work, and you'll follow me in?"

"Correct."

"And you don't think you'll stand out, creeping about behind me dressed like that?" Riley, who looked elegantly businesslike in a smart-casual trouser suit, blouse and moderate heels, looked sideways at Palmer's casual slacks and battered jacket, his fit-all outfit for blending in. He rarely wore anything different on the grounds that after years as a member of Her Majesty's Royal Military Police, he had done with being pigeonholed by dress or dictate, preferring the to-hell-with-it look. Somehow, though, she had to admit, it went with his easy smile and the way his fair hair seemed to flop into place without benefit of gel or effort.

"What's wrong with it?" Palmer checked his clothes with a critical eye. "They're decent threads, I'll have you know. I paid good money for these." He fluttered his eyebrows. "Anyway, I told you a long time ago, I have the power to merge in anywhere and become as one with the scenery. Especially when preceded by a pushy blonde with a cheesy smile and all her own teeth, to act as a distraction."

Riley raised an eyebrow. "Yeah, I know – Frank Palmer, the original west London ninja. But thanks for the compliment, even if you don't mean it."

"Distract the receptionist," he continued, ignoring the barbs, "long enough for me to get past her. She has a panic button which lights up in every office when anybody official shows up. With a bit of luck I'll catch Gillivray with his laughing gear wrapped around a cup of Starbucks' finest and –" He produced a digital camera from his pocket. – "get a shot of his ugly mug in the process."

"What if the receptionist doesn't play ball? I'm no security expert – I can barely remember how to lock my own flat."

Palmer curled his lip. "You're an investigative reporter; it's not like you'd ever run out of things to say, is it? Come on." He walked through the entrance and faced a large, middle-aged security man in a dark suit and blue shirt, sitting behind a steel-topped desk. Both it and the man had seen better days. The rest of the foyer was empty, functional and bland, as welcoming as a bus stop.

"We've an appointment with Mr Gillivray at Stairwell Management," said Palmer briskly. The security man, busy leafing through a copy of the *Sun*, stood up sharply and pushed two adhesive badges across the desk.

"Right, sir." His eyes assessed the two visitors, flicking away to give Riley the barest of glances before switching back to Palmer. "If you'd fill out the book and these badges, sir, Stairwell's reception desk is on floor six." He indicated a pair of lifts to the rear of the foyer, and flipped open a visitors' book.

Palmer scribbled in the required boxes and did the same with the badges. Handing a badge to Riley, he nodded to the security man, then walked over to the lifts and pressed the call button.

"Did I miss something?" asked Riley, as the doors closed behind them and the lift began its upward journey. "Or did you hypnotise him?"

"What do you mean?"

"Just now. You had that poor man standing to attention as if he was on parade."

Palmer shrugged. "Beats me. Habit, I suppose." He began to hum as the lights flashed through the levels, and gave her a quick smile, something he knew had the ability to annoy her when he was being obtuse. When they reached the sixth floor, the lift stopped and the doors opened to reveal an identical space to the foyer downstairs, but without the welcome desk. At one end was a glass wall, with letters spelling STAIRWELL MANAGEMENT marching impressively across it in plain black script, and beyond that, a polished wooden counter where a small block of wood sprouted a clutch of international flags. A receptionist was sitting behind the counter, one cheek bearing a dinky little mouthpiece the size of a match-head.

Palmer ushered Riley ahead of him out of the lift. "You're punting for work, that's all," he reminded her. "If it gets sticky, bail out and we'll meet down in the street."

Riley stared at him. "Sticky? You never mentioned sticky. Or bailing out."

But Palmer had already reached past her to thumb the entry button beside the glass-panelled door. There was a buzz as the locks disengaged and the door clicked open.

"Can I help?" The receptionist smiled automatically, taking in Riley's no-nonsense make-up and sleek blonde hair. She switched her attention to Palmer, who smiled and raised his eyebrows, but showed no reaction. Assessment over, she relaxed and pulled back her hand which had been hovering out of sight below the counter.

"I rang to speak to your human resources director," said Riley. "He wanted to talk about internal security –" She broke off as she noticed the receptionist's attention was suddenly riveted on something just past her shoulder. When she looked round, she saw Palmer had doubled up, clutching at his stomach, his face red and strained. He coughed, and a dribble of spit oozed from his lips and ran down his chin.

"Palm–" Riley yelped and instinctively dodged sideways, caught unawares. Palmer waved a hand and clamped a handkerchief to his face.

"Quick... I need a washroom," he mumbled. "Sorry – food-poisoning."

The receptionist looked horrified at the prospect of Palmer being violently ill right in front of her. Flicking away the tiny mouthpiece, she jumped up and flapped a carefully-manicured hand towards a corridor to one side. "Down there... right at the end. Quickly..." She glanced at Riley as Palmer hurried away down the corridor, hand clutching his gut. "Is he all right? He's not having a heart attack, is he?"

Riley shook her head. She would get even with Palmer

for springing this on her. Not that she could fault his acting; he'd genuinely looked as if he was having a nasty turn. Now all she had to do was display the same degree of talent until she got tossed out on her ear or Palmer returned and gave her the sign to bail out.

Palmer found himself in a corridor that ran arrow-straight to the end of the building, then turned sharply to the left. He could hear the soft buzz of conversation and the burr of a phone beyond the wall on his left-hand side, and wondered where Gillivray had his nest. Somewhere at the back, no doubt, with a fire escape conveniently close by. People like Gillivray rarely conducted their business up front, preferring to avoid the cold scrutiny of their victims should they come calling.

He ignored the washroom door and followed the corridor, tucking his handkerchief into his jacket. More doors on the left, and to the right, a row of windows overlooking a tiny inner courtyard filled with heating and ventilation equipment, speckled with pigeon droppings and a layer of airborne city dirt.

A door opened to his left, and a woman stepped out juggling a large pile of computer printouts. Palmer moved to one side and flapped his wallet with a smile.

"Is Doug about? I've got his wallet. Dozy bugger left it in my car."

"Oh. Yes." The woman smiled vaguely over the printouts and shuffled sideways, using her chin to indicate a door further along. "He's in there." She smiled again and disappeared with her burden, heels clacking on the bare tiles.

Palmer put his wallet away and checked his digital camera was ready to shoot. He took a long, white envelope from his inside pocket, then pushed open the door and marched up to the bulky figure of Doug Gillivray, who was standing on the other side of a plain mahogany desk, counting out a pile of notes. He was short, stocky and dressed in a tight, pin-stripe suit, with a garish, spotted tie held against his lower chest by a gold clip. His pudgy fingers flashed with heavy rings as he flicked through the money with the practised ease of a bank clerk, and Palmer wondered how much all the gold weighed.

"Doug Gillivray?" Palmer stood in front of him.

Gillivray stopped counting, mouth open in annoyance, and automatically took the envelope. "What's this?"

As Palmer aimed the camera and fired off two quick shots, Gillivray's expression changed from surprise to anger. "Here, what the hell are you doing? Who let you in –?"

But Palmer was already on his way out, closing the door behind him and striding back down the corridor. He smiled as a loud bellow followed him, no doubt signalling Gillivray's discovery of the envelope's contents.

Riley was still in conversation with the receptionist, who seemed to be steadfastly holding her ground against her pleas to speak to someone about security. Grabbing Riley's arm, Palmer stabbed the exit button on the door and smiled at the receptionist. He hoped she wasn't about to get fired, unless she was related to Gillivray and knew what he was up to, in which case she probably deserved it.

Fortunately, the lift was still there. They got in and Palmer thumbed the button for the ground floor.

"Someone sounded cross," murmured Riley, as the lift rumbled slowly downwards.

Palmer tried to look innocent, but failed. He waggled the camera in triumph. "Yeah, well. Shit happens."

The lift stopped at the first floor and three men stepped in. When they saw Riley and Palmer, they cut short their conversation. Leading the way was a man in shirt-sleeves. Slim, fair-haired and clean-shaven, he looked to be in his forties. Alongside him was an older man, thin to the point of gauntness, with tanned, leathery skin at odds with the climate outside. He had dark, piercing eyes surmounted by bushy, grey eyebrows, and was conservatively dressed in a grey suit.

The third man trailed in their wake, plainly with them yet somehow disconnected. He was younger, with dark, glossy hair atop a broad, almost Slavic face. His eyes flicked briefly across Palmer and Riley, then moved away, disinterested.

Palmer noticed vaguely that none of the men wore visitors' badges.

When the lift reached the ground floor, the three men got out first. The younger man crossed to the entrance and surveyed the street, leaving his companions talking. For a moment, as they stood in profile, something about the older man with the suntan triggered a flicker in Palmer's mind. An image stirred, fleeting and surprising, then was gone.

"Palmer?" Riley glanced at him. "You're not really ill, are you?"

Palmer shook his head and dropped his badge into the security man's outstretched hand. "I'm fine. A flashback, that's all. A ghost, maybe. Come on, let's get out of here." He led the way out of the building, resisting the temptation to turn and look back.

With an odd feeling of unease, Palmer knew it was no ghost; he had seen the older man before.

3

"Well, that went really great, Riley. Thanks for your help – you were a star. I must get you to help me again sometime, then heap endless praise and gratitude on your head." Riley's voice dripped with sarcasm as she steered her Golf skilfully through a tangle of stalled traffic, narrowly missing most of a line of cones around a breached water main. A stray one rattled off the front wing, wobbled promisingly, but stayed upright. If Palmer noticed, he made no comment.

They were on their way back to Palmer's office in Uxbridge. He hadn't said much since leaving Gillivray's office, intent on scowling up at the roof of the car instead, his head back on the seat rest. Even the cigarette between his lips remained unlit, which was a relief and a puzzle. Palmer being thoughtful was something Riley wasn't really accustomed to. Quiet, yes; even half asleep was fairly normal. But not thoughtful. He usually left that to others.

"Do what?" He looked at her, then nodded. "Oh, right. Yes, you were great. Thanks." Then he went back to his thoughts, staring out at the passing scenery and whistling quietly.

When they reached his office, situated above a row of shops and small office suites, Riley switched off the engine and turned to face him. "OK," she said. "Out with it. Something's bugging you. Tell Auntie Riley or I'll have to get out the electrodes."

But Palmer climbed out and stood by the car door. "It's nothing, don't worry."

"What is it, Palmer?" she insisted, peering up at him. "You haven't even taken chunks out of me about my driving.

You're not going through the male menopause, are you?"

"Of course not," he replied, tapping the roof of the car. "Just got a couple of things on, that's all. Thanks for your help earlier. How about I spring for a meal? Say, day after tomorrow?"

Riley nearly laughed, relieved that he seemed to be shrugging off his earlier mood. "God, you're offering to buy me food? You're on. Come round to my place at seven – I know a great new Italian restaurant. The lights are so low they print the menus in Braille."

Palmer looked sceptical. "You're not getting all romantic on me, are you?"

"No way." She slipped the car into gear. "The bad light means I can be seen with you without ruining my reputation." She stuck out her tongue as he closed the door, and pulled out into the traffic, leaving Palmer standing on the pavement, deep in thought.

Riley turned her thoughts to her own work schedule and headed north towards the outer reaches of Hertfordshire. It was an assignment she had left pending for too long, but needed to fill in some background information before deciding whether to continue with it or dump it as a dead loss. A rumour of an unlicensed landfill operation involving the illegal disposal of asbestos and oil waste near a primary school was now looking less and less likely, and much too thin to stand up to detailed scrutiny. While she didn't mind going in to bat for the occasional good cause, especially if the authorities were showing a reluctance to listen, being used as a loaded gun in what was looking more like someone's private dispute over a local use of land was a no-win situation.

She came to a long line of traffic at a set of road works

and tapped the speed-dial on her phone. Time to check in with her agent. Donald Brask, fat, gay and as busy as a bee on steroids, was her main source of income. He represented a string of journalists, media personalities and a handful of entertainment 'names', and regularly found reporting assignments for Riley, freelancing for magazines and dailies when extensive digging and an investigative eye for detail was required. He also put occasional work Frank Palmer's way, of the sort needing a former military cop's particular talents. It was how Riley and Palmer had met. So far the arrangement had worked a handful of times and suited them both.

"Sweetie," murmured Donald, as soon as she identified herself. "How's that horrid dumping business? Are we going to get an exclusive this side of Christmas or should I plan on early bankruptcy?"

Riley smiled and edged the car forward in the line of traffic. Donald had a waspish tongue whenever deadlines were concerned, and was openly insincere in many ways. But beneath his cutting manner was a warm heart, especially towards her. He occupied a large Victorian house in north London, surrounded by enough computer and communications equipment to run a NASA space station. It was his centre of operations, and enabled him to keep in contact with clients and contacts around the world, day or night. Since he rarely seemed to sleep like normal people, it meant he was apt to call when most humans were fast asleep. Riley often thought the worst thing that could happen to Donald would be a total power failure. Unless he had a standby generator in the basement, he'd be utterly lost without the phones, faxes and computers which provided him with a constant flow of uninterrupted information and news every minute of the day.

"It's looking thin, I'm afraid," she told him. "I think there's a hidden agenda somewhere that we haven't been told about. I'm on my way to give it another try, but if it still looks doubtful, I'll have to kill it."

"Consider it dead, buried and decomposing, sweetie," Donald muttered flatly. "I've been hearing things, too. It's hardly a headliner. Never mind, I've got two more jobs, if you're interested. I'll email you the briefs in a minute. One of them may require the additional talents of that roughneck, Palmer. I'll send him the details, too. You can compare notes over a cup of camomile."

"OK. I'll be at home." Riley clicked off and at the first opportunity, headed back to west London. She was quietly relieved to have got rid of the dumping job, even if it was lost income. But she was looking forward to something fresh to get her teeth into – although it might mean some element of risk, hence the need for Palmer's help. The main advantage of working freelance was the variety in her working life. It was something she had learned to appreciate early on after starting out on a small local newspaper with little in the way of excitement, when the idea of working to the same format or deadlines every day had lost its appeal very quickly.

She climbed the steps to the front entrance and saw Mr Grobowski, the ground floor tenant, watering some plants in the communal hallway. As self-appointed neighbourhood watch officer and concierge, he rarely missed anything, especially Riley's comings and goings. He straightened up now with a friendly smile on his craggy face.

"Miss," he yelled happily. "How are you doings? Busy days, I bet." Mr Grobowski was built like a blockhouse, with a head topped by a flat mat of coarse hair which refused all attempts to tame it. With a mild-to-serious case of deafness, he presumed everyone else had the same problem and spoke at maximum volume. In addition, sixty years of living in London had not diminished his Polish accent, and he constantly mangled the language with cheerful abandon. He also insisted on calling Riley 'Miss' in spite of her numerous attempts to get him to use her name.

"Fine, thanks, Mr G," Riley replied. She looked for signs of her cat, the only non-human tenant of the building. She hadn't yet got round to giving him a name, in spite of inheriting him from a former neighbour in Fulham some time ago. Mr Grobowski had tried calling him Lipinski, after a famous Polish violinist, but the cat seemed supremely unimpressed by this honour, answering only to the signs and smells of food. With one of Mr Grobowski's interests being a part-time volunteer worker, cooking for his fellow countrymen at the local Polish community centre, this was something he always had in abundance.

"Tchah! Is no good looking for Lipinksi," he warned her mock-grumpily. "He eat like a horses and never say a thank you. He most likely visiting his womens friends in other buildings, I bet."

"If that's so," Riley told him cheerfully, "he's living on memories. He had the chop last year." She left the old man to his watering, and made her way up to her first floor flat. As usual, there was no sign of the old lady she referred to as the dowager, who lived on the third floor. She was almost never seen in daylight and seemed to live the life of a bat.

She checked her email. Along with the usual collection of spam messages promising a life of unrelenting fulfilment, she found the promised attachments from Donald. Her phone contained five voice messages, none of them urgent or interesting except one from John Mitcheson. He had called from his home in sunny California, with the teasing sounds of surf and music in the background to remind her of what she was missing.

While she waited for the printer to spit out Donald's email and attachments, she dialled Mitcheson's number. She could never quite figure out what the time difference was, but with luck, he should be lining up his second glass of OJ after completing his customary early morning run.

Thoughts of John always left her feeling unsettled. Currently hanging on by their fingertips to a tenuous and long-distance relationship, with Mitcheson living in the States where he was running a security company, it was hardly an ideal situation. After having become involved with other former soldiers in a vicious gangland feud masterminded by a murderous old woman named Lottie Grossman, John was *persona non grata* in the UK. Although there were no active charges against him, and the evil Lottie had since disappeared, probably killed off by her many rivals in the underworld, they had decided it was better for Mitcheson to go into self-imposed exile until further notice. Now, when they met, it was always too fleeting, usually confined to a snatched few days wherever and whenever the two of them could match timetables.

"Swine," she muttered calmly, when he answered. He sounded half asleep and she wondered if he'd had a late night. After years in the army, he was, like Frank Palmer, something of a night bird and kept unusual hours.

"What did I do?" he protested, the pleasure of hearing from her evident in his voice.

"More like what you haven't done," she said earthily, wandering around the room, "And I need a holiday. I suppose there's no chance of you coming over this way soon, is there?"

"I'd like to," he replied with feeling. "Let me look at some dates and I'll get back to you. How's Frank?" He always made a point of asking after Palmer, something for which Riley was grateful. She used to think it might have been a touch of jealousy on his part, knowing as he did that she and Frank often worked together. But she had finally come to the conclusion that it was genuine interest, coloured perhaps by the fact that Palmer had saved him from arrest after the gang business.

"He's OK. Actually, a bit weird." She briefly related the morning's events, until a distant doorbell at Mitcheson's end led him to cut short the conversation.

"Sorry, kid," he said regretfully. "Gotta go. I'll call you."

Riley put down the phone and went to study the two briefs Donald Brask had sent her. It was work, but way better than dwelling on her various frustrations.

One assignment was a simple reporting job with minimal legwork, involving a National Health Service trust manager suspected of having financial links to a large and successful chain of funeral homes. The fact that the company's name seemed to figure with unusual prominence on a number of hospital lists, to the exclusion of others, implied he was not suffering too much from any conflict of interest. Given the right approach and the waving of some documentary proof, Riley was sure she might be able to get him to fold. It wasn't a headliner, as Donald would have called it, but being NHS, it was interesting enough to be picked up for the news value.

The other was, as Donald had hinted, on the heavy side, and involved the hiring and importing of gangs of fruit pickers from eastern Europe. The suspicion from other pickers and gangs was that some of them were being used to bring in more than just their strong backs and their abilities with a fruit knife.

She decided the latter assignment had more immediate news potential and dialled Palmer's number. If they were to be working together on this, they'd need to go over the details. Which meant bringing forward their dinner date.

There was no reply from Palmer's phone. Probably already out on one of the jobs he'd mentioned. She hung up and looked at the cat, sitting pointedly in the doorway to the kitchen.

"Looks like it's you, me and the NHS for the rest of the day," said Riley, heading for the fridge. She added as a warning: "Although I'm not sure you're going to like this, not after Mr Grobowski's fancy cooking…"

"We could have a small problem. There was a man in the lift earlier. I've met him before. I think he might remember me."

The speaker was in an office on the first floor of the block in Harrow, and was staring out of the window at the advancing evening, hands thrust into his pockets. The up-glow of lights from the street was throwing an unearthly haze across the horizon, and down in the street, the throb of traffic was building to its customary frenzied pitch as commuters made their way home. As if echoing the scene outside, doors slamming in the building and the whine of the lifts heralded the same activity.

The office was large and neat, furnished comfortably with a well-stocked fridge in one corner and a scattering of soft chairs and discreet lighting. It was adequate for the man's needs. He was too old for anything more humble, the days of roughing it for Queen and country long gone; but a more lavish base would have attracted unwanted attention, something he had always worked instinctively to avoid.

His name was Arthur Radnor, and he had just concluded a lengthy telephone conversation. He turned to look at a younger figure leaning against the wall by the door, hands clasped across his middle in a relaxed pose. His name was Michael Rubinov and, unlike Radnor, whose skin was tanned like old leather after a lifetime in foreign climes, he was ghostly pale, emphasising the dark sheen of his eyes, his black hair and habitual dark suits and highly-burnished shoes.

"Where do you know him from?" Michael's accent was slight, the words polished and precise. It took a keen ear – or someone who cared – to spot that his origins were from several hundred miles away on the eastern side of an expanding Europe, deep in what had once been Soviet Russia.

"Germany, some years ago. There was a shooting on the east-west border – I mentioned it to you?" Michael nodded, remembering, and Radnor continued: "He was one of the military policeman who attended the scene."

"Ah." Michael understood. "That's not good."

"No." Radnor agreed. "It's not."

"What do you want me to do?"

"Nothing yet." Radnor picked up a glass of whisky and finished it in a gulp. Michael's character had long ago been formed by his membership of a sub-directorate of the old KGB. The word 'do' in his vocabulary carried a variety of connotations and, as had happened once or twice in their shared past, often ended in spilled blood. While there were times when this approach had undoubtedly proved useful, it had occasionally caused problems. "Just watch him for now. Check his background. If he looks like taking too close an interest… well, we'll do whatever is necessary."

Michael shrugged, as if that was no big thing. "OK. Military policeman, you say? He didn't look ex-military."

"He was a British Redcap. He wasn't much of one at the time – he was young and inexperienced. But he wouldn't have stayed that way; they train them too well." He shook his head. "Not that it matters. His name's Palmer. Frank Palmer. And the way he looks doesn't come into it. Once a cop, always a cop." He reached for the whisky bottle and poured a fresh shot, surprised his memory should still serve him so well after all these years. "Find out why he was here, what he was doing. It could be nothing, but I'm not prepared to take the risk."

4

The following morning, Michael approached the security desk with an almost inaudible tread. As a tenant, he could ask whoever was on duty anything he chose, and he asked to see the visitor's log from the previous day.

The security man shrugged and slid it across the desk. He wasn't overly polite, but Michael appeared not to notice.

He had spent the morning checking on the man Radnor knew as Frank Palmer. Getting his address had been easy, but the details had been sparse, which was what he'd expected from a former military man. If Palmer the civilian had much of a life, then it wasn't very evident from any of the normal signposts. He earned a living as a private investigator and security consultant but spent little; he belonged to no organisations that advertised the fact, and so far had either avoided breaking the law or had friends well placed enough to erase any records. To Michael, the latter made perfect sense; in his experience it was the norm to use one's position for advantage, whatever the circumstances. Among neighbours where he lived, Palmer was rumoured to have a relationship with a young woman in uniform – assumed to be police. That was something Michael decided not to pursue. Taking too close an interest in members of the police was best left for now.

In all, he had unearthed sufficient information to know that they were not dealing with some seedy amateur, and that the man had been well trained by the British military, ending his career in the Special Investigations Branch. This alone, according to Radnor, made him a potential threat.

Even so, Michael's own brand of logic told him that if

Palmer was all that special, he would not be pursuing his line of business on the margins, scraping a living from what appeared to be little more than odd jobs. Still, better to be sure. He ran his eyes up the page for the previous day until he came to the approximate time entry he was after. There was no Frank Palmer listed, nor anything resembling such a name. But then he hadn't expected it. Just a vague scrawl which could have been anything. He looked at the security man and spun the book round so he could read the name.

"This visitor. Do you remember him?"

The security man looked down at the name and appeared to give it some thought. There had been relatively little traffic over the past twenty-four hours, and each face was still fresh in his mind. "Yes, sir. Is there a problem?"

"Have you seen him here before?"

"No, sir, can't say I have. Seen the type, though."

"Type?"

"Yes, sir." His eyes slid down Michael's face to his smart suit and back again. "Ex-army, if you know what I mean." His expression seemed to imply it was unlikely, and therefore a distinction Michael would never warrant, no matter how smartly he dressed.

Michael ignored it, wondering what kind of subtle signs Palmer gave off which displayed his background. He turned the book round again and read across the page. "It says he was visiting Stairwell Management. What do they do?"

"They're on the sixth floor, sir. Don't really know much about them. A bit of this and a bit of that, so I've heard." His tone suggested that whatever they did, it was unlikely to be entirely legitimate. "The appointment was with a Mr Gillivray," he added helpfully, hoping it would make up for the fact that the name was illegible and he should have checked it before allowing them up.

"A police matter?"

"I doubt it, sir. They didn't look like police to me – none of the local ones, anyway."

Michael nodded, then looked up sharply. "They?"

"Sir?"

"You said 'they.'"

"That's right, sir. There was a young lady. He filled in the book for her and they went up together."

Michael looked again at the book. The line beneath the one Palmer had filled in was in the same handwriting. Another illegible scribble, but it confirmed Palmer had brought someone with him. Then he remembered the woman in the lift: attractive enough, young, blonde, well-dressed… If he'd given it any thought at the time, he would have assumed she was merely an office worker leaving the building for some reason. Only that wasn't the case. So who was she? Girlfriend, wife or colleague?

Whatever. They had been here for a reason and, unless they had laid a careful blind to fool him and Radnor, that reason appeared to lie up on the sixth floor. He nodded to the security guard and took the stairs back to the first floor at an easy trot, his mind processing questions and possibilities. His instincts told him Palmer's presence in the building had been a coincidence. He and Radnor had been very careful so far, keeping their heads below anybody's radar, the way they had been trained by their respective employers. But instincts could sometimes prove faulty. He decided it might pay to look into the people who called themselves Stairwell Management, to see what could have brought Palmer and his friend to this particular building. Whatever the Stairwell people were into, they had drawn the attention of an investigator. And that was something he wanted to avoid at all costs.

Riley spent the morning filling in background details on Trevor Creeley, the NHS manager with the dubious funeral service connections. She wasn't sure if he was stupid, sloppy or simply arrogant, but a drive-by of his home on the north-westerly edges of rural Essex showed a man who was living more than extremely well. From the background notes Donald had sent her, Creeley came from humble beginnings, with no record of family or inherited wealth. Yet he lived in a smart, opulent detached house set in two acres of prime land, with trimmings which included a paddock with two ponies, a large, new summer-house in the rear garden, a swimming pool and a Porsche Boxter driven by his apparently shopaholic wife.

At lunchtime, Riley was parked just along the road from Creeley's workplace. When she saw a late-model executive Jaguar nose out of the car park, she slotted in behind it, leaving two vehicles between them. It was soon apparent that Creeley was heading towards home. He drove fast and with a level of aggression that spoke of either a bad morning or a barely-concealed lack of tolerance towards other drivers bordering on the suicidal.

Enquiries at the local village shop had added gossip about two daughters at an expensive boarding school, exotic holidays and weekends away, with the description of a coastal villa in Portugal thrown in for colour. Even allowing for local petty jealousies and rumour, it was an impressive portfolio. Riley would have to check out the facts anyway, along with Creeley's credit ratings, but even this low-level study revealed a man living well above the salary of a National Health Service employee.

She checked her map. It was probably too late to start on the fruit pickers assignment. Their base was in Huntingdon, which she guessed gave their teams easy access to various work sites in Kent, East Anglia and the east Midlands. But clocking the people involved would necessitate an early morning start to identify the various faces, and she guessed she would need Palmer to help with that one. According to Donald's information, the gang masters who brought in the foreign workers each year were deeply suspicious and possessed of an acutely-tuned radar for signs of anyone taking too close an interest in their operations.

She headed for home, trying Palmer's number on the way. It might be worth getting together with him before their dinner date, so he could make a start on getting close to the Huntingdon site. She had no doubts that it would be difficult penetrating the gang's operation, but if anyone could find a way in, it would be Palmer.

5

Palmer yawned and slid down in his car seat, jockeying for a more comfortable position as he watched the office block. He winced and retrieved his mobile, which was digging into his hip, checked it was still switched off and dropped it on the passenger seat. Next to it lay a barely-touched flask of coffee and the insipid remains of a chicken sandwich bought from a snack wagon an hour ago. It was as much to help break the monotony of a lengthy surveillance session as any desire to eat. In any case, drinking while on any kind of stake-out usually led to the need for regular exits from the car, which meant running the risk of being spotted by your target, or worse, having them disappear while you were otherwise engaged.

Seeing the familiar face in the lift the previous day had unsettled Palmer more than he cared to admit. Having shrugged it off after leaving the building, dismissing it as one of those odd coincidences in life, he'd found the image returning with the persistence of a nagging toothache. He felt bad about not confiding in Riley; she deserved better. They had become close while working together, and while there were not many people Palmer had learned to trust over the years, Riley was high on the list. Indeed, she had once saved his life at considerable risk to her own, and that was something he could never repay. But until he could come up with something solid to show it wasn't just a figment of his imagination, he decided to keep it to himself. Time enough to tell her when he was certain.

Lounging at his desk with his feet up the previous evening, he had shuffled through his mental filing system of faces and names, searching for a hint of where he might have seen the man before. To help his thought processes, he reached for a notepad and doodled.

Three cigarettes and a coffee headache later, he sat bolt upright, spilling ash down his front. His trawl through the mental archives had unleashed a leaden feeling in his stomach, followed by a flurry of images that began to unravel as the memories grew clearer. He stared down at the notepad, on which he'd made some random jottings. If he was right, and his memory wasn't playing tricks, this went even further back than he'd thought. He shook his head. This was insane. But even as he thought it, he knew there was no mistake. Germany, 1989.

He lit another cigarette and mulled it over. The older man's face belonged to a time when Palmer had been a young and inexperienced member of the RMP on his first posting to Germany. Assigned to a forward base close by the East-West border, Palmer had been hooked up with a veteran, Sergeant Reg Paris, and was expected to settle in quickly and start learning on the job. Fortunately, Paris had been a good teacher, because the learning curve had proven a lot steeper than either of them imagined.

Several mornings into the posting, a coded phone call had come in to the base security post. It was very early, still almost dark and with the cold bite of winter hanging in the air. There had been a fatal shooting along the border, the caller had coolly informed them: a runner spotted crossing to the west had failed to stop when ordered by the East German border guards. Now his body was lying just inside West German territory and needed to be retrieved. Reg Paris had been sour-faced with scepticism; it happened every now and then, when some poor soul made an attempt to escape to the affluent and free west and tried to run the gauntlet of mines, dogs and security alarms. They failed more often than not, and the civil police usually dealt with the tragic results. But this one was different. The caller was asking for RMP backup, and quoting an authorisation code with which there was no arguing. Minutes later, Palmer and Sergeant Paris had buckled up and were driving out to secure the scene.

Two days later, Reg Paris was dead, the victim of a freak autobahn accident which had reduced his pool car to a tangled mess of crushed metal. And with him, seen climbing into the car by Palmer himself, had been the man he had just seen in the lift in Harrow.

But that was impossible.

He adjusted his thinking, reverting to cool logic. Once you took out all the variable explanations of a problem, he reminded himself coolly, you were left with either an absurdity which took you nowhere, or alongside it and most likely well hidden, the only possible explanation. The trick was spotting the difference.

He decided to go back to basics, which meant when in doubt revisit what you know. Since he could hardly return to the scene of the car crash, it left him with examining the most recent information he possessed. Taking another look at the man he had seen might at least confirm that he wasn't imagining things.

Now, from his position in the shade of a generous elm tree, and with the freshness of a new day to help him, Palmer had an uninterrupted view of the rear of the office building. It included a private parking area with space for a dozen vehicles, a narrow loading bay with double doors, and two rubbish skips. There had been little movement in the area so far, save for the occasional arrival or departure of cars, postal deliveries and a sandwich vendor, and the irregular appearance of a figure in a dark uniform and blue shirt, walking unhurriedly around the site, checking the doors and windows and pausing for a cigarette break. Palmer recognised the security desk man from their earlier visit. He was replaced later by another man of similar appearance, who moved in the same measured, purposeful manner. Neither gave the impression of being particularly zealous in their routine, but Palmer doubted they would miss much between them.

He checked his mirror for signs of a traffic warden or a roving community support officer. He had discreetly fed the meter, but there was always a risk that an eagle-eyed resident might have noticed his presence and phoned it in. Arguing with a uniform about his right to use a parking space for longer than the allotted time was hardly guaranteed to help in discovering more about the men on the first floor of the office building down the street.

The loading bay doors opened and a figure in a dark suit appeared, carrying an armload of packaging material. Palmer felt a prickle of interest. It was the youngest of the three men he had seen in the lift.

The man walked to the edge of the bay and threw the packaging into the nearest skip. Brushing off his hands, he stood looking around as if taking in the fresh air.

Palmer froze, recognising the signals. It was the slow, careful scan of someone acutely aware of his surroundings, ticking off visual checkpoints in his mind. For a brief second, Palmer was sure the man was looking right at him, and felt a momentary chill of apprehension when the eyes appeared to dwell just a fraction too long on his location. But the young man turned away and moments later disappeared inside, closing the door behind him. Palmer allowed himself to breathe again.

A cab swung into view at the end of the street and turned into the parking area. It was a cream Mercedes with a small pennant flapping from the radio aerial. On the roof was a white plastic pyramid with the words WHITE TOWER in black lettering. Private hire. Minutes later, a slim figure appeared at the rear door of the building, clutching a briefcase in one hand and the front of his lightweight coat in the other as a gust of wind threatened to snatch it away. The tanned skin looked even darker as the man scowled, and Palmer felt a renewed shock of recognition.

He hadn't been mistaken.

The man turned and climbed into the cab, slamming the door behind him, and the vehicle drove out of the car park and turned down the street in Palmer's direction.

He stayed where he was, his mind in free-fall, trying to work out the inexplicable. Just in time, as the cab approached, he remembered to snatch up his mobile and clamp it to his ear, hoping this small subterfuge and the dappled shadow of the tree would be all the camouflage he needed. He watched in his wing mirror as the cab disappeared down the street, before dropping his mobile on the seat beside him. Then he turned the ignition and drove away in the opposite direction, deliberately taking an easy pace. If his memory and instincts were correct, it was possible the man's younger colleague might even now be watching from an office window to check vehicle movements in the area. A car pulling out and sitting on the older man's tail would be noticed immediately; a vehicle moving the other way would not merit the same attention.

The moment he hit the end of the street, which was in a blind spot from the office building, Palmer floored the accelerator. He had an imprint of the street layout in his mind, and if he followed a simple box system, he should be able to catch up with the cab. As long as he didn't run head-on into it or remain on its tail for too long, there was every chance he might find out more about the man he was after.

As he turned a corner on to a main through-road, he saw the cab ahead of him, pulling out of a side road, the triangle on the roof just visible. He settled in behind it three cars back, the pennant on the cab's aerial a helpful marker in the shifting jumble of traffic.

The journey was shorter than he'd expected. After little more than a mile, the cab stopped outside Kenton underground station. Palmer hung back, watching as the man left the cab and disappeared into the station without looking back. He automatically noted the man's gait and build, adding to the picture he already had, and wondered why he had chosen to come to this particular stop, when he could have walked from the office block to Harrow-on-the-Hill station in two minutes. Maybe he didn't like walking. Or maybe he was going somewhere specific to this station.

He gave it ten minutes, watching the entrance in case the man re-emerged, then called it a day and headed west.

Back at his office, he consulted his new Rolodex, finding comfort in the spin and clatter of the cards. He had begun filling it in a few days ago, starting with immediate and current acquaintances, like Riley and Donald Brask, then gradually trawling wider to include occasional and past contacts, people he might need to call sometime. He stopped at a name he had discovered in an old diary and almost rejected, then decided at the last minute to leave in. He hadn't been sure that he would ever need to call on the Frankfurt offices of an international enquiries agency, but his work occasionally took him down some strange paths. Maybe the truth in that was about to be proven most aptly.

He picked up the phone.

Five minutes later, he had a name and another phone number belonging to a man in a private office in a town called Schweinfurt, one hundred kilometres to the east of Frankfurt. He hoped the subscriber's English was better than Palmer's German, or he was in for a hard time.

While he waited for the number to answer, he checked his watch. Six-fifteen. After this he would go home and grab an early night. He had a busy day tomorrow. He lit a fresh cigarette. Riley would have given him a hard time for smoking too much, but it helped him think. And thinking right now was all he had. Because unless there had been some astounding advances in medical science recently, dead men simply could not come back to life.

6

As the rush-hour traffic leaving London's westerly sprawl slowed to a trickle, a large saloon pulled into the kerb before a row of shops and offices in Uxbridge. The driver cut the engine and waited, eyes on the interior mirror, finger gently tapping out a rhythm on the wheel. The passenger in the rear was holding a mobile phone and keying in a number. After six rings an answer machine cut in, and a tinny voice asked the caller to leave a message.

The passenger switched off her phone and peered out of the window, then gave a brief nod to indicate all was clear. The driver slid out from behind the wheel and clicked the door shut. As he walked across the pavement, he rolled his shoulders to ease his muscles, cramped after an hour spent in the confines of the car.

The driver's name was Szulu. He was tall and slim, with strong shoulders and powerful hands. A ring of shiny dreadlocks framed an ebony face and grey eyes. He walked with a loose-limbed grace, and this, coupled with an air of strength, meant he was often treated with caution among those who didn't know him. The one thing Szulu was not accustomed to was acting as an errand boy, which was how he felt right now. But he needed the money to settle some outstanding debts. Failure to pay very soon meant he would receive a visit from men who knew little of his reputation and would care even less if they did.

He approached a single wooden door set between two anonymous glass-fronted commercial premises. Beyond these on one side was a dry-cleaning shop, which was still open, and on the other a bookmaker, which was not.

He pushed open the door, which needed a paint job, he noticed, and stepped into a gloomy apology for a hallway, with just enough room for a hard chair and an empty waste bin. The air smelled damp. A narrow stairway covered in curling carpet tiles led upwards to a glass-panelled door at the top. A box of rubbish teetered on one of the middle treads, a clutch of yellowed newspapers spilling out from a gash in the side. Szulu listened, head cocked to one side. All he could hear was the hum of an occasional vehicle outside and the sound of a radio from somewhere nearby. He flexed his shoulders again and willed himself not to look back at the car. He didn't need an imperious flap of the passenger's hand urging him to get on with it; he'd had enough of that already and it did nothing to make him feel better about himself.

He walked up the stairs, treading lightly, hands held loosely by his sides. All he had to do was go in, check the place, then give the passenger the all-clear signal. Easy enough. Unfortunately, as he knew from experience, it was the easy jobs that most often led to disappointment or pain.

There was no name on the frosted-glass panel. He already knew from the briefing his passenger had given him two days earlier that his main item of interest was a private investigator named Frank Palmer. And this was Palmer's office. He tried the door, but it was locked. He took out a bunch of keys and selected a few, trying them one by one. The fourth worked with a smooth click and the door swung open. The dull atmosphere of the staircase gave way to the dark reaches of a small, stuffy room heavy with the fog of recent cigarette smoke and typical office smells.

He switched on the overhead light. Two minutes later, he heard the downstairs door open and slow footsteps on the stairs. He cut the main light and pulled the blinds, then switched on the desk lamp. It didn't do much to improve the scenery, but was sufficient for what they needed.

The passenger appeared in the doorway and Szulu stepped over to the window where he could watch the street through a crack in the blinds. It also meant he didn't have to look the woman - his temporary employer - in the eye.

"Have you touched anything?" Her voice was soft, with signs of wheezy breathlessness after the stairs, and awoke in Szulu unhappy memories of a particularly malevolent and asthmatic nun who'd taught him maths when he was eight.

"No." he said curtly. "You said not to."

The woman nodded and stepped into the room, her nose twitching at the smell. She looked gaunt in the throw of the desk light, and moved carefully, as if she was trying to keep herself upright in spite of a particularly bad back. She wore expensive shoes and jewellery, and was wrapped in a heavy coat tightly belted at the waist in spite of the warm weather. Szulu thought the coat was hideously dated, but since he knew nothing of fashion and the woman was no longer remotely young, he assumed his views would count for little. His mother wore a coat all year round, but he put that down to her coming from Antigua and because she, too, was as old as the hills. Old people felt the cold.

The woman pulled open a filing cabinet and rustled through the contents, her wrinkled hand with its bright red fingernails racing across the tops of the drop-files like a large, gaudy spider. She selected two or three, briefly scanning the sheets within, then replaced them carefully where she had found them. The drawers closed with a *thunk*. From there she moved over to the desk and worked her way through its contents. It didn't take long, and she gave a small sigh of irritation. Next she turned her attention to a notepad on the top of the desk, covered in meaningless squiggles. She picked it up, scanned it, then dropped it back on the desk.

"You want me to help?" Szulu offered finally. She was staring at a battered PC monitor sitting on the desk. The tower was beneath the desk, the green power light glowing in the shadow. He wasn't great with computers, but he could generally find his way around them. It would be better than standing here like a lemon – and quicker.

"Are you an IT specialist?" she asked, eyes swivelling towards him. It was like coming under the gaze of a bad-tempered rat, and he could feel the tension coming off her in waves. He couldn't help it: he flinched. And shook his head.

"Then you can't help." She reached across and pulled at a Rolodex sitting alongside the PC monitor. She spun it round like a dealer shuffling a pack of cards. When it stopped, she stabbed a long fingernail at a point in the index and unclipped a card. She studied it for a few seconds before dropping it on the desk. "Remember the details then put the card back."

She moved away to the window, where a small pot plant stood on a coffee table. The plant looked neglected and close to death, with the tips of the heavy leaves yellowed and beginning to curl. The soil around the base was dry and cracked, and edged with a white fuzz. Alongside the plant was a small plastic watering can with a long spout. It was empty, and still had a sales ticket stuck to the base. The woman took the can to where a kettle sat on a tray, and transferred water from the kettle, then carefully poured a trickle around the plant, using the handle of a teaspoon to turn over the soil and help the moisture penetrate.

Szulu watched in astonishment as she tidied up some spilled soil, and wondered whether this woman was for real. Didn't she realise they'd get caught if the owner came back? Yet here she was playing *Gardeners' World*. Maybe she was nuts.

She finished what she was doing and wiped off the spoon with a tissue from her coat pocket. Replacing the spoon near the kettle, she walked out of the office and down the stairs, leaving Szulu half-hoping she might trip on the way down.

He checked the card she had dropped on the desk. The surface bore the indent from one of her chisel-like nails. There wasn't much on it; a name, address and a phone number. He slid it back into the pack, then turned his attention to the PC. He touched the tower, which felt warm from recent use. He wondered if he should take a quick look, anyway, then dismissed the idea. The woman hadn't told him what she was looking for, and hanging around here too long was asking for trouble. Without thinking, he reached down and flicked off the power button.

He pulled the door shut behind him, instinctively reaching for the keys to lock it, then changed his mind. He liked the idea of this Palmer person knowing someone was watching him; that someone had entered his domain because they felt like it. And, what the hell, the old woman didn't own every decision he made, in spite of her money and her evil eye. As he walked back down the stairs, he found himself thinking about the Rolodex card, and wondering who Riley Gavin was.

7

Early next morning, Palmer was once more outside the office block in Harrow. This time he was facing the opposite way down the street, and parked close to the rear entrance, within sight of the loading bay. The cover here wasn't ideal, but it was likely he'd only need to be here for a short while. After his revelation the previous day, he needed one more look; one more sighting of that face to confirm that he wasn't losing his entire sense of perspective.

Fifteen minutes later, after watching a procession of early workers, deliveries and the usual comings and goings related to an office building girding itself for the day's business, he saw a White Tower cab turn the corner and slide into the kerb. One passenger got out and closed the door without looking back, and the cab pulled away. No goodbyes, no indication that money had changed hands in the usual way. A regular user, then – most likely an account-customer.

The tanned skin and gaunt look confirmed it was the man from the lift.

Palmer took a digital camera from the glove box and fired off a couple of shots. With the face already imprinted on his memory, he wouldn't need to refer to the camera again. The photos were purely for backup, a hangover from his days in the Special Investigations Branch of the RMP.

The man approached the rear of the building and punched in a security code on a small black box to one side of the door. There was no audible click from this distance, but by the way the man barely checked his step, the delay was brief and the procedure something of a habit. It showed he had been coming here for some time, and had settled into the comfortable routine of a regular.

As soon as the door closed behind him, Palmer called a number he'd stored in his phone the previous evening. He hadn't been confident enough to do it yesterday, but now he had no hesitation.

Reg Paris had come from a small village near Trowbridge in Wiltshire. It was the seat, the tall NCO had once joked, of the Paris family ever since they had first been discovered living under a rock. Coming from a family of farm labourers, Reg had displayed the raw-boned strength and build of his forebears, a fact, Palmer recalled, that had proven useful in promoting an air of calm among trouble-some squaddies around the pubs and clubs.

With no current information to go on, Palmer had, the previous evening, dialled up his account with a directory search engine and keyed in the name and the largest town, Swindon. The first result had produced a blank. He'd tried other county towns, wondering whether he was being over-optimistic, before finally hitting on three references and phone numbers. The first two had been unhelpful. The Paris family, it seemed, was no longer as close as it had once been. The third number, however, had led to gold in the form of a younger brother. Although wary at first, the man had finally given Palmer a phone number for Reg's widow, Marjorie. She had answered after three rings. By now long remarried, she was surprised to hear from any-one about her former husband's death.

"It's been years," she said calmly. "I thought that was all over and done with."

"Just tying up some loose ends, admin-wise," Palmer told her, playing the diligent civil servant. "I was wondering whether you were ever given any details of the accident?"

"Details? What… you mean how it happened?" There was a pause before her voice came back laden with suspicion. "Here, this isn't going to affect my pension, is it? Only I was told at the time there was no problem with the pension, seeing as how he'd been killed on duty, like."

"No, it's nothing like that. I was wondering if you were told anything specific, that's all."

"No. I wouldn't have wanted to, neither. They said Reg was on his way to some civil police court to make a statement, and he got hit by a big lorry that was going too fast. It happens, over there, with those German roads, doesn't it? They should have a speed limit, same as we do. Why are you asking?"

"Just clearing up some bits and pieces before sealing the documents, that's all. Umm… did anyone mention the other man in the car?"

"Other man? Are you sure you're looking at the right papers, love? There wasn't nobody else with Reg. They told me he was on his own."

Palmer thanked the woman and hung up, his chest drumming. It wasn't what he'd been expecting to hear, yet perversely it came as no surprise. He dropped the phone on to the seat and chewed over what he knew, trying to picture once again the man who had turned up at the base two days after the shooting and informed Sergeant Paris that he, as the senior British RMP present, was required to make a statement to the civil authorities in Frankfurt about the scene of the shooting and what he had observed. There had been the usual display of authorisation, followed by a confirmation phone call to the CO, and Reg had marched out with a flat face to the car pool, closely followed by the man in the coat. They had climbed into the first available car, Paris taking the driver's seat and hitting the gas before his passenger had fully closed the door. Palmer hadn't heard the exchange between them, but Reg had muttered to the guard on the gate that he had to accompany the man to Frankfurt and would be back the following day.

It was the last time Palmer had seen him.

After another twenty minutes and two more calls, including one to a sniffy *hausfrau*, Palmer switched on his ignition and drove away. He was experiencing a shimmer of excitement which he recognised of old: the frisson of the chase, that stirring of the blood and sinews when a subject was in the frame and he was focussing on the detail and procedure necessary to lock on to the target. It was what he was good at.

In his pocket were his passport and a small bundle of euros. An overnight bag sat on the floor by the passenger seat, containing a change of shirt and underwear and some other essentials. He might give Charlie a ring later today or tomorrow, just in case his immediate plan didn't work out. Riley, too. Thinking of her reminded him of their dinner date. He swore. He'd have to call her. She'd no doubt play hell when she discovered he'd been working on something without keeping her in the loop, but for now, he wanted to see how far wrong he was before he made a complete spanner of himself. He checked his watch. He had plenty of time to get the flight he wanted. With luck he'd be back again by evening. He pointed the car towards Heathrow.

Riley was becoming seriously concerned about Palmer's unavailability. She had called him several times during the morning to talk about their new assignment, but his mobile was constantly off and his answer machine had given up taking messages. She didn't expect him to be waiting at the end of the phone for her, but being out of touch this long without a word was out of character. She would never claim to know the former military policeman completely; he wasn't exactly an open book, and rarely talked about himself, preferring to hide behind humour and dry wit. But she felt she was as close to him as anyone else, and knew he would not drop out of sight or contact without good reason.

She had already discarded the idea of driving over to his place to see if he was there. If he was busy and simply keeping his head down for some reason, he wouldn't thank her for chasing him around the capital like a mother hen. Instead she had occupied her time doing her accounts, shredding unwanted files and half-heartedly cleaning the flat, her least favourite activity. When that had failed to hold her interest, she turned her attention back to the assignments from Donald, especially bringing a close to the information on the NHS manager with the platinum card life-style. With a bit of luck and a fair wind, she would be able to confront him with the evidence and see if he would admit to receiving financial inducements from the funeral chain in return for the guaranteed business he was suspected of putting their way. The clincher so far had been her discovery, under the guise of pursuing an insurance claim against a hotel for lost baggage, that the last family holiday in the Caribbean had been paid for by a company called RestPlan, which turned out to be a subdivision of the funeral chain. If such a glaring oddity didn't prove sufficient to unnerve the man, he was tougher than she'd imagined and she'd have to rethink her strategy.

She rang Donald Brask. The agent would have been chasing Palmer about the fruit-picker brief, too, and might have spoken to him. He'd probably confide that Palmer was slumped in his car somewhere, running surveillance on some corporate drone suspected of having his hands in the company piggy bank.

But she was in for a surprise there too. "Sorry, sweetie," said Donald. "I haven't heard a peep. I've tried raising him a couple of times, but his mobile's switched off. Unusual for him, I must say." For once, Donald sounded concerned, reflecting what Riley was already thinking: Palmer dropping off the radar without leaving word was seriously odd. "Perhaps he's found love, do you think?" Donald added waspishly, ever ready to trade gossip.

"I wish I knew," said Riley. She thanked him and switched off, mystified. Hell, maybe Donald was right and Palmer had found love. Now, that might make him lose his sense of perspective and keep his head down.

The cat wandered in and sat in front of her, eyes half-closed, paws treading the carpet. Riley shook her head in disgust. "This is getting bloody desperate, cat. It's looking like another night in, one man beyond reach in sunny la-la land and the other... well, wherever." She stood up and walked through to the kitchen, where she spooned some cat food into a dish, then placed the dish on the floor.

"Sorry, cat," she said, collecting her car keys and jacket. "I'd be terrible company anyway. If Palmer shows up while I'm gone, scratch his ankles for me. See you later."

8

Riley slotted the Golf into a space outside Palmer's office and checked his window for signs of life. Knowing Palmer, he could be fast asleep over his keyboard, lulled into unconsciousness by a lengthy surveillance session and a heavy takeaway. Unless Donald had been right about love, of course, in which case his office was the last place she should expect to find him.

She walked up the stairs and dug out the key he had given her a long time ago. Fretting about him the previous day and his brief call cancelling dinner had produced a suspicion that whatever was ailing him wasn't good. Palmer simply didn't take off like this; he was a creature of habit and rarely allowed anything to disturb his routine. As a friend she needed to know what was going on, even at the risk of incurring his annoyance.

As she inserted the key in the lock, the door swung open. She was greeted by stale, smoky air and the sharp tang of warm plastic. Well done, Palmer, she thought; you've left your office unlocked and your machinery switched on. One day you'll come back here and find it stripped bare or a smouldering skeleton, the remains of your desk having trickled through to the ground floor in a fine shower of grey ash.

She looked around, subconsciously checking details. Same desk, same filing cabinet, same PC, tea and coffee stuff, coffee table, neglected pot plant and grungy carpet. Palmer's empire in all its impressive glory. Still, for all his carelessness, it didn't look like he'd been burgled, not unless the place had been dismissed as beyond temptation by the local criminal cockroaches.

A fine layer of dust covered everything, testimony to the rarity of any cleaning schedule. Riley had once suggested an occasional cleansing might make his clients feel more welcome, but Palmer had ignored her, saying anyone who walked through his door was more interested in his ability to solve problems, not how he kept his office.

She checked the desk, which held a notepad covered with doodles and hieroglyphics; just the standard squiggles that would be of interest only to Palmer's shrink, if he ever had one. A few numbers were dotted about around the edges, and what could have been dates and questions marks circled or underlined. Most looked old. But down at the bottom of the sheet, Riley noticed the words *Sgt, Reg* and *Paris,* and *Meiningen...border.* It obviously meant something to Palmer but did nothing to tell her what he might be up to. Instinct made her tear off the top sheet and fold it into her pocket. She could always replace it if necessary.

A quick check of the desk drawers revealed an unused diary still in its cellophane wrap, a bundle of cheap pens in a rubber band, a box of paperclips, mostly interlinked, and a collection of stale breadcrumbs.

She noticed the Rolodex and smiled. She'd bought it for him as a joke, following a wistful comment that private eyes always had a Rolodex and he'd have to get one in which to file the names of his underworld contacts, friendly cops, bar owners and hot, available blondes. When she produced one a few days later he'd been delighted, and sat there flicking it round like an executive toy.

As she pulled it towards her, one of the cards slid out on to the desk, skidding through the thin patina of dust. She turned it over.

The card bore her name and address.

She clipped it back into place. Typical Palmer, casual

to the last. At least it proved he was using it. She flicked through the rest of the cards, which were mostly unused. When she saw a familiar name in the C section, she thought for a moment, then on impulse made a note of the details before replacing it.

She wandered around the rest of the room, eyeing Palmer's computer. There might be something in it other than games of solitaire and minesweeper. Or maybe not. Palmer always claimed not to be the most computer-literate soul on God's earth, but she knew he'd had training in basic IT skills in the army. He simply chose not to use them much. She craned her head to peer at the tower beneath the desk, expecting to see the green power light glowing, but it was switched off. Wow, Palmer, she thought. I'm impressed.

As she turned away, her eyes fell on the plant pot, evidence of a past attempt by her to add some soul and colour to the masculine drabness of the place. It had been pearls before swine. Palmer's eyes had glazed over the moment she'd taken it out of the bag and placed it on the desk. Plants of any kind really weren't his thing, unless they could be fried and eaten or their containers used as an ashtray. Still, he'd promised to try and keep it alive, although she'd guessed it might be by swamping it with endless dregs of cold tea.

She frowned, bending closer. The plant looked sick, which was no surprise, but that could be down to the stuffy atmosphere up here. Yet the soil showed signs of having been watered recently. She touched it with the tip of her finger. It was definitely moist. Maybe she owed Palmer an apology for this, too. And there was only the faintest trace of soil spill on the table top, as if it had been wiped clean. The last time she'd watched him water the thing, he'd created a mini tidal wave, sloshing water and soil every-where like a kid in a sandpit.

She left the office and locked the door. The small landing was as airless as the office, but as she walked down the stairs, she thought she detected traces of a distinctly feminine perfume she had missed on her way up. Sweet, almost cloying, the smell reminded her of an elderly aunt who doused herself liberally in cologne without realising its effect on those around her.

Outside, she stood and looked around, undecided on her next move. She was torn between concern for Palmer and the knowledge that if he was simply caught up in a job he'd forgotten to mention, he could be anywhere. After all, he was a big boy and could do what he liked.

"Miss?" A male voice came from a doorway to her left. It was a dry-cleaning shop, the windows covered in gaudy special offer stickers and the smell of chemicals and hot air wafting from a vent over the front door. A man was standing in the entrance, holding a cleaning cloth in one hand. She vaguely recalled seeing him when she'd visited Palmer before. He'd been squirting some liquid over the glass from a plastic atomiser when she first arrived, then rubbing at the glass with a fixed frown. He was plump and swarthy, with a heavy moustache and receding hairline, and showed a flash of white teeth as she turned towards him. "Miss. You looking for Frank?"

"Yes, I am." Riley stepped across the pavement towards him. "Have you seen him?"

"No. Not recently." His accent was middle-eastern with a thin American overlay, his smile easy and apologetic. "But I know you. You're Miss Riley, right?" He nodded and waited for her to agree. "Frank tell me."

Riley nodded, wondering what else Frank had told him. "That's right. Riley Gavin."

The man slapped his chest and smiled happily. "I am

48

Javad. I come from Iran. I know Frank Palmer well. He likes my coffee. Very strong. He says 'Iranian coffee thick enough to float a dead horse.'"

"Sounds like him, right enough," Riley agreed. Frank Palmer, coffee and quaint sayings a speciality.

"Sure thing. He tells me you work together, busting cases, right?" He laughed. "I like all cop shows. Bloody good action." Then he frowned. "But you're not…" He clapped his hands and rubbed them together. "…not a twosome, I think." The idea seemed to disappoint him a little, although it didn't diminish the twinkle in his eye. Maybe he liked the idea of everyone being happy together.

"No," said Riley, figuring that gossips were the same the world over, be it Tehran or west London. "We're not a twosome." She turned to leave, but Javad stepped out of his doorway and gestured up at Palmer's office window.

"Maybe Frank's busting a drugs case, huh? Needed to go underground."

"Drugs?" Riley looked at him. She had a feeling Javad was just a little too fond of cop shows. Next thing, he'd be asking to see her gun and firearms permit.

"Sure." Javad nodded energetically, then stepped close and looked around, the sign of cautious gossips everywhere. "I'm not racist, you know, but the black with the…" He flicked his fingers up and down the sides of his head. "…the dreadlocks. He could be up to no good, right?"

"Black? Oh, a black man. What about him?"

"Yesterday, seven thirty or forty in the evening. I was closing up, doing my cash. Not a bad day, God be praised, but not great. Weather not yet hot enough to need clothes cleaned. A big car arrives, and I think, maybe a late customer. So I wait. You never know. But it wasn't a customer. A tall black gets out and goes to Frank's office.

I didn't get a good look, but he looks very fit, you know – like one of those footballers. And he walks arrogant, like he owns the street. He had a ring of dreadlocks around his head. You know dreadlocks?" He waved a dismissive hand. "Hah. Should be for girls, these things, not men."

"What then?"

Javad shrugged. "He go inside, but I can't see him after. I have to count my cash, see, or I lose count and start all over again. Then the car door opens in the back and a woman comes out. She walks across the pavement and goes inside, also."

"You're sure they went to Frank's office?"

"Of course. Only place to go. The offices either side, they are closed. So, a client for Frank, I bet. All investigators get clients at strange times, right? Bang on door, walk in and say 'Find me this person damn quick!'" He chuckled at the idea. "But why the big black, huh? Bodyguard, maybe? Enforcer, perhaps." He pulled a face and tapped his chest. "Where I come from, only presidents and bad people need bodyguards." He gave a snort of laughter. "Sometimes one and same people, of course."

Riley thought about it. She knew most of Palmer's work was picked up by word of mouth or through Donald Brask. But that didn't mean he never had walk-ins looking for instant solutions. Desperation didn't always follow conventional channels. "Did you see what the woman looked like?"

"Sadly, no. She had on big coat, and she walked like she was old woman. Stiff, you know? And short. That's all."

"How long were they up there?"

Javad stared into the distance for a moment and puffed out his cheeks. Then he shrugged expansively. "Five minutes, not more. I count quick, so I know it's not long. By the time I finish cashing up, they are down again and gone. Nice car. New Volvo, I think. Or was it Japanese? All look same to me. Anyway, solid as brick shithouse." He smiled disarmingly, evidently unaware of the word's position in polite conversation.

Riley remembered the trace of heavy perfume in the stairwell and the watered plant; an older woman with a dreadlocked minder. So who were they? A Yardie with a taste for horticulture? An elderly or infirm woman with a tame gorilla dropping by to do Palmer a favour? Both seemed about as unlikely as Palmer becoming eco-friendly.

"Thanks, Javad." She took a card from her pocket and handed it to him. "If they come back, this woman and the man with the dreadlocks, would you call me?"

Javad nodded eagerly, happy to be of help, delighted to be in on something exciting. "Of course, Miss Riley. Sure thing. You think Frank's all right?"

"I'm sure he is. He's probably... you know – working undercover for a while." She shook his hand and walked back to the car, her mind now in overdrive at this latest development. Still, she now had the eagle-eyed Javad watching the place, so maybe he'd turn up something.

From Palmer's office she drove the short distance to his flat, which was in a quiet, two-storey block in a leafy back road. She parked out front and walked into a tiled foyer surrounded by frosted glass. It was deserted and silent, with a fresh smell of lemon in the air. She walked up the stairs to Palmer's front door on the first floor and rang the bell. No answer. She counted to ten and tried again. Nothing. There was no mail-slot in the door, so no way to peer inside. With fingers crossed that none of the other tenants would choose that moment to happen along, she bent down and put her face to the tiled floor, trying to see beneath the door. Nothing there, either, save for a slit of daylight and some dust.

She nudged the door with her shoulder. It was solid and unyielding. The jamb was tight, which meant she could forget about trying to use her credit card or any of those other clever tricks to get inside, even if she knew how.

Frustrated, she went back downstairs and looked at a rack of metal mailboxes on one wall, one for each flat. They were gunmetal grey, secured by serious-looking locks, and seemed too sturdy for her to spring the door with an unladylike kick or nudge. She slid her fingers into the slot and immediately encountered a ridge of paper inside. It was just too far down to get hold of, but felt like an envelope. Next to it was the softer surface of plastic film covering a catalogue or brochure. She dug deeper and found more envelopes. Then she realised something was touching the back of her hand. She turned her hand palm up and felt around with her fingertips. It was a newspaper – probably a local freebie – and felt as if it had been jammed in across the top of the box. She worked at the paper with her fingers, trying to dig her nails in to pull it loose, and felt it begin to move.

Suddenly the front door rattled, and a cough sounded from outside. It was the dry hack of someone elderly and female. Riley stepped back and pulled out her mobile, pretending to be waiting patiently while it rang. All she needed now was for some Neighbourhood Watch trooper to yell for the police and it would really make her day.

An old woman appeared, steadying herself by leaning on a wheeled shopping basket as she stepped through the door. She looked at Riley with wide eyes and kept the basket between them, then limped away with a peculiar rolling motion, moving up the stairs without a backward glance.

Riley stepped back to the mailbox. With a quick tug, she pulled the newspaper from the box and checked the date. Two days old. It meant the rest of the mail had been there at least the same time.

Eighty yards away, tucked into the kerb behind a large rubbish skip spilling over with builder's debris and broken furniture, the man named Szulu sat in his car and watched as Riley walked out of the block of flats and drove away.

He yawned and wished he'd brought something to drink. He'd been watching the place for several hours now, hoping Palmer might put in an appearance. After finding no clues to Palmer's whereabouts at his office, his home was looking just as empty. The vigil had so far proved fruitless; only a couple of men had crossed his line of vision, both of them too old by about thirty years to fit the old woman's description of the investigator. He judged he was on the outer limits of spending any more time here before arousing suspicion.

Although he hadn't been able to get inside Palmer's flat, and had been forced to make do with a couple of swift forays up to his front door and out again, Szulu had an instinct about these things. If Palmer hadn't shown up by now, he probably wasn't going to any time soon. Not unless he'd managed to transform himself into a little old lady with a shopping basket and arthritic hips, or a fine looking blonde chick with nice legs and a frown, like the one just leaving.

He gave it ten more minutes, during which a couple of locals gave him the evil eye, so he started the car and drove away. As he headed south, he wondered how to go about telling his employer that she was wasting her time and money.

9

"I don't like the sound of this." Arthur Radnor drummed his fingers on the top of his desk and stared hard at Michael. "Not a bit."

"I agree." The Russian was sitting on the other side of the desk, casually flicking a trace of something from his trouser cuffs. If he felt he was at the focus of Radnor's comment in some way, he gave no indication. "I think we should try to dissuade this man Palmer. Just in case."

Radnor sat back with an irritated flick of his hand, and loosened his tie, a rare sign that he was under pressure. From what Michael had discovered, the company on the sixth floor, Stairwell Management, had suddenly surfaced as a problem right on their own doorstep. How much of one he wasn't sure right at the moment, but his instincts told him that if they didn't find some way of controlling things, it could get badly out of hand. "I'm not sure. Is Gillivray a conman? Is that it?"

"It's all I could find. He has been convicted of petty offences so far, mostly to do with businesses which do not exist, or at least, do not provide what they offer."

"What sort of businesses?"

Michael shrugged. "Take your pick – he has tried so many; mail order schemes, website design, advertising, printing services, site management. He sets up a company through a PO box or a temporary mailing address, advertises in local papers and draws in some customers looking for a cheap deal. He takes their money, then closes the company. None of the companies are legal, or course, but by the time the customers find out, it is too late and they are untraceable. He has had some clients track him down, possibly through bad luck or carelessness, but he seems to have handled things by buying them off. One or two have threatened violence, but nothing serious." Michael pulled a face. "He is a nothing – a minor criminal."

"He may be a nothing," Radnor snorted, "but if he's attracted the attention of people like Palmer, that's too close for comfort. Who knows how many others are watching him? What did Palmer want with him?"

"Palmer apparently gave some legal papers to him, which made him angry."

"Served papers," Radnor corrected him. "It means a solicitor is after him on behalf of a client. Christ, that's all we need; next thing we know the police will be sniffing around, followed by Customs and Excise and the Inland Revenue." He threw his head back, agitated at the idea of their previously peaceful existence being threatened by the arrival of men with summonses or arrest warrants – and most of the traffic going past their front door.

"You worry too much," Michael said easily, trying to inject a measure of calm. He was aware that Radnor had been under a great deal more pressure than this in his chequered past, including the danger of imprisonment or worse in various parts of the world, and was therefore surprised at this level of agitation.

"Well, someone has to," Radnor snapped. "I've had a feeling something wasn't right for a while." He stabbed a finger into his stomach. "A feeling in here. It's gut instinct – and it hasn't failed me yet. We've got too much invested to have it turned upside down at this stage. There are shipments coming in which we can't stop."

"The shipments won't be affected," Michael countered reasonably. "We let them go to the usual place. We just move this part of the operation somewhere else instead, away from Palmer's focus. There are plenty of other offices to rent."

"It's not that simple, though, is it?" Radnor sighed and made an effort to calm down. "We can't operate from some crummy lock-up, or it'll look as if we can't compete. And if we start moving around and changing addresses, it'll make the others jittery. They'll think we're not stable, and we can't risk that."

Michael nodded. As he knew only too well, their suppliers, based in some of the more inhospitable parts of the former eastern bloc, seemed fixated on the idea that their 'partners' in the west should have every sign of respect-ability, as if that would, by association, enhance their own standing. They also had appallingly low tolerance levels for sudden change, and tended to regard any minor deviation from the norm as a sign of bad faith. If they detected what they thought was a show of instability in their business contacts, even as a precautionary measure against some perceived outside threat, they might not react in a reasonable manner. And among men who traditionally settled disputes with alarming finality, the effect could be disastrous in more ways than merely financial, even this far removed.

"So what do you suggest?" He smiled coldly, and made the sign of a gun with his forefinger and thumb, adding a cocking sound. "Where I come from, it would be a simple matter. No more Gillivray."

Radnor gave him a baleful look, but for once, did not discount the idea out of hand. He finally shook his head. "It's risky. This is Harrow – not Kabul."

If Michael minded this reference to his past employment with the Soviet security forces, he gave no sign. "OK. So I deal with Palmer instead. Nobody would know."

"That wouldn't work, either. The solicitors would simply hire someone else. Before we knew it, we'd have even more people nosing around – someone we didn't know."

"Then our options are limited."

"I know. I know." Radnor stood up to pull on his jacket, and picked up his briefcase. He walked over to the door. When he spoke again, he sounded calmer. "I have to go to Hayes to inspect the latest shipment."

Michael nodded with a smile, recognising that it was going to be left to him to come up with a solution to their problem. Radnor merely needed to be persuaded into saying so. "What are you saying?"

Radnor shrugged, the final act of hand-washing. "Do what you think best."

Michael waited ten minutes after Radnor had gone, running over the range of options available to him. He dismissed them one by one, invariably coming back to the same idea that had been building ever since the Palmer problem had shown up. Then he stood up and left the office, locking the door carefully behind him. He walked down the back stairs, footsteps echoing on the tiled floor, and emerged by the twin doors to the loading bay. The space was clear except for a collection of packaging material, a strapping machine and some spare pallets. The area wasn't much used except by him and Radnor, so he was accustomed to coming here without bumping into anyone save the occasional security guard doing his rounds.

He opened one of the twin doors and stepped out on to the raised bay, scanning the car park and the street beyond. It was quiet out here. There were one or two vehicles in their bays, indicating that some of the building's tenants were still at work, but that was all. It was something to be mindful of.

His eyes lit on a silver Audi TT parked with its nose to the building. He checked the registration number against a scrap of paper in his pocket. Satisfied it was the one he was looking for, he walked down the concrete steps to the parking level, pausing to check that he was not being observed. The angle here was such that only someone leaning out of an upstairs window would see him, although the chance of that happening was remote. True, there was always the chance appearance of a tenant going to a car. That might be a problem, depending on how late it was. But he could adapt to suit the circumstances; it was what he was good at.

He stepped up close to the Audi. It was Gillivray's car, a gleaming, highly-polished toy, and carried enough optional extras and gadgets, such as an impressively obvious satellite navigation screen, to show the man believed in conspicuous wealth. He shook his head at the stupidity of some people. Men like Gillivray deserved to fail.

Taking out his door keys, he took another look around. This had to look real, in case he couldn't finish it this evening. He jabbed the keys viciously into the Audi's wing, gouging a deep line into the paintwork just above the rear offside wheel. The bay next to it was empty, and the anyone seeing the damage would assume the departing vehicle had clipped the Audi as it reversed out.

Satisfied, he went back upstairs, but instead of returning to the office on the first floor, he continued on up to the sixth level and pressed the bell outside the Stairwell Management suite. Through the glass, a young woman was just slipping her bag over her shoulder and flicking off switches ready to leave. She paused and buzzed him in.

"Hi," he said smoothly. "Does anyone here drive an Audi TT?" He made a show of glancing at a piece of paper in his hand and read off the Audi's registration number, although he now knew it by heart.

The girl nodded. "Yes, that's Mr Gillivray's car. Is there a problem?"

Michael shrugged. "Well, not for me, exactly. But somebody just hit it and I thought he'd like to know. I work downstairs, by the way. Nasty scrape… such a pity with a beautiful car like that."

The girl's mouth made an O, and she bent and pressed a button on the switchboard panel. When a gruff voice answered, she said, "Doug? There's a man here from downstairs, name of…?" she looked up at Michael expectantly.

"It's Mike," he said.

"His name's Mike, and he says somebody's hit your car."

There was a muffled curse, and she put the phone down and looked at Michael with a grimace. "Oops, doesn't sound like he's too happy. He loves that car."

"I'm sure," said Michael sympathetically. "I wouldn't be happy, either."

Seconds later, a short, stocky man bustled into the reception area, his face thunderous and ready for trouble. He was dressed in a flashy suit and a loud tie, which seemed to fit with Michael's idea of the over-optioned vehicle in the car park downstairs. "What's this about my car?" he demanded, and fixed Michael with a suspicious glare. "Who hit it – did you see?"

Michael deflected the none-too-subtle accusation with ease, wondering if the man knew how, in other circumstances, he would have received immediate retaliation. However, he'd been prepared for this reaction; it made what he'd planned all the more enjoyable. "I'm afraid not. I just noticed the damage, that's all. If it was my car, I'd want to know about it." He smiled sympathetically, and wondered how long it would take for the receptionist to decide to go home. "I could show you, if you like? Maybe act as a witness for the insurance claim."

Gillivray looked surprised by his generosity, but nodded eagerly. "Sure. Why not? Let me get my jacket."

"Doug." The receptionist stepped forward and pointed to her watch. "Do you mind if I go? I'll miss my train. Everybody else has left."

"Of course. You go," said Gillivray, flapping a vague hand. "I'll lock up, don't worry." He turned back to Michael. "Hang on, will you, um… Mike?"

"Sure." Michael smiled easily. An empty office, no witnesses. This was going to be easier than he'd thought. "Take your time – I'm in no hurry."

He stepped across to the door and opened it for the young woman, then closed it carefully behind her. He waited until she stepped into the lift and the doors closed, then he turned and followed the stocky figure of Gillivray along the corridor.

10

The man whose name and phone number Riley had found on a card in Palmer's Rolodex was waiting for her in the foyer of the Mandeville Hotel, just off Wigmore Street in London's West End. Charlie, who did not offer his surname, was a former army colleague of Palmer's. Riley had never met him before, but his appearance fitted his own description: pale, thinning and out of condition, all brought on by too much work, a killer mortgage and a serious lack of sunlight, something which went with his job as a civil servant. She was aware that his job description wasn't quite as bland as he made out, and that he had some connections with the security authorities, so was therefore to be approached cautiously. But he was a friend of Palmer's and that was enough for her.

He had agreed with a mild show of reluctance to meet her for coffee, but on the condition that it was away from his normal place of work in Whitehall. Riley recalled Palmer once describing his friend as one of the Ministry of Defence's tunnel rats working in military records, and therefore security-conscious by instinct and training rather than paranoia.

She knew Palmer had once used him to check on some military personnel records when they had first worked together investigating a gangland feud - the investigation that had led to her meeting Mitcheson.

She nodded at Charlie and sat down across from him.

"Miss Gavin."

"Call me Riley, please."

He was about to speak, but stopped as a couple of guests

dropped into armchairs just across the foyer within ear-shot. He glanced towards the door and gestured behind him. "There's a bar in back. It's quieter there. We can talk."

Riley followed him through to a bar, which was deserted except for a yawning young man in a waistcoat and black uniform trousers, polishing a wine glass with a cloth. He clamped his mouth shut with a muttered apology and put down the cloth and glass.

Charlie looked questioningly at Riley, who said, "Coffee, please. I need the caffeine."

He placed their order and joined her at a corner table. He sat facing the doorway, then leaned on his elbows and looked at her. "Frank speaks very highly of you. What's up?"

Riley was surprised by his directness, but appreciated him getting to the point. It was better than going round the conversational houses and wasting time on banalities. It also sounded about as close to approval as she could get.

"I might be jumping the gun," she began, already feeling foolish at dragging Charlie away from his desk. "But I'm worried about Palmer. I've been trying to get hold of him for a couple of days, but his mobile's switched off. I've checked his office and flat, but there's no trace of him."

Charlie sat back as the bartender brought a pot of coffee and put it on the table, along with milk and sugar. When he was out of earshot, the former army man said, "Could be he's on a tricky job. You know Frank – he goes into operational mode sometimes. Or maybe he's got a new girlfriend. It happens – even to Frank."

"I'd have known. Believe me."

Charlie poured coffee for them both and stirred sugar into his own cup. She caught him taking a surreptitious glance at his watch. "What makes you think there's anything to worry about? He's been OK otherwise, hasn't he? Not ill, I mean?"

Riley bit back a retort that she wouldn't be wasting her time here if she thought he was lying in a hospital somewhere. Charlie, after all, was merely reacting the way any reasonable person would. Which, on the face of it, was more than she was doing. And how many days had Palmer been out of contact? She shook her head doggedly. "I'd have known about that, too." When he looked doubtful, she explained, "Love and illness to some people aren't very different. Anyway, Palmer's not that much of a dark horse. If he was unwell, I'd have spotted it. He's a man, and you lot don't hide your problems as well as you think."

Charlie grunted good-naturedly. "Point noted. So what do you know for sure?"

She told him about her visit to Palmer's flat, which revealed he had not checked his mail for a couple of days. She also described her impressions of his office. "I got the feeling someone had been in there recently. Someone other than Palmer, I mean."

Charlie looked sceptical about both, but she sensed he was wary of upsetting her by being too dismissive.

"Palmer doesn't do horticulture," she said, after describing the state of the pot plant. "He'd only water that damned thing if I was standing over him with a gun. Yet the soil was damp, and someone had cleaned up afterwards. I know you army boys can be fastidious, but this is Frank we're talking about. And he doesn't employ a cleaner."

He said nothing for a long while, idly drumming with his thumb on the table. "OK. So he hasn't been home in a while, nor checked his mail. He's not at his office, yet he's either broken the habits of a lifetime by watering a pot plant you bought him, or somebody did it for him while he's away. Is that it?"

Riley felt ridiculous hearing it laid out in such stark

terms. "God, you make it sound so wet. I'm sorry." She began to think that she'd been too quick to cry wolf. What the hell was Charlie going to say to Palmer when they met up next?

"Don't be," he replied, surprising her. "It's the mundane that often hides something. If the fact that he's not shown up is unusual, then where is he?" He puffed out his cheeks. "Anything else strike you as unusual? Daft or not," he added kindly. "Makes no difference."

It was sufficient to make Riley grasp at her last straw. "Only that his computer was switched off."

Amazingly, Charlie frowned. "Bloody hell. That is unusual."

"Are you taking the mick?" She glared at him, but he raised a defensive hand.

"No, straight up. That's Frank – he never switches anything off. At least, he never bloody did it when I worked with him. He was always walking out and leaving electric fires on. I told him he'd have a blaze on his hands one day, but it never made any difference. What else?"

"His office looks dusty. OK, it's always dusty, but this is worse than usual – especially the desk. At least when he's there it gets stirred up a bit. I don't think he's been in since I dropped him back three days ago. And Palmer enjoys sitting at his desk, especially for his morning coffee. It's one of his... his things." She felt disloyal, describing this as if it was some odd quirk of his character that was best left unsaid. But Charlie merely nodded, eyebrows floating upwards.

She described how her card had fallen out of the Rolodex; that it hadn't bothered her before, but thinking about it now, why would Palmer have needed to look at her card? He knew the details by heart.

"And he'd had a woman visitor recently. I could smell

the perfume. And before you say a girlfriend, this was an older woman's scent. Sickly sweet. Expensive."

Charlie sipped the last of his coffee. "Could be a suspicious wife wanting a round-the-clock check on an errant hubby who travels. That'd certainly keep Frank busy enough. Standard work for someone in his line of business. Maybe he got a friend or neighbour to pop in to water the plant. Does Frank know any older women who like gardening?"

"I've no idea. I doubt it. The other thing is, a local shop-keeper mentioned seeing a large car out front the other evening. He said a tall black man with dreadlocks went in first, followed by an older woman. He couldn't see enough detail for a description, though, and couldn't swear that they went into the office."

"Could have been anyone." Charlie pushed his cup away. "Pity you haven't got more. I mean, you and I might think it's odd, but it's a bit thin."

Riley thought about the business at the office block where Palmer had seen the familiar face from his past. She still wasn't convinced it was anything other than coincidence, but in her experience, it was ignoring the apparent nothings which often led to mistakes.

"There's one other thing." She told Charlie about their visit to the office in Harrow, and Palmer's reaction. "It was immediately after seeing some men in the lift. He got slightly weird after that, and went quiet on me. When I asked him about it, he said he'd had a flashback. *A ghost* was the term he used. He tried to brush it off after that, but he didn't sound convincing."

"And that's it?"

"Yes. I don't know if it's connected, but I found this in his office." She took out the sheet of paper from Palmer's office notepad and unfolded it. Seeing it now, it simply looked like a sheet of paper covered in doodles, and she wanted to snatch it back.

Charlie scanned the sheet, eyes flicking across the doodles. When he reached the bottom, he went very still.

"What is it?"

He shook his head. "Dunno. 'Sgt' is an abbreviation for sergeant. 'Reg' could be short for regulation. But 'Paris'? There's only two of those that I know of: one in Texas, the other in France. Frank has been to neither, as far as I know, unless it was on a dirty weekend."

"What about Meiningen? I haven't had a chance to check, but could it be a place name?"

Charlie nodded and folded the paper, sliding it into his inside pocket. Something in the casual way he did so made Riley feel uneasy.

"What? What is it?"

But his face was expressionless. "It sounds German. Frank spent some time over there, that's all. I'll look into it."

She realised that was all she was going to get out of him and decided not to press him further. "I feel disloyal talking to you like this," she said, wondering if he thought her actions were crossing some invisible line of confidentiality between colleagues. "Like it's private."

"Rubbish," Charlie replied bluntly. "Just because Frank's a secretive, obstinate git, doesn't mean we have to be." He chewed his lip. "This Gillivray character you called on in Harrow: could he have got heavy with Frank for dropping papers on him? Gone after him, I mean?"

"I don't know. I doubt it. Frank didn't seem worried. He said he was a low-level conman, but maybe there's more to him than that." Riley ran through the possibilities in her mind. She hadn't given the idea any serious thought, principally because Palmer had seemed so relaxed about it. She was pretty sure that if he'd thought there was a chance of heavy retaliation, he never would have involved her.

"You're probably right." Charlie glanced at his watch and said: "I've got to go." He levered himself out of his seat and smoothed down the front of his jacket. "Look, don't worry. I'm sure Frank's OK. But I'll see what I can' come up with. If you think of anything else, give me a call." He dug out a card and scribbled down a phone number. "That's my mobile. If he turns up in the meantime, give him hell."

He gave a reassuring smile and disappeared through a side door into the street.

Later, Riley was in her flat finishing some preparatory notes on the annual migration of fruit pickers and their gang masters, when her phone rang. It was Charlie. The sound of traffic was heavy in the background, accompanied by the noise of a roller door closing nearby and the harsh clatter of a motorbike engine.

"You should go into business with Frank full-time," he told her. "You've got a good eye for detail."

Riley felt her stomach tense. "How do you mean?"

"Those doodles you found on the notepad in Frank's office. I fed the words into a database, and came up with some hits. By themselves, the words meant exactly what we thought they did, which was 'sergeant', 'regulation' and the French capital. Meiningen is a small town in what was eastern Germany, just over the border."

"Oh. I wondered if it might be significant."

"It might well be, but I haven't figured out why yet. I'm sure I've heard of it before, but it could be through work stuff. When I put the words together, I still got a lot of odd hits, but then one connection jumped off the screen at me.

There was no link to Meiningen, but the most obvious hit for the others was that in February 'eighty-nine, a Sergeant Reginald Paris, RMP, was killed in an RTA on the autobahn near Frankfurt. That's about the same time Frank was in Germany."

Sgt. Reg. Paris. It explained the notes Palmer had made. Riley said, "He must have served with him. But why would he be thinking about him now?"

"No idea. Before my time, I'm afraid. I was hoping there would be some notes to go with it, but there's nothing other than the report of the death. The bloke's officially dead – recorded and confirmed."

"Could there have been a mistake?" Riley's immediate thought was that Reg Paris and the man in Harrow were one and the same, wild as that sounded to her. But Charlie's response seemed to counter it.

"I doubt it. The army doesn't make mistakes like that, not when it comes to paying out pensions and stuff."

"How did it happen?" Riley wondered if Palmer had been involved, which might explain his reference to ghosts.

"His car was totalled by a Merc transporter travelling in the same direction. The report says Paris was driving a pool Opel and must have wandered across the lanes, like he'd fallen asleep. Some of those pool cars weren't that good; they got hammered to a standstill, mostly, so there wouldn't have been any speed under the foot, see, to get out of the way. The truck couldn't stop and went through him like wet paper. The civil cops had to make the identification from army records. It couldn't have been pretty."

"Was anyone else killed?"

"No. He was travelling solo."

11

Walter Unger was a tall, slight man in his late fifties with glossy, grey hair and perfectly tanned skin. He was dressed in a green waxed jacket, corduroy trousers and brown brogues, and in spite of the rolling German countryside behind him, looked more British Home Counties than mainland European. He was puffing on a small cigar and leaning against a dark blue BMW parked in a lay-by.

Palmer cut the engine of his rental car and climbed out, easing his shoulders with a wince of relief. He was stiff after the flight from Heathrow and the long drive from Frankfurt airport, and pleased to be on his feet again. It had been a while since he'd driven any distance on the right and still had not adjusted. He glanced around and breathed in deeply, relishing the fresh air. The scenery was lush and green, and looked very different from when he had last been here. The sun had broken through the cloud and he caught a flash of reflected light in the distance. From his mental map, he guessed it was over by the former East German town of Meiningen.

"Mr Palmer." Unger stepped forward to greet him with an outstretched hand. "I recognise you from the photo you emailed me. My apologies for that little precaution, but it helps avoid… problems. We live in uncertain times, after all."

His English was impeccable, displaying only a trace of an accent, something that had been more pronounced over the phone. Palmer's surprise must have showed, because the German smiled and explained: "I did a language course at Oxford. I gained five kilos, a love of English beer and, so

I'm told, an accent which has served me well with British and American clients." He chuckled at his good fortune and gestured with his cigar out across the open countryside behind him, where the fields and dark shadows of woods rolled away to the horizon. "This is the area you said you were interested in seeing. You would need to have been born here to see precisely where the border used to be, but I understand you have a good idea, anyway."

"It's changed a lot."

Unger nodded energetically. "That's correct. For the better, I have to say. The farm you mentioned is still here, of course. Still owned by the same family." He reached in his coat pocket and consulted a notebook, although Palmer suspected he had the details memorised by heart. "The current owner is Oscar Hemmricht. He is the son of the original owner. He was a boy here back then and has agreed to speak to you." He looked up, his face serious. "There is still a problem here for people to be easily open, Mr Palmer. Too much history, too much suspicion. So I don't think we need to worry too much about this matter being discussed widely by anyone else. Memories are still fresh with the way things were. The towers and the wire may have gone, but there are still shadows. And some ghosts, too."

"You mean I shouldn't jump in with both feet," said Palmer.

"Well, if you do," said Unger dryly, "make sure they land softly. I've already prepared the way with a brief explanation about what you are seeking, but if you will allow me to make the introductions first, then I'll step back and let you get on with it." He turned and reached into the BMW and handed Palmer a buff folder. "This is all the information I managed to discover about the incident you mentioned. It is not much, but I cannot say I am surprised; not all such incidents were recorded as well as they should have been." His expression suggested that such carelessness was an unfortunate product of the times. "It gives us the name of the person who died, and a little of his history from justice ministry files. He was under suspicion, which may explain his actions."

"You've gone to a great deal of trouble." Palmer was referring to the fact that Unger had indicated over the phone that he would not be seeking a fee for his assistance, merely a consideration of any future business Palmer could put his way. It was a remarkably generous offer, and one Palmer wasn't about to turn down.

"Not at all. This was a small amount of work for me. I am keen to build up my business internationally, and would welcome any introductions you can make. Besides…" He smiled and cocked his head to one side. "I am also intrigued, and it is a change from my usual work. Legal transactions can be so boring."

"Fair enough. I'll see what I can do. For now, you might like to contact this man." He handed Unger Donald Brask's card. "He's in the information business. I'll recommend your name."

Unger nodded gratefully. "That is very kind."

"No problem. How does this business about the border sit with you?" He had already explained in cautious terms what he remembered from when he was here, but had left out certain things he felt Unger did not need to know.

"As a lawyer, you mean, or a German?" Unger shrugged, seeming to read his mind. "The same. You have an interest in a matter related to what happened here in 'eighty-nine. I'm guessing you have not told me everything, but I understand that. All lawyers deal in half-details and economies of the truth. For myself, if we tried to address every incident that happened in this country over the past decades, we'd

71

all run out of time and friends. What I hear today stays with me. Believe me, I have enough to do elsewhere." He nodded towards a low huddle of buildings in the distance. "That's the farm you mentioned, and beyond it in the distance is Henneberg. We proceed along this road for half a kilometre before turning left. The track is OK, but you should take it easy." He nodded and climbed into his car, flicking away his cigar as he did so.

Up close, the farm seemed neater than the vague glimpse Palmer remembered from years ago, and showed signs of recent rebuilding. New farm machinery stood in a large barn to one side of the main house, and a few cows were clustered in a paddock surrounded by a modern run of freshly painted wooden fencing. The overall impression was of improvements being made gradually, now that the looming shadows of the wires and border towers were no longer cast over the land.

The two men had barely climbed from their cars when the door to the house opened and a young man appeared, squinting in the sunlight. He had obviously been awaiting their arrival.

Unger made polite and careful introductions. Oscar Hemmricht was tall, rawboned and dressed in a check shirt and heavy work pants. He looked carefully at Palmer before shaking hands, then invited them both to sit at a heavy kitchen table, while he poured fresh coffee from a cafetière.

"He does not speak English," said Unger. "Sorry – I should have said. Obviously, I'll translate for you, unless…?"

"I'd be grateful." Palmer's German was passable, but not for this kind of thing. There was too much danger of missing something important, and Unger would be better able to judge how things were going if he was involved first-hand.

Unger spoke for a few minutes, during which Palmer picked up references to the *Volkspolitzei* – the border police – and the *Ost* – the East. Oscar Hemmricht listened, nodding and occasionally looking at Palmer, then cleared his throat and asked a question.

"He wants to know if you were here before," said Unger. "He says you have the look of the military."

"Yes," replied Palmer, looking directly at the farmer. There was no benefit in avoiding the truth. "I was a military police-man in 'eighty-nine. I came out to this place with a colleague when the shooting was reported. It was the only time."

Oscar nodded but said nothing, so Palmer decided to ask him a direct question. "Your father ran this farm back then, is that correct, Herr Hemmricht?"

Hemmricht spoke and Unger translated: the old man had died five years ago of pneumonia, leaving the farm to his only son. It was a good farm now, with more land and lots of opportunity, but still difficult to make it pay.

"Were you all here on the night of the shooting?"

Hemmricht frowned and shook his head. "No, we were asked to leave two days before."

"You recall that period, then?" Palmer felt a sense of relief. At least it wasn't a complete non-starter. He'd been worried the man would draw a complete blank.

"Of course. Very little happened here." Unger conveyed the farmer's wry shrug. "I was a boy... these things were interesting. What do you want to know?"

"Did anyone say why you had to leave?"

"A man came. From the British. There was a military exercise coming through, and so close to the border there were dangers for civilians. My father was not pleased, because of the farm, but he agreed to go. They said it was the law."

Unger looked sour at what he plainly saw as a misuse of military and local powers at the time, and explained: "What they meant was, they did not want to risk having to pay compensation if anyone got hurt. It was probably cheaper to pay for the family to stay in a spa thirty kilometres away until the exercise was over."

"Really? I've never heard of that happening before."

"Nor me," said Unger.

Palmer said nothing, but watched Hemmricht's body language as Unger was translating. The man kept shooting nervous glances at him and curling his roughened hands around his coffee cup. Palmer thought he might be holding something back, but Unger appeared not to have noticed. He asked one more question to make absolutely sure.

"Did you keep animals here back then?"

Hemmricht nodded and held up his hands, fingers spread, happy to be on safe ground once more. "Nine cows," confirmed Unger. "And a few chickens. They did not have much."

Palmer smiled before saying casually, "And you fed them on the night of the shooting?"

Unger looked surprised, but put the statement to the farmer. Hemmricht, in turn, became guarded, and there was a heavy silence, during which Palmer kept his gaze firmly on him. Eventually the man sighed and spoke briefly and Unger translated. "He says he was here. How do you know this?"

"Because his father had been here since he was a boy, am I right?"

"Yes."

"And no British army exercise was going to be allowed to risk what few animals they had in the world. So the old man told his son to stay behind and lie low while the exercise passed by, and to make sure the animals were fed and watered. I'm no farmer, but it's what I would have done."

Unger translated, then looked at Palmer. "He says you are correct. His father was very insistent that the animals should not be left alone. Two cows were in calf, and the money from the calves was important to them." He paused, then said apologetically. "He says his father did not trust the soldiers."

"But there was no British army exercise, was there? I'm only guessing, but I think I would have known about it at the time. I was a military policeman and it would have been my job to know. There was nothing."

Unger's translation received no response from the farmer, save for a pulse beating in his throat.

"What did he see?" Palmer insisted softly. "Tell him there will be no recriminations. I would like to see justice done, that's all. To put right a serious wrongdoing."

Unger spoke again, and Hemmricht got up and refreshed their coffees, then sat down again. He avoided their eyes, but as he spoke, it was clear that the passage of time had not diminished the strength of his boyhood memories.

The farmhouse and adjacent buildings were in darkness. He had been awakened by the sound of an engine moving along the track from the road, heading towards the border area. Speaking softly to calm the animals, he had peered out through a crack in the wooden side of the barn, but all he could see was a set of headlights bouncing along in the dark. He couldn't understand why any car would be going over there at this time of night; it was just a track to some fields. Beyond that was the border and the open expanse of ground where only motorised and dog patrols and the truly desperate ever set foot. Not even the game birds seemed to congregate there, as if recognising the inherent dangers posed by man. He decided the vehicle must be an advance party for the military exercise they had been told about, although it was surprisingly close to the border. Even as a boy, he was aware of the tensions surrounding where they lived.

He had never seen an exercise before, although he had heard tell of the vast array of tanks and personnel and, being a boy, was curious to see the soldiers. There was a dry ditch running in a zigzag fashion from the farm over towards where the car had stopped, where he sometimes used to take his dog, rooting for rabbits and rats. Although close to the border, it was safe as long as he did not venture beyond it. He considered it now. It was easily deep enough to hide in, so he slipped from the barn and crept along it until he was as close as he dared go. Then he settled down to watch.

He waited for two hours, during which the car's lights went out and nothing stirred. An occasional sound came from the border tower, the sharp bark from a dog or a laugh from one of the guards, but beyond that, nothing. No tanks, no armoured carriers, no trucks, no jeeps, no flares. Perhaps, he thought, they had taken a wrong turning. Not a good sign for a military exercise.

He had fallen asleep for a while, he explained, until dawn began to tinge the horizon. It was bitterly cold, but he was accustomed to it. The cows in the barn started to shuffle around, and he was on the point of going back to feed them, when he noticed movement by the vehicle. Three men, he said, got out and were looking towards the wire and the open ground. It was as if they were waiting for somebody. One of them had a long object hanging from his shoulder – a bag of some kind.

Then he spotted a flicker of movement in the one place he had not expected it, in the area his father had once called the killing ground. He recalled his father impressing on him that only the truly desperate came through the wire, and their chances of survival were almost nil. He rubbed his eyes and peered through the gloom, and made out the figure of a man inching forward out of a thin scattering of brushwood, right on the border by the fence. He couldn't see any detail, but the man must have been there for a while. It was amazing that he had not been seen or heard by the guards. He guessed the man had crossed to the halfway point just after dusk, when there was a changeover of guards and the chances of being seen were reduced by the fading light.

When he looked over at the three men again, the one with the bag had slipped it from his shoulder and was tugging at one end. Then he realised what it was. His father used to have one just like it. It was a canvas rifle bag.

There was a movement by the fence. He watched in amazement as the man coming from the East suddenly jumped to his feet and began to run, his body crouched over like someone very old. Yet he ran quickly, although it could not have been easy over the rough ground.

With his heart pumping, Hemmricht had glanced at the tower, and saw that the guard had turned away, his head thrown back in a yawn. Then he saw movement from the three men, and saw that the one with the rifle was taking aim. But before anything could happen, there was a shout and a searchlight light came on. There were shots and the runner fell down. He did not get up again.

Hemmricht stopped speaking. There was a long silence, during which the three men sat looking anywhere but at each other.

Unger was the first to voice his thoughts. "It's crazy!" he

whispered. "The man with the rifle was going to open fire on the border guard? What madness! I've never heard of such a thing. It would have started an international incident!" He shook his head at the enormity of the situation and fell silent, clearly unable to voice the potential for disaster that had come so close.

"I don't think so," said Palmer, who had been watching Hemmricht all the while Unger was speaking. The young farmer was clearly still disturbed by what he had witnessed, and was shifting in his seat with barely suppressed agitation. No doubt having to relive those scenes was stirring up unwelcome memories. Then Hemmricht nodded emphatically and said something, stabbing his finger in the air, and Unger looked even more shocked.

"The man with the rifle wasn't going to shoot the border guard, was he?" said Palmer, guessing what the farmer had said. He looked directly at Hemmricht for confirmation. "What do you think he was going to do?"

For the first time, Hemmricht seemed to understand fully without needing Unger's intervention, and gave a loud sigh. It was as if the information was long overdue and he could now finally let it go. He stared down at his hands with an air of deep sadness, and when he finally spoke, Palmer needed no translation.

"*Ya.* He was aiming the rifle right at him. At the running man. I think the man with the gun was there to shoot him as he came across. But he didn't need to."

Palmer nodded and thought back to the face he had seen in Harrow. Then he realised something that sent a dart of ice right through him. It was something he hadn't even given a thought to. Palmer had recognised the man immediately, even after all these years. But what if the man had recognised him, too? If so, given what he had just heard, then he and Riley might be in more danger than they could possibly know.

He excused himself and took his phone outside, where he dialled Riley's number. Engaged. He waited a few minutes and tried again. Still engaged. He rang Donald Brask, this time getting an answer, but the signal died before he could say anything. He swore and went back inside to finish the interview with Hemmricht.

Thirty minutes later, he was on his way back to Frankfurt airport, having said his goodbyes to Unger and Hemmricht. But it wasn't until he was walking through the departure lounge that he was finally able to leave a warning message for Riley. He hoped it wasn't too late.

12

Riley tried Palmer's mobile again, followed by Charlie's number, but both were switched off. It was probably too early to be chasing Charlie, anyway. Unlike Riley or Palmer, Charlie was constrained by layers of officialdom, prone to conducting audits on the movements and workings of its officers just in case one of them might be toiling away diligently on overthrowing the elected government of the day or trying to steal the keys to the tea money. Charlie would get to whatever information he could dig up, she figured, when he got to it and not before. She hoped it was sooner rather than later.

She called Donald, but he had no news, either. Eventually, concentration eluding her, she closed her laptop, threw on some jeans and a suede jacket and picked up her car keys. When all else failed in an investigation and the dots didn't link up, you went back to the beginning and started again. Palmer's favourite dictum.

"See you later, cat," she told the sleeping animal in passing. But it ignored her. No support there, then.

She made her way across north London and found a parking space a short walk from Gillivray's office. The weather was warm but blustery, and she wondered what it was doing wherever Palmer was.

The same security man was on duty behind the desk, a copy of the *Sun* spread out before him. The foyer was deserted. She nodded and approached the desk, and watched his face working through the process of recognition.

"Morning, Miss," he said neutrally, and opened the visitor's book for her. She wondered if the fact that his other hand was resting by the phone on the desk was mere coincidence or a touch of paranoia on her part. She'd soon find out.

"Do you remember me?" she asked him.

He nodded. "Of course. Three days ago, wasn't it? You were here with the gentleman. An appointment with Stairwell Management, I believe. Floor six, Miss...?" He waited, eyebrows raised.

"Gavin," Riley supplied instinctively. "Riley Gavin."

He spun the book round and flicked through the pages, then nodded again with a dry smile. "If you say so, miss. You and Mr Gavin, was it?"

His tone was pointed enough to make Riley look at him. "I'm sorry?"

He placed a finger on the page, and when she saw the way Palmer had filled in the boxes, understood why.

"Oh." Damn Palmer. She hadn't thought to check what he'd written. It was a squiggle, like a doctor's writing, only less decipherable. But certainly not Gavin.

The man waited for her to speak. When he saw she wasn't going to, he asked, "How can I help you, miss?"

On the way here, Riley had rehearsed what she was going to say. She had concocted a plausible-sounding story about fraud and identity theft: one that, in her own mind, had him hanging on her every word and eager to help. Now, faced with the man's austere look and the realisation that Palmer had not given their names, it all seemed so unlikely, she fell at the first fence. She wondered how she could explain it. Was he looking at her with just more than professional interest, or was she simply suffering from an attack of the wimps? Oh, what the hell, she thought. How about telling him the truth? Well, part of it, anyway.

"My... colleague," she began, "said you were in the army. Is that right?"

"That's correct, miss. Royal Artillery. Twenty-three years. Him, too, I'd guess?" His questioning tone lobbed the ball fairly back into Riley's court. She had been hoping to skirt round exactly what Palmer had done, but there was no way to bluff her way past this man. She had a feeling he might simply see right through it and toss her out on her ear.

"Yes. But he was an MP."

His eyebrows went up a fraction, but instead of the hostility she'd been expecting from a former soldier, he grunted and gave a ghost of a smile. "I should have known. My brother was a Redcap, too." He pulled a mock-sad face. "He always was the divvy of the family. How can I help?"

Riley experienced a rush of relief mixed with astonishment. "What is it with you guys?" she asked. He looked puzzled, and she went on, "Do you have some kind of secret code between you, like masons?"

He rocked on his heels. "You mean the army thing?" He shrugged. "Never thought about it. Takes one to know one, I suppose." He stood up and beckoned Riley to follow him across to the window, where he stood with his arms folded, facing the lifts. "OK, so what were you doing here?" he said softly. "You and the Redcap?"

"The truth?"

"It's a good start." He gave an encouraging smile. "The name's Nobby, by the way."

Riley took a deep breath. There was nothing else for it. She described the three men they had seen in the lift, and Palmer's strange reaction. She followed this by relating how, alarmingly out of character, he had subsequently dropped out of sight.

"You think something happened to him?"

"No. At least, not the way you mean." Riley blinked. She hadn't even thought along those lines. "Frank's too... solid.

He's always watching his back."

"Fair enough. So why come back here? You think he's in the area?"

She shook her head. "If he is, we won't see him. I was just trying to figure out if his… reaction was anything to do with the men he saw in the lift, that's all. I keep thinking about it, and it all seems to stem from there. I thought maybe you'd know something about the people, so I could figure out what was going on."

Nobby shook his head. "Can't help you there, I'm afraid." He raised a placatory hand. "Not because I don't want to – I've only been here a couple of weeks, so I haven't got to grips with the place yet." He seemed to consider his words carefully, then continued: "There's only ever three of them go up to the first floor – mostly an older chap and a pasty-faced Russian. There's a tall fella comes and goes, but he's some sort of accountant or book-keeper. The other office on that floor is vacant. "

"Did you say Russian?" Riley was surprised.

"Yes. Well, something like that, anyway. He has the look about him. A cold fish. The other fella's British, although he looks like he spends a lot of time on the sunbed."

"What's their company called?"

"Azimtec Trading. No idea what the Azimtec stands for, but they get parcels into the loading bay at the back about once a week, then ship them out again. That's all I know, I'm afraid." He paused. "This may seem a daft question, but your colleague, Frank, is he on the level?"

Riley looked him in the eye. "I'd trust him any time, no question. Why?"

"Because the Russian fella was down here, asking about him. And you."

Riley felt the ground shift beneath her feet. It was the last thing she had expected to hear. What on earth could have prompted one of the men to ask about her and Palmer? Unless...

"What did he say?"

"He wanted to know who your friend was and why he was here. Then he realised you were together." Nobby looked pained. "Sorry – that was my fault. I couldn't tell him your names, though, but I had to tell him you were visiting floor six."

It was Riley's turn to look sheepish. "I'm sorry. Did we get you in trouble?"

He waved a hand. "Nothing I can't handle."

"Did he say why he was interested in us?"

"No."

"Oh. Are Azimtec and Stairwell connected, do you know?"

"No, not from the way he was talking. He asked me what they did. I told him they were into various things."

She was about to thank him and leave when he said, "Hang on a second." He walked back to the desk, dug out a piece of paper and a pen from a drawer and scribbled something down.

"You need to speak to my predecessor, Jimmy Gough. He knows everything there is to know about this place. And he's got no love for that lot up there. They kicked him out on the pretext of his age. He's sixty-seven, but the truth is he's a damned sight fitter than I am. Personally, I think they're control freaks; they like to know who's who." He handed Riley the scrap of paper. "I'll let Jimmy know you're coming. He has lunch every day at the Gold Platter. It's a greasy spoon about half a mile from here. Not bad if you're into the Atkins diet, but don't touch the shepherd's pie. Tell him if he doesn't help, I'll tell my sister." He gave her a wicked smile. "He's a bit soft on her, see. Scared, too.

84

She's a big girl is Eileen."

The Gold Platter was the kind of establishment that would have had a professional nutritionist foaming at the mouth. The windows were heavily steamed from top to bottom and displayed a range of signs offering almost anything, it seemed to Riley, as long as you liked chips. The *plat du jour* was an all-day breakfast. It was cheap and simple, which probably explained why it was so busy.

Jimmy Gough was a short, heavily built man with close-cropped hair and a shiny face, and he appeared to occupy the corner table as if he had been born there. He was neatly dressed in the manner of many former serviceman of his era, and stood up as soon as Riley approached.

"Pleased to meet you, Riley," said Jimmy, when she introduced herself, and gestured with a nod towards a phone on the wall, beneath a large sign advertising a Pensioners' Special. "Nobby called to say you were coming. You fancy a cup of something?" He pointed to his own mug and signalled to the girl behind the counter to bring another one. "It's nothing special, I'm afraid, but it'll kill most known household germs. I come in here because the grub's cheap." He sat back down. "Nobby said you needed some dope on the people at Azimtec."

"That's right. I'm not interrupting your lunch, am I?"

"Nah. Just finished." He smiled and looked round at the other patrons, most of them men around the same age, and all trying to pretend they weren't ferociously intrigued by Riley's meeting with Jimmy. He leaned forward and confided softly: "I have to say, love, you coming here to see me is doing my street cred no end of good. The minute you're gone, these buggers'll be all over me like a rash, wanting to know who you are. Nosy lot, but I won't tell 'em nothing. Do 'em good, know what I mean?" He chuckled wickedly.

Riley smiled, warming to him, and explained why she was there. He listened carefully, nodding occasionally, holding up a hand to stop her when her tea arrived, then urging her to continue once the waitress was out of earshot.

When she had finished, he pulled a face. "Azimtec aren't the only iffy ones in that building, love. But they're the only ones who keep such a tight lid on what they do. Not that their security is that good." He sipped his tea and explained: "They import fine art from eastern Europe. At least, that's what I reckon. I've never seen much, mind, but they get lots of crates that look as if they might hold pictures and such. And I found some old frames in the skip out back one time. They'd been damaged beyond repair and chucked out. Then one night I was doing my rounds and they'd wedged the lift door open so they could bring stuff up without having to call it each trip. I stuck my head in to say they were breaking safety regs, and saw a load of packing material on the floor and a couple of icons on a table."

"Icons?"

"Yes. Nice stuff, too, though I'm no expert. I was in Berlin with the army years ago, part of the military liaison team. I got to see quite a lot of museums and suchlike in my spare time. My missus thought it might improve my mind and give me a taste for culture." He looked around the café and grinned. "Guess it didn't work, did it?"

The mention of icons reminded Riley of what Nobby had said about one of the men in Azimtec. She asked Jimmy what he thought.

"Yeah, he's right. He's either Russian or Bulgarian, but I don't know which. Calls himself Michael, but it was probably Mikhail or something like that originally. Creepy little bugger, he is. Eyes that look right through you. He walks like he's on air most of the time – you can't hear him coming. Reminds me of some of the KGB or *Stasi* bods that used to follow us when I was doing playground duty in Berlin."

Riley looked at him. "*Stasi*. The East German security service?"

Jimmy nodded sourly. "That's right. Hundreds of the buggers everywhere, like fleas on a hedgehog. Spying on us, spying on the Yanks, but most of the time spying on each other. Hell of a way to live, you ask me."

"And playground duty?"

He laughed. "Sorry. It's a trade term. We had a few kids on attachment to the embassy while I was there. Young women, mostly, in the secretarial pool. Nice girls but green as grass, most of them, and whenever they went walkabout in the city, one of us had to tag along to make sure they didn't get into trouble. The Russians and East Germans were always up to something in the hopes of compromising one of our embassy staff and getting them to turn. Honey traps they called them."

Riley felt her pulse quicken. "What about the older man – the one with the tan?"

Jimmy shook his head. "No idea, love. British, I think. He seems to be the boss man, but who knows, eh? Now what's his name?" He hesitated, screwing up his face. "Radnor, that's it. Blimey, thought my memory must be going for a second. Arthur Radnor. Strange bloke. Never says much." He sniffed derisively. "Not that I'd trust him, either. It was him or Michael who got me pushed out."

"What for?"

"Search me. It wasn't long after I spotted the icons in their office. Maybe I saw too much."

"And the tall man – the one Nobby says might be an accountant?"

"He doesn't come in very often. I don't recall his name. Nobby's right – he's a number-cruncher. Freelance, I think. Local, anyway."

Riley sipped her tea and wondered if she wasn't being dragged down a blind alley. On the surface, it didn't add up to much. Even if the creepy Michael was Russian, he was hardly the only one now living and working in London. And if they were bringing in artwork from eastern Europe – and there was nothing to say it wasn't completely legitimate – why wouldn't a Russian be involved? He could be a middle-man responsible for initiating the contacts and acquisition over there, with Radnor the salesman on this side.

"So where does all this artwork go?"

He shrugged. "Couriers come and collect it. I've never seen the labels, but I hear the States is a real hot market for that stuff. Lots of Russians over there now – stinking rich some of them, like Abramovitch, the Chelsea bloke. Maybe it reminds them of home, being able to buy up stuff from the old country instead of football clubs."

Riley took out a card and handed it to him. It might be worth looking further into it, but she still had to find out what Palmer was doing. At least now she had a name to give him.

"Thanks, Jimmy," she said gratefully. "You've been a great help."

He smiled. "No problem, love. I'm always here if you need anything else."

Aware of the interest from the other customers, Riley leaned over and gave the old man a kiss on the cheek. He immediately struggled to his feet, flushing a deep red. But his pleasure was evident in the broad smile stretched across his face.

Riley found a parking space just around the corner from her flat, and was approaching the gateway leading to the front entrance, mulling over what Jimmy had told her, when a tall figure suddenly appeared in front of her. She gave a start and stepped sideways, muttering an automatic apology. The man carried on by, showing a flash of teeth as he passed. She was barely able to take in the dreadlocks and piercing grey eyes before he was walking away with long, athletic strides, his manner gracefully unhurried.

She wondered vaguely who he had been visiting, before hurrying upstairs to see if there were any messages waiting. He was probably one of the local community outreach workers visiting Mr Grobowski. The elderly Pole was involved with various local matters. As soon as she stepped in the flat, she noticed her answer machine flashing. She hit the playback button.

It was Palmer's voice, sounding tense. The message kept breaking up, with gaps between the words. *"Riley? Sorry… bunking off…that. …few things…check urgently. Listen, I'm…back to London…man I knew…careful who…answer door…Bye."*

Among the intermittent background noise, Riley heard a two-tone chime followed by the crackle of an announcement. She wondered where Palmer was calling from. Was it a railway station? An airport? *"Back to London."* Did that mean out of the city – up north, for example? Or out of the country? And what was that about answering the door? She replayed the message a couple of times, and finally worked out what the announcement in the background was saying. It came as a surprise.

It was a woman, and she was speaking German. Damn you, Palmer – what are you up to?

Ten minutes later her mobile rang. She snatched it up, ready to tear verbal chunks off Palmer for not keeping in touch. But it was Jimmy Gough. He sounded worried.

"I thought you should know," he said without preamble, "There's been some activity at the office in Harrow."

"Activity?"

"Nobby just dropped me the nod. Asked me to pass it on. I hope your mate hasn't been back there since you last called."

"Why, what's happened?"

"A bloke named Gillivray – wasn't he the one you called on? Bit of a wheeler-dealer, if you know what I mean. Anyway, he didn't turn up for work this morning. He's usually in about mid-morning, regular. His colleagues rang down, said they were worried about him, 'cos he wasn't at home and they wanted to know if he'd rung in. Nobby said he hadn't seen the bloke, but his car was in the car park. He's got one of those fancy Audi TT jobs. Anyway, a bit later, Nobby was doing his tour of the outside, checking doors and stuff, same as usual." Jimmy's voice went flat on the final words, as if he was hoping he didn't have to finish what he was saying.

"Go on."

"He found him round the side of the building, in a soak-away. That's a gulley round the building. You'd never see it unless you walked round there. From where he was lying, it looks like your Mr Gillivray took a dive right off the sixth floor."

13

Riley thanked Jimmy for the information and immediately rang Donald Brask. After what Jimmy had just told her, a leaden feeling was growing in her stomach. This was turning into a potential disaster. First Palmer saw a ghost from his past. Then he went walkabout – to Germany, if her guess was correct. Now a man they'd called on to serve some papers, tricking their way into his office to do so, had died after plunging from a sixth-storey window. The police were going to have a field day with that one. She hoped Donald was still there; he'd know who to call to find out what was happening.

Donald answered after two rings, and she told him about Jimmy Gough's news.

Donald sounded incredulous. "And you think Palmer –?"

"No way. Why would he? Anyway, he's been somewhere across the water." She related his brief if incomplete message. "But the police will probably make the connection sooner or later. Even I could hear Gillivray shouting as Frank left his office, so plenty of others will have done. And friendly as the security man was, he'll have been forced to give them a description. Unless there was a whole procession of people that Gillivray upset that day, Palmer's probably heading the list of candidates."

"Maybe not. If he's been overseas, it might be his best alibi. Even so, I suppose it could be sticky for him. OK, sweetie, leave it with me." She could hear Donald already tapping out a number on another phone. "I'll get back to you." He disconnected, leaving her feeling strangely useless and adrift.

It was three hours before he called back. He sounded subdued. "Sorry, sweetie. I've been unable to get hold of my usual contacts. So far the police haven't issued any names or details, but they've got several leads they're looking at. That's all I could find out."

"It doesn't look like suicide, then?"

"Unlikely, from the noises they're making. There was only one clue: Gillivray was a bit of a gambler on the side. He'd booked a weekend in Monte Carlo not long before he died. You don't do that if you're considering killing yourself."

"I suppose not."

"It seems he didn't have the widest circle of friends, and owed serious money in some very murky quarters. A source inside the building told the police of two visitors within the last few days, one of whom they said had some sort of argument with Gillivray. Beyond that I couldn't find out more."

"A source? It must be the receptionist."

"Probably. When Palmer does surface, tell him to keep his head down. In the meantime, the police might stumble on who really did push Gillivray into space."

"I'll do that. You'll keep me informed?"

"Of course." Donald paused for two heartbeats. "One way or another, this story is looking as if it might have legs. I know you're concerned about Palmer, but you might bear that in mind."

Riley sighed. "Donald, you're all heart." But she knew he was right. There was a story here, even in the death of the late, probably unlamented Doug Gillivray. And if it should turn out to be connected in some way with the men on the first floor, there was no way she could ignore it. There was also the question of Donald's invaluable support; he had resources she might need to get to the bottom of this.

"So why exactly are you so interested in this Palmer guy?" Szulu glanced in the mirror and caught the eye of the woman in the back seat. They had been sitting in the car off Holland Park Avenue for over an hour, and her sickly perfume was beginning to clog up his airways. He eased down the window a fraction, grateful for the near-inaudible hum of the vehicle's electrics, and breathed in some fresh, exhaust-laden city air.

They were just down the street from a house divided into three flats. The area was quiet here, with just a few passing cars and fewer pedestrians, none of who gave the car a second glance. There was no sign of life on the two upper floors of the house they were watching, but a lot of light was spilling out from ground level. The old guy who lived there, Szulu figured, didn't have much to hide, otherwise he'd have used his curtains more. Maybe he liked living in a goldfish bowl. What was his name…? Grobowski, that was it. Polish, a shopkeeper down the street had let slip. "He done you on a deal or what?"

"The why doesn't matter," replied the woman. "I just want him found."

"Then what? Only, one thing you should know, right, I only get driver's money."

"So?" The response was a long time coming.

"So it doesn't mean I do other stuff."

"What do you mean?" The street light reflected off the woman's glasses, momentarily blanking her eyes. It made her seem sinister and unfriendly, like a large, malevolent fly.

"Breaking arms, that kind of thing." Szulu shrugged easily. "Don't mean to say I can't, right? Just that there's a rate for the job." He grinned, though he felt nervous. "Like a plumber."

"A plumber." Her voice echoed back at him, heavy with what sounded like contempt. He felt a rush of heat. This old bitch was really starting to push his buttons, talking to him like this. Come to think of it, she wasn't actually talking at all. Not like other people he'd worked for. They had at least filled him in, making sure he knew what the score was. Treated him with respect. Not like her.

"That's right. A plumber would want to know what he was into, wouldn't he? Then he'd tell you how much it would cost." He nodded, pleased at the comparison. "Me, I know nothing. Just find this – what's this bloke – Frank Palmer."

There was silence in the car, and Szulu wondered if she was about to take a .357 Magnum out of her bag and let him have a bullet in the back of the head. Or maybe she'd use a Glock, which was lighter. Now that would never have surprised him. But she didn't move.

"All right," she said finally. "You want to know more, I'll tell you. But I'll keep it short – you wouldn't be able to handle the full version." She shifted in her seat. "Frank Palmer did me a great harm a while ago. He disrupted some important plans and caused the deaths of at least two valued employees... and my dear husband."

"What?" Szulu turned his head in surprise. He began to wish he hadn't started this line of conversation. Getting mixed up with hit men was a whole different thing. Low-lifes and druggies he could handle, but people who killed for a living – now there was an irony – was something else. "He kills people? You never said nothing like that before."

"I didn't see the need." The woman's voice was sharp, cutting through his objections. "I said he caused the deaths, I didn't say he killed them. Not," she added, "that the distinction will help him." She paused for a moment, then continued in a whisper, as if voicing her thoughts out loud. "I've waited a long time for this. Too long, in fact. But no longer." She looked at him. "It's now time, before it's too late."

"So it's pay-back, yeah? All this?"

"That's right, Mr Szulu. Pay-back. You're acquainted with the concept?"

"Damn right." Szulu understood perfectly. Getting even was what kept some people going. That and fear. What he didn't get, though, was how utterly cold this woman was. Revenge was something you did when you were fired up and white-hot, and nothing was going to get in your way. Revenge was all about blood and honour and not being seen as weak. The way this old crone spoke, it was like it was a discussion in a school class or something. Matter-of-fact, almost. Scary.

"So it's just him, then, is it – Palmer?"

"No. There was a young woman as well. She lives right there." He glanced back to see her nodding towards the house up the street. The one where she'd earlier told him to sniff around and check out who lived there. All he'd come up with was the old Polish guy, a pensioner on the top floor whom nobody ever saw, and a journalist – the one called Gavin. He remembered the name from Palmer's Rolodex.

"You never mentioned no young woman." Szulu's words carried an unmistakable tone of accusation, too late to rein in. This old witch still wasn't telling him everything. It was like she was drip-feeding him. Then it hit him. "Hey – wait. You mean Riley Gavin is a *chick's* name? Shit, *that* would have been good to know." He felt his stomach lurch as he recalled the young woman he'd nearly bumped into as he was leaving the house. Christ – that must have been her. And he'd seen her somewhere before, now he thought about it: coming away from Palmer's place! He opened his mouth to tell the old woman, but thought better of it. Maybe it wasn't such a good idea.

There was movement in the back seat and he smelled her breath on his neck, sour and heavy with a hint of long-dead peppermint. When he turned and looked fully at her, he saw eyes like cold slate. Old as she was, and undoubtedly frail, too, so much so that he reckoned it would take no more than a quick grasp of her chicken neck to snuff out her lights, he still felt a palpable sense of threat coming off her.

"Do you need a reminder of how I found you, Mr Szulu?" she said quietly. "Found out you were… available?"

Szulu shrugged, trying not to care. But he felt something inside him cringe with what she was driving at, and hated himself for it. He tried to block out any further thoughts and was relieved she couldn't see his face.

"Next time you feel like questioning me," she continued, calmly goading, after he'd had time to digest the question, "perhaps you'd like to give Mr Pearl a call."

Pearl. The cold worm of fear broke through in the pit of his stomach at the mention of the name. Ragga Pearl was bad fuckin' news of the worst kind. He was nuts, for one thing. Cold, no messing, clinically insane. And given to taking out his frustrations, real or imagined, on anyone who crossed him. He even made those LA gangstas with their craze for gold-plated MAC10s and Uzis look socially acceptable.

"We can leave the Ragga out of it," he said quietly, hoping she couldn't see the tic thumping in the side of his neck. Unfortunately, Ragga Pearl had somehow got it into his head not long ago that Szulu had been disrespectful to him. He hadn't, actually – it had been a misunderstanding that Szulu thought had long blown over. But crazy-as-a-fruit fly Ragga Pearl didn't work on the normal human level; one minute he could be all smiles with you, the next you were in a war zone. Worst of all, he had a habit of suddenly calling up remembered hurts long past their sell-by date. And when he did that, if you'd ever looked at him the wrong way, shown disrespect, called against him, then you better head for the Arctic or some such remote place, as far away from his kingdom in south London as you could get.

And the worst of it was, it had taken one phone call from the Ragga, and here he was saddled with this mad old bitch – and she was *white*! Man, the world had gone crazy. He looked round and the woman smiled, her rouged mouth twisting in a way that made Szulu want to slap her. Not that he was into hitting women, but he was beginning to think there was always a first time. "No need, right?"

"Good. As long as you do your job, I'll keep Mr Pearl and his demands off your back. And as for any extra duties… well, I think we can start with one this evening. I'll pay, of course."

He shrugged, but any sense of victory was blanked out by a sick feeling in his gut. For a couple of days, he'd been able to push all thoughts of Pearl out of his head. Now he was back, like the freak of nature that he was. And all it would take was one phone call from this woman…

He wondered how much the Ragga had charged her, his pride hoping it was an extortionately high rate.

"What do you want me to do?"

"Send them a warning. Just for starters. No violence, though. Not yet."

"OK." Szulu dragged the word out, not sure where this was going. She was asking him to put the frighteners on somebody. He was willing to bet it was the woman. Fair enough. He'd deal with anything more if it came up.

"But be warned, Mr Szulu," she added quietly. "I will not tolerate disloyalty. I never have. If you cheat me, if you try to short-change me in any way, I will speak to Mr Pearl."

Yeah, yeah. Whatever. Jesus, this woman and the *Ragga*? He still couldn't get his head round that. It was criminal.

"There's one thing," he said quietly, trying to get his mind on to something more pleasant, and to demonstrate that he wasn't bothered by her threats.

"What is it?"

"What do I call you? Your name's not really Fraser, is it? Only, I've used it a couple of times, and you didn't reply. I need to know what to call you, right?"

"How observant of you, Mr Szulu." She considered it for a few moments. "Very well. You might as well call me by the name Palmer and Gavin know me by."

"Which is?"

"Grossman." Her eyes glittered with an unpleasant light. "They know me as Lottie Grossman."

14

Riley watched the cat patrol the outer edges of the living room and settle down in the kitchen doorway, eyeing her with a flat gaze. It was the usual ritual if she failed to feed him within what he considered the allotted timescale. She sighed and got up, her thoughts still on Palmer and what the latest developments of Gillivray's death might mean for him. For both of them, really; she had, after all, been in the building with Frank when he'd confronted the man.

She opened the fridge. Damn. No cat food. It was on her list of things to buy. Had been for three days, in fact, although the ever-dwindling supply of cans had clearly proved insufficient to remind her.

She threw on her jacket and grabbed her purse. She would have to go to the corner shop. "OK, OK," she muttered, riddled with guilt at the way the cat was now staring at her and following her progress to the door. "I'll spring for something special, if that makes you feel any better. God, you're such a bully."

She stepped out on to the landing and closed the door behind her, patting her pockets to make sure she'd got her mobile. She could hear Mr Grobowski's television downstairs, turned up to super-loud, and guessed he was busy cooking tomorrow's Polish Community Hall lunch while tuned into the soaps.

She was back inside five minutes. As she reached the top of the stairs and leaned to slip her key in the door, she caught a flicker of movement out of the corner of her eye. It came from slightly above her on the stairs leading to the second floor where the reclusive dowager lady lived. Riley opened her mouth to utter a greeting, although without expecting a reply, when she realised the shape was too tall and slim for the tenant upstairs.

Riley froze, the bag containing the cat food dropping from her hand and rolling across the landing. A man was standing there, not moving, not speaking, utterly still. Even though he was in shadow, she sensed him gazing down at her with frightening intensity.

She tried to speak but nothing came, and felt angry and impotent at her failure to respond. Was this the instinct for flight nullified by fear? It was like a dream she'd had as a child, trying to outrun danger, yet treading through what felt like treacle, her legs unwilling to obey, her voice strangled into silence.

Then the man moved. But instead of coming towards her, he turned and went upstairs, taking the steps two at a time. It was enough to break the moment, and Riley shouted something unintelligible and questioning, before sliding to the floor, legs weak and body trembling.

When she looked up again, he had gone.

She was there, slumped against the wall, when Frank Palmer arrived two minutes later.

"Riley?" He knelt by her side and took her hand. "What happened?" She was shaking but otherwise seemed unhurt. He peered into her eyes and guessed she was in shock.

"A man," Riley said softly, pointing towards the upper stairs. "He was standing there, just watching me. I came out to get some cat food and..." She swallowed hard and shook her head as if trying to force herself back to reality. "Tall, dark... something about his head... I don't know. Christ, Palmer, I just froze like some silly kid."

"Get inside," Palmer instructed her calmly, "and lock the

door. I'll be right back." He handed her the bag she had dropped, then ran up the stairs. The landing was empty, but a slim side window was open. He looked out and saw two stretches of sloping roof, one below the other. He guessed from the height that it was only a small jump to the ground. From there, access to the street was simple.

He locked the window and went back downstairs. Riley had evidently followed his instructions and disappeared inside her flat, taking the cat food with her. He went out the front door and followed the path to the street, his mind already tracking ahead to where the intruder might have come out. He was betting the man was mobile, but even on foot, he'd need a stretch of clear ground to get away from here.

He reached the end of the street and rounded the corner, then sprinted for the next, which would take him into the street running parallel to the one Riley lived in. A man walking a small dog jumped out of his way with a startled shout, dragging his companion with him.

Palmer spotted a flash of movement ahead, about fifty yards away. A tall figure was crossing the pavement. A car door slammed followed by the urgent stutter of an engine. Lights came on and a dark saloon surged away from the kerb, revving hard towards the far end of the street and the eventual safety of Holland Park Avenue, leaving a heavy haze of exhaust smoke hanging in the air.

Palmer slowed, waiting for the car to slip under the glow of street lights. When it did, he noted the number. He also saw something else: the driver, hunched over the wheel, was suddenly outlined by the headlights of a vehicle coming towards him. Around his head was a swirl of movement, too heavy to be loose, yet too defined to be any kind of headgear.

Palmer reached for his phone and retraced his steps to Riley's flat.

When she opened the door to his knock, she had the safety chain on. She had evidently recovered her composure, anger now replacing the shock. Mostly, he guessed, the anger would be directed inwards.

"Don't beat yourself up," he said, as she let him in. "He was on your turf right where you didn't expect it. Got any whisky?"

The matter-of-fact approach seemed to work, and talk of the mundane, such as a glass of whisky, made her drop her air of smouldering fury.

"Yes, of course." She looked at Palmer and shook her head with a wry smile. "Sorry – I was about to get stupid for a moment, wasn't I? It's just that, he was there and – " She sighed and walked into the kitchen, where the cat was gorging itself and purring contentedly. Riley took a bottle and two glasses from a cupboard. "Did you see anyone?"

Palmer gestured with his mobile. "Saw him, got the number, phoned it in." He scratched his head. "Didn't you get my message?"

She frowned for a moment, trying to compose her rattled thoughts, then nodded. "Yes, but it was a terrible line. Not much of it made sense. Why?"

He shook his head. "Never mind. I was warning you to be careful about answering the door. I was a bit late. Sorry."

She poured two generous measures and handed him a glass. Her hand was trembling slightly, he noted, but with a brief tilt of her glass in his direction, she threw it down and poured another. "What do you mean?"

"I'll tell you later. It's about the man I recognised in Harrow."

She looked at him. "You think my visitor just now was

something to do with him?"

"Could be. This one was tall and thin and looked like his hair was in dreadlocks. I couldn't be sure of the car model, though."

Riley's eyes widened in understanding. "Dreadlocks? I didn't recognise what they were in profile. It was a vague shape around his head... the light wasn't that good." Then, with a start, she remembered something else. "Wait. I've seen him before – at least, I think it was him."

"Where?"

"Here – outside the house, earlier this evening. He was just leaving and I assumed he'd been calling on Mr Grobowski. Mr G talks to lots of other community people, like outreach workers." She took another sip and pulled a face. "Christ, why am I drinking this? Do you want coffee?"

Palmer shook his head and relieved her of her glass. He tipped the contents into his own and murmured, "Waste not, want not, as me sainted old mum used to say." He took a sip and studied her closely. She still wasn't her old self and was probably suffering flashbacks. He was annoyed with himself for not having anticipated the speed with which the man in Harrow would track them down, yet puzzled as to how it had been done. "Don't worry about him. We'll find out who he is and I'll get someone to beat him to a pulp."

His attempt at lightening the atmosphere didn't quite work. Riley banged her hand furiously on the worktop, catching a cup and sending it skittering away. "How dare he? Coming into my own home like that! Christ, if I'd had a gun...!"

The cup teetered for a moment on the edge of the worktop, before tipping over and crashing to the floor. In the silence that followed, a car horn hooted.

"A gun's no answer," Palmer said evenly. He spoke instinctively, the ex-military man's automatic response to the use of firearms. He was unprepared for the strength of her response.

"Really? You think so?" She glared at him, her face colouring with outrage and anger. "You'd be bloody amazed at what I think is the answer right now, Frank!"

He returned her look without comment. The rare use of his first name was an indication of her anger and shock. Not that he blamed her entirely. "Picking up a gun is easy," he said after a moment or two of silence. "It's a lump of metal, that's all. No big deal. But shooting someone? You have to point it, first. Decide where you want to hit them: head, stomach - maybe just a wingtip. Shoot to wound or shoot to kill? Most people aren't that good. Most guns aren't that accurate, either – not unless you get up close. That's when they do the damage. You might hit a main artery or blow off their arm. Have you ever seen anyone gut-shot? It's pretty nasty."

Riley looked stunned by the flat brutality of Palmer's words and the images they painted. "Palmer, for God's sake –"

"I mean it." His voice was utterly calm now, but insistent, drilling into her. "Pulling the trigger… it takes almost no pressure at all. One small squeeze and it goes off. *Bang.*" Riley blinked at the harsh sound. "But once you do it, once that gun goes off, it'll change your life forever."

The sound of the cat's claws tapping on the tiled floor broke the spell.

"Talking from experience, Palmer?" Riley could have bitten her tongue, the words out before she could stop them. "I'm sorry. I didn't mean that."

"Forget it," he said easily. "I thought you should know, that's all."

Riley nodded guiltily and touched his arm. "I'm grateful, too. Just sounding off a bit. Ignore me." She took a deep breath. "There's something you should know. Gillivray's dead." She told him about Jimmy's call, and he looked puzzled.

"A disgruntled victim, maybe?"

"I've no idea. But you could be in the frame, you know that?"

Palmer shrugged. "Then I'd better keep my head down, hadn't I?"

"Yes. Talking of police, who did you call just now to find the car number? Your friend in the Met?" She was referring to a contact Palmer had made some time ago, somebody who could access useful information whenever he needed it. Riley still didn't know the person's name, only that it was a woman and the mere mention of her could bring a silly smile to Palmer's face.

"Not this time," he said enigmatically. "I got Donald on to it. He's got a back door to the DVLA. He said to give him an hour or so."

"Fine." Riley reached for the phone on the wall, glad to be doing something. "In that case, while we're waiting, how about a large pizza with all the toppings and a bottle of red? I need some serious stodge. Then you can tell me where you've been the last day or two and what that man means to you."

15

"As we came down in the lift from Gillivray's office," Palmer reminded her, disposing of the last of his pizza, "three men got in on the first floor. One in shirt-sleeves, another young, smart, with black hair. The third older and thinner, with a deep suntan."

"His name's Arthur Radnor," said Riley, and grinned at the surprised look on Palmer face. "Come on, Batman, you think you're the only one with contacts?"

Palmer rolled his eyes. "OK, what else do you know?"

"Only that the young man is called Michael, possibly Russian, and the third man is a part-time book-keeper or accountant. They're in the import-export business, bringing in works of art from eastern Europe." She paused, her face solemn. "Michael was asking about us the following day, about what you and I were doing in the building."

Palmer's face grew serious. "How do you know that?"

Riley filled him in on her return visit to the office block in Harrow and her talks with Nobby and Jimmy. He listened without comment, then sat back and stared at the ceiling, puffing out his cheeks. "Damn," he said mildly. "So he did recognise me."

"If you want a cigarette," said Riley, "go ahead, smoke. You look as if you need it."

But Palmer surprised her. "No, thanks. If I'm right and Radnor remembers me, it might explain the visitor on the stairs." He scowled at this latest development. "What I said about guns and shooting people? Forget it. There are some people you should shoot, preferably more than once."

"What do you mean?" When he didn't reply, Riley

leaned forward and tapped the coffee table. "Palmer. You're worrying me now. Why the face?"

"Because if your visitor was from Radnor, they've traced your address. Only I can't figure out how. I didn't put our real names in the visitors' book."

"As I discovered," she said dryly. "You could have warned me. Luckily, the security man on the front desk was a former boy scout, like you."

Palmer looked guilty. "Sorry. I didn't expect it to become an issue. It was meant to be a one-time visit."

"The bad news is," said Riley, "he's got your address, too." She told him about her talk with Javad, who had seen a man and woman arrive by car, and her own impression the following day that someone had been in Palmer's office. "Tall and black with dreadlocks, according to Javad. It has to be the same man."

"Yeah. Was anything missing?"

"Not that I could see. You'd know better than me. But how does the woman fit into it? Javad said she looked old."

He frowned. "Beats me. The timing's all wrong, though, to be connected with Radnor. They can't have popped up so soon after the Harrow thing. And the last old woman I knew was my Auntie Dot. And as far as I know I haven't upset the local Coalition of Pensioners and Cool Dudes in any way."

"So," said Riley. "are you going to tell me where you've been?"

Palmer gave a long sigh. "OK. Germany, nineteen eighty-nine. I hadn't been out there long. I was a junior RMP, feeling my way around. I'd been assigned to a forward base. One morning there was an incident involving the border police. A man tried to cross to the west and the guards shot him. At least, that was the story."

"You didn't believe it?"

"I did – I didn't know any different. But my sergeant was sceptical. He'd seen stuff like it before and reckoned there was probably more to it."

Riley tried to rethink her history but couldn't remember the date. "Wasn't the border open by then?"

"That was later, in the November. Until then, it was business as usual for both sides. If you wanted out of the GDR bad enough, you attempted a crossing. If you were a member of the *Volkspolitzei*, your job was to stop runners. Some got away with it - if they were young enough and lucky. Mostly they didn't."

"And Radnor was involved?"

Palmer nodded. "He was a witness to the whole incident, so he claimed. He had someone contact the nearest RMP post, which was us, using an authority code I'd never heard before. My sergeant had, so he checked with the CO. He was told to attend and assist, but to keep it quiet. That meant minimum involvement by anyone else, no word to the local police unless they came calling and everything was to be dealt with as if nothing had happened. The US Cavalry had a strong presence nearby, but this was on our sector. Reg, my sergeant, was even more convinced that it pointed to an intelligence connection. He didn't like it, nor did the CO, apparently, but there was no way out of it."

"Spies, you mean? Does the army get involved in that stuff?"

"Not normally. Sometimes it can't be avoided. When it does blow up, everyone keeps a tight lid on it and there are more reminders of the Official Secrets Act flying around than scales on a goldfish. Anyway, I was on call, so I went out with Reg to secure the scene. It was right up against the border, with pretty much open countryside all around. It was starting to snow and was bitterly cold. There were some old farm buildings not far off which looked abandoned, but that was it. By the time we arrived, there were three men there. One was British, I don't know about the other two – they were younger and stayed in the background. Local gofers, probably. They'd already been out and recovered the body, which was unusual. Reg wasn't impressed."

Riley debated whether to reveal that she knew about the existence of Reg Paris, but Palmer was in full flow. "Why?" she asked.

"Because the usual form when a runner got shot was to leave them out there while each side did their share of posturing and arguing about who did what. Understandably, nobody from our side wanted to walk out and collect them – the East German border guards were far too twitchy. It needed open clearance from all sides before anyone dared step out on to neutral ground. The political implications of serving military personnel being shot by the other side were mental."

"So these men jumped the gun."

"And some. Anyway, since the body was now clearly on our side, and there didn't seem to be any doubt about what had happened, we offered to get it taken to the base. But the Brit wouldn't let us. He said he'd get his men to deal with it."

"So why did he get you out there in the first place?"

"I can only think it was to give it an extra security gloss in case of witnesses. The sight of British army MPs would have warned anyone off and stopped any questions. We filed a report to the CO and that was it." Palmer drummed his fingertips on his knee. "Reg said they were spooks and it was better I didn't get involved. He wouldn't even tell me the man's name. Said he'd clear it with the CO and I should keep my head down. So I did."

"The spook being the man in Harrow. Radnor."

"Right. A couple of days later, he turned up at the base, looking for Reg and waving some paperwork. He said the German police had got wind of the shooting via a man on the other side. As the senior military cop on the spot, Reg was required to make a deposition to them about what had happened. After that, they'd handle it. The army wasn't about to argue, so Reg had to fall in line."

"What then?" Riley thought her voice unnaturally loud in comparison to Palmer's soft tones.

"They took off in a pool car. Reg was driving. Later that day, on the autobahn near Frankfurt, they were hit by a Mercedes truck."

Riley said nothing.

"The pool car blew apart under the impact." He looked at her. "There were no survivors."

16

"But that's impossible." Riley now knew what had affected Palmer so acutely. Seeing a face from the past, knowing that face should no longer exist, must have been world-shattering. At least it hadn't been his former colleague, Reg Paris, that he'd seen. "Did you see the car?"

"No. A couple of guys who did said it had been ripped apart like a wet paper bag. Not even the seats were recognisable. Whatever was left of the bodies was flown back to England once the inquest was completed. Two days after the crash I was assigned to embassy duty in Stockholm with orders to leave immediately. When I got there I rang my CO to ask about the funeral. He said the family had requested a private ceremony and it was none of my concern. Done and dusted." He gave a thin smile. "I didn't think to ask about the other man, and was junior enough to do as I was told, so I forgot about it."

Riley nodded, thinking it was time to mention her meeting with Charlie. Hopefully, Palmer would see she had been trying to help. As usual, however, Palmer was sharp to catch on.

"You know, don't you?" he accused her. "You weren't the slightest bit surprised by my mention of Reg Paris."

Riley tried to look apologetic but failed, because she wasn't. "Sorry, Palmer, but I was concerned when I couldn't contact you. I contacted your friend Charlie. He looked up the accident report."

Palmer looked puzzled. "Christ, that was a shot in a million, wasn't it?" Then he nodded. "My notes." He stared at her. "You've been in my office."

"Guilty as charged. I happened to see Charlie's name in your Rolodex. He was the obvious person to ask. I gave him the notes off your desk, thinking it might be a clue to where you were. You'd made doodles which included Reg Paris's name, although I didn't recognise it at the time. Charlie used some whiz-bang search engine to check the database and came up with the accident report."

Palmer put on a look of feigned disgust. "Christ, you can't trust anyone these days. So much for the Official Secrets Act." He half smiled. "But thanks for the concern. I'd better give Charlie a ring. He'll never forgive me for not telling him."

"So who was he?" asked Riley after a few minutes. "The man killed on the border? I suppose that's why you went to Germany?" She added by way of explanation, "I heard the airport announcement when you rang me."

Palmer sat back and linked his hands behind his head with a deep sigh. "Actually, I'm not sure why I went back. Seeing that face again stirred it all up. I suppose it wasn't buried as deep as I'd thought."

"You wanted answers. You thought the man was dead. It's natural."

"Yeah. I don't know what I expected to find, but the border seemed the best place to start. I figured if I discovered what had really happened, including who the runner was and why this man - Radnor? – was there, I might discover the reason for the deception." He took out his notebook to refresh his memory. "Unger, the lawyer I met over there, filled in the gaps for me. The runner's name was Claus Ulf Wachter. He was in his forties, a middle ranking bureaucrat attached to the East German Ministry of Arts and Culture, responsible for museums and galleries."

"What connection would Radnor have had with them?"

"No idea. The Intelligence community normally confines its interest to other things. But who knows what devious paths they pursue? Could be Wachter knew someone with access to useful information in the military field. In any case, he was probably skipping out before he got caught."

"Doing what?"

"Hands in the till, from the information Unger dug up. At the time, a lot of state-owned artwork, especially by Soviet artists, was going missing and finding its way to the west. There were no reliable inventories, so it was fairly easy for stuff to be siphoned off. Wachter was thought to be involved." Palmer shrugged. "They were desperate times for some people. Who would miss what they didn't know about? It would have been easy work with someone on the inside. Then with the collapse of communism and the Wall coming down, there was a flood of people getting out and the system simply unravelled. This time though, the new people weren't coming out through tunnels, across the wire or in small boats. They were leaving legitimately. And lots of them had access to money and weren't shy of using it. Once they got out, they wanted mementoes of the Homeland."

"With Wachter as the source? But he was killed before the Wall came down."

"There's where I got lucky. One thing about the East Germans: their museum inventories may have been full of holes, but they kept detailed records on people – especially the likes of Claus Wachter. Some interior police transcripts named Wachter among several officials who were under suspicion for theft of government property. I think he knew his time was up. Maybe he got greedy and was moving too much stuff, and came to their attention.

They were all being watched at that time, with *Stasi* spies everywhere."

"So if he was working for Radnor," said Riley, "he'd have instinctively turned to him for help. It would explain why Radnor and his men were there that night."

"It might," Palmer agreed. "But it doesn't explain why one of Radnor's men was ready to shoot him." He related Hemmricht's story, and Riley listened in astonishment.

"Couldn't Hemmricht have been mistaken?" she said. "He was just a boy at the time. It would have all been… I don't know – soldiers and guns and stuff."

Palmer shrugged. "What other reason was there? They wouldn't have been ready to take on the border guards; that would have been tantamount to starting World War Three. For some reason, Radnor didn't want Wachter to make the crossing. Makes me wonder what he wanted to hide."

Riley chewed it over. Something had suddenly begun tugging at her memory. Connected with Radnor. Was it something she'd heard or just an assumption? She poured more wine. "Rewind a moment," she said, closing her eyes. "Something you mentioned just now hit a nerve."

"East Germans," Palmer recited, going along with her. "Border guards, Wachter, Hemmricht. Shooting, farm animals, ditch."

Riley shook her head. "No. Further back than that. It might have been something else… keep going."

"Farm, winter, military exercise, compensation."

"No. Keep going."

"*Stasi*, museums, artwork, Reg Paris–"

"Artwork." Riley opened her eyes. "There was something about artwork… something recently." She snapped her fingers, searching her memory. "Jimmy Gough – the retired security guard. He said he walked past Radnor's office one

114

day and saw some icons on a table. He knew what they were – he served in Berlin. They'd just brought them up in the lift and unpacked them. He probably wasn't meant to see them."

"Now, that makes sense." Palmer sat forward and looked at Riley. "It would tie in with Wachter's job. Radnor indulging in a spot of free enterprise while working for the government, making a bit of extra money on the side for his pension. Or is that too easy?"

"It might explain why he didn't want Wachter to come over." Riley felt a ripple of excitement in her stomach. "Having an East German official blab to the authorities about what one of their spies had been up to on the side would have been difficult to explain. I don't suppose the chief spooks encourage that sort of sideline."

Palmer nodded. "If Wachter had half a brain, he'd have known deep down what Radnor's real job was. There was certainly no way any ordinary Brit could make trips to East Germany at that time. Wachter might have even let slip that he knew, just to ratchet up the pressure to get him out. Radnor would have had no other choice, because if Wachter got caught by the East Germans, he would have blown Radnor's cover anyway." He rubbed his eyes with his knuckles and sighed. "Or are we moving too fast, here? This could be so wide of the mark."

"Go with your instincts," suggested Riley. She hadn't known Palmer seriously express doubts before. He tended to cast them aside and go for direct action.

Before he could answer, his phone rang. It was Donald Brask. Palmer listened carefully for a minute or two, scribbling in his notepad, then thanked Donald and hung up.

"Your visitor was using a hire car," he said shortly. "Registered to an executive rental company near Heathrow.

Donald did some extra digging. The vehicle was hired for a minimum of three days by a woman named Fraser. She lives overseas but is registered at a hotel near Windsor. The driver was a local hire. His licence checked out clean." He looked up. "Described as tall and black, with dreadlocks."

"It's him. But what does that tell us?" asked Riley.

"Only that there's no obvious connection between them and Radnor." Palmer looked mystified and added darkly: "apart from us, that is. I need to take a closer look at the office."

"I doubt that will help. I didn't see anything that would be a clue… unless you can figure out why a woman named Fraser from overseas would water your pot plant for you."

Palmer shook his head. "Not my office. I meant the one in Harrow."

In a warehouse on a small commercial estate to the west of London's main sprawl, the man called Michael stood by a newly-arrived consignment of wooden crates and sipped from a bottle of mineral water. He had just arrived to help Radnor go through the shipment, and report on something he had discovered.

"Palmer and the Gavin woman are being watched," he told him. "An old woman and a black. The black has long hair, braided like a girl."

Radnor sniffed with distaste. "They're called dreadlocks. So?"

"He was chased from Gavin's house by Palmer, but he got away."

"Interesting." Arthur Radnor stared at his mobile phone, which he'd been using before Michael arrived. "Maybe an old pigeon come home to roost."

"What do you mean?"

"Old enemies, perhaps. I had a contact in the police look at Palmer. A while ago, he was suspected of being involved in the death of a London gangster in Malaga. More recently, he was close by when two men, one an American, died in a vehicle fire. The American was a bogus priest heading a ring of blackmailers. He targeted runaway kids, dug up some dirt, and blackmailed the parents. If they didn't pay, he killed the kids. The report suggested he was probably alive when he burned."

Michael shrugged and stubbed his toe against one of the crates, which was coated in heavy green paint. "Sounds as if he had it coming."

"Possibly. But on both occasions Palmer was working with the Gavin woman. It means Palmer's no pushover, and the woman is clearly no shrinking violet." He gave a grunt of irritation. "I don't like it. They're professionals and plainly not frightened off easily. If they come after us, it could ruin everything."

"You worry too much. I have it under control."

Radnor wondered if he did, and felt a twinge of unease. After a lifetime in the deception game, he had developed a mental antennae tuned to signs of danger. Occasionally, the threats had been unfounded. But there had been too many times when he had listened to good effect, and he wasn't about to dismiss the warning signs now. He was still trying to come to terms with the potential implications of having the police swarming all over the building in Harrow, investigating Gillivray's death. It wouldn't take much for them to wonder about the other occupants, and to scratch beneath the surface, which was something he wished to avoid. The Azimtec paperwork and cover were perfectly good, and would withstand most cursory inspections. But experience told him that even with the best operations, there was always a chink somewhere. Michael, true to form, appeared oblivious to the results of his actions, and seemed merely intrigued by unfolding events, as a meteorologist might be curious about the movement of air.

"We can't afford to brush this off too easily," Radnor said finally, making a decision. "Palmer could be trouble, directly or indirectly."

"What are you suggesting?"

"We should move. Another base, away from Harrow. Let the dust settle. In the meantime, the black and the woman watching Palmer might be a useful smoke screen to keep his attention diverted."

"What if they aren't? What if Palmer and his friend get in our way?"

"That's your job. Make sure they don't."

17

From inside Riley's Golf next morning, parked in the same spot Palmer had used on his first survey of the office block, they sat and watched a procession of police and forensics personnel buzz around the area. Whatever commercial activity normally went on inside the building appeared to have been suspended; there was little sign of the usual ebb and flow of corporate visitors or staff, and one or two arrivals were clearly put off by seeing a uniform at the door.

They watched Nobby do a brief tour of the outside, carefully avoiding a taped-off area to one side of the building where the police activity seemed to be focussed. From the concentration and position of the forensics team, Gillivray had fallen from a side window, landing close to the building in dead ground just outside their view.

"Odd place to jump from," said Riley.

Palmer nodded and studied the building through a small pair of binoculars. "Especially since the windows don't look that big. No way you'd fall out of there by accident."

"So you're thinking what I'm thinking?"

"Somebody helped him out," Palmer said flatly. He put the binoculars away.

A police constable left the car park and strolled along the street towards them, inspecting vehicles. He spoke occasionally into his radio, no doubt passing on registration details for vehicle checks. Riley sank down in her seat.

"If he comes close, I'm not going to snog you, Palmer," she warned.

"Thank God for that," Palmer murmured.

Just as they thought they were going to be spotted, the constable stopped barely thirty yards away and listened to his radio, then turned and hurried back to the building.

Riley looked at Palmer. "Go on – you're relieved, aren't you?" she accused him. Then she sat up as the rear door of the building opened and the familiar figures of Radnor and Michael appeared. They were carrying briefcases and coats, and headed towards a cab which had pulled into the rear car park.

"Stroke of luck," said Palmer. "While the cats are away…"

"You're not saying we go in there now?" Riley checked to see if he was serious. "The police are all over the place."

"It's the best time." He opened his door. "The world doesn't stop just because some low-life has taken a one-way ticket to the Great Beyond." He picked up a leather dossier case on the way out of the car, and Riley scrambled after him, holding a plain, black briefcase she had been given as a present several years ago but rarely used.

They were stopped at the front entrance by a uniformed officer. "Can I ask what your business is, please?" he queried.

Riley showed him her business card and told him they had an appointment with Azimtec on the first floor. Hopefully, he was unaware that its two main members had just left by the rear door. He studied them both for a moment, then nodded and stood aside.

They approached the desk where Nobby sat waiting, barely managing to control a faintly bewildered expression at their arrival. Across the foyer stood two men in suits, talking quietly. They bore the distinct air of police officers, but didn't look at the newcomers.

"Sir. Miss," said Nobby, standing up and assuming a non-committal expression. "Sign the book, please?" He pushed the visitor's book towards them, followed by two badges. This time Riley filled in the spaces using their own names; the chances of being stopped and asked for ID were too strong. They had decided to go in under cover of Riley doing a speculative piece about art imports from the former Soviet Bloc, with Palmer stringing along as an advisor. It might not fool anyone for long, but since it involved half-truths and would be impossible to disprove, it was as good a story as any.

"You know where to go," said Nobby, for the benefit of the police, before sitting back down and picking up his paper. Clearly, said his body language, nothing unusual was going on here. As if to reflect that, the two men turned and walked towards the rear of the building, one of them holding a set of building plans.

Riley had a sudden thought and leaned across the desk. "Can you contact Jimmy and ask him a question for me?" she said quietly.

"Sure. What is it?"

"Ask him if he ever saw a tall black man with dreadlocks going up to the first floor, or if he ever knew of Azimtec employing a driver who was black?"

Nobby nodded and reached for the phone. "The police have been through the building interviewing everyone. They did Azimtec half an hour ago."

Riley smiled her thanks and followed Palmer, who was on his way past the lifts and up the stairs, fingering the badge clipped to his lapel. He flashed the back of it to Riley. Behind the badge was taped a key. Once they were out of sight of the security cameras by the lifts, he ripped it off and headed for the solid wooden door of Azimtec Trading.

Seconds later they were inside, listening to the silence of an empty office and, from outside, the hum of traffic in the street and the muted sound of voices from the forensic team. Palmer locked the door.

He stood still as if absorbing the atmosphere around him, then slipped the key into his pocket and pulled on some thin rubber gloves.

"What are we looking for?" asked Riley.

"Not sure yet. Don't touch anything. Just use your eyes. If you see anything interesting, let me move it and you remember its position."

They were standing in an area approximately twenty feet square. It was in the same position as the one they had seen on the sixth floor, but with no reception counter and no chairs. Thinly carpeted, it contained only a plain desk against one wall, and a side table holding a single telephone. There were no pictures on the walls, no signs leading to other offices and no indication that it ever welcomed visitors.

"Friendly atmosphere," muttered Palmer. He nodded towards a door to their right. "This way." It opened on to a bare, uncarpeted corridor. The first door on the left was to an office containing a desk, wastebasket and a small cupboard. It smelled unused, with a thin layer of dust over everything. It was the same with the next room and the next, each roughly ten by ten.

They retraced their steps to a door on the opposite side of the foyer. This opened into a well-appointed office, with decent carpeting, pleasant décor and comfortable furniture. A large desk in the centre of the room was blank save for a telephone, a wire correspondence tray, a small clock and a blotting pad. A bookcase stood against one wall, the shelves lined with a selection of volumes interspersed with statuettes and some glassware. A small fridge stood in one corner next to a table holding some glasses and a bottle of mineral water.

Palmer tried the desk drawers. They were unlocked and full of office desk clutter from notepads and paper to paperclips, spare pens and personal detritus. He was about to flick through them when he noticed the way in which the contents were so evenly scattered. Everything looked just a little *too* casual, *too* neat, as if it had been set up to look like a million other desk drawers.

He carefully closed the drawers and moved over to the bookcase, where Riley was using a pen to shuffle aside each book, checking for items in between. They were standard office tomes on company law, administration and accounting, all too old to be of current use and plainly bought by the yard. But one looked out of place, with a glossy cover and cantered at an angle to fit into the shelf space. Palmer took it down. It was a hardback edition of *A Guide to Russian Imperial Art*, and looked well thumbed, with yellow post-it notes protruding from the edges of the pages.

He flicked through it. The notes highlighted an array of icons, portraits, glassware, gold and silver, all elaborately decorated and set against a backdrop of display cases lined with plush material to highlight the rich colours. One or two pages had neat notations in the margins, in Russian, so Palmer couldn't read them.

Close to the back, he found two slips of paper. One could have been a shopping list, containing references to page numbers in the book. The other was smaller and heavy in texture, with a glossy feel. It had jagged edges, as if torn from another, larger piece. He slipped this into his pocket, and replaced the book exactly as he had found it.

In the fridge, they found two bottles of lager, a bottle of vodka and one of whisky, with six small tins of tonic and soda. A plastic tray of ice cubes. No peanuts, no chocolates, no little nibbles. Whatever Messrs Radnor and Michael were into, they didn't lean towards the wild side when it came to alcohol.

"This isn't where they do their main business," said Riley. "Is it?" She was staring round with a grim expression. "It's too blank."

"Right," Palmer agreed with her. "It's a place to hang, that's all. A cover. No working office is this bare – not when there are two of them and they come in here every day. They haven't even got a computer. When was the last time you saw an office without one?"

"Laptops," Riley guessed, nodding towards a coiled power cable on one of the shelves. "Safer than leaving a PC lying around. With the right hardware, they can make a connection to anywhere they like." Even the phone had a thin covering of dust. "But what about the stuff Jimmy said they bring in from time to time? And the packing stuff in the skips?"

"More cover. My guess is, they move a bit of stuff through here, just to keep it real. If so, it's probably genuine and clean. I'd like to know where the other place is."

"Could be they've flown." Riley thought back: when Radnor and Michael left the building earlier, they were carrying briefcases and coats, but hadn't seemed in a hurry. But then, if Radnor was who Palmer thought, he would have been trained not to give anything away, and to act normally, especially if he thought he was being watched.

Palmer walked over to the window. Standing to one side, he peered down at a couple of forensics officers, who were studying the ground in minute detail, while a young woman took shots with a digital camera.

He wandered back to the desk. Something about the contents had rung a small alarm bell. It wasn't simply the layout, which was too contrived to be normal, but something else. He slid the top drawer open again, careful not to disturb anything.

"What is it?" Riley knew Palmer's body language fairly well and realised he had noticed something.

"Without touching anything," he said, "tell me what you see." He turned away and stared out of the window.

Riley turned to the drawer and studied the contents. "OK. There's a stapler, paperclips, elastic bands, pens, pencils, ink cartridges, a book of stamps, scissors, sticky tape, some string, a gold something – could be a tie clip – some euros, a retractable craft knife, earphones, a pen-torch–"

"Go back." Palmer turned and joined her at the desk. He looked down. "Where's the gold tie clip?"

"There." Riley pointed to where a small bar of gold with a clip attached to one side was sitting in one corner of the drawer, partly concealed beneath a stapler. The clip was bent back away from the main bar.

"Damn," said Palmer, with a faint look of surprise. He'd been concentrating so hard on the layout of the drawer and not leaving clues, he'd missed the obvious. "Well, now we know who killed Gillivray."

Riley stared at him. "Radnor?"

"Michael looks more the type."

"But why? I wouldn't have thought they even knew each other."

"They probably didn't. You said yourself that Michael was asking questions about us. The visitors' book would have shown who we were calling on – even if your chum Nobby hadn't told them. It's a short step from there to wondering what we were doing here, and following the trail up to the sixth floor. Radnor must have got worried and set Michael on to them, to find out what they were up to. Knowing Gillivray, he probably told him to shove off. After that, it was a link they couldn't leave, in case he blabbed."

"Killing him's a bit extreme."

Palmer wasn't so sure. It went with the background of people like Radnor. "It's what they do, covering their tracks."

Suddenly the phone rang. They stared at it, both rooted to the spot. Palmer let it ring four times before reaching forward and picking up the receiver with his fingertips.

"*Incoming!*" The voice was Nobby's, speaking from the front desk. "*Twenty seconds – half a minute, tops.*"

18

Palmer replaced the phone and gently eased the desk drawer shut to avoid disturbing the contents. Riley was already making for the door.

"Across to the other side." Palmer said quietly. "First door on the left."

They crossed the foyer to the opposite door. Just as Palmer closed it behind him, he heard a key turning in the front door. He followed Riley into the first office and clicked the door shut behind him.

They heard the newcomer close the front door, whistling tunelessly as he moved away from them across the foyer. Then came the sound of the door to Radnor's office opening.

Palmer turned to look at Riley, to warn her to be ready to go, but she was peering into the wastebasket by the side of the desk. Ten seconds later, footsteps approached and the door to the corridor was flung open. Palmer readied himself, but the newcomer walked on by and disappeared down the corridor and through another door, humming tunelessly.

Riley looked at Palmer and mouthed the question, "Toilet?"

Palmer nodded and opened the door, then beckoned Riley to follow, silently thanking the God of weak bladders.

Thirty seconds later, they were downstairs and crossing towards the desk where Nobby sat waiting, his face drawn with worry.

"Christ, that was close!" he breathed. "I was waiting for him to start screaming blue murder." He stood up and came round the desk. "I spoke to Jimmy, like you asked. He said you've got to be joking about the black guy."

"Why?" Riley asked.

"A cleaner here was fired two weeks after Azimtec moved in. They complained he was incompetent and implied stuff had gone missing. He was black. When an Asian took over running a sandwich service into the building, they stopped taking food from him. They also insisted they'd only use white cabbies. Jimmy says from other comments they made, if those two on the first floor aren't card-carrying members of the British National Party, they should be."

Back in the Golf, Riley and Palmer watched the building for signs of alarm. The police presence appeared to have been scaled down, and only one or two uniforms were in evidence around the outside, with an occasional glimpse of forensics personnel. But it was soon clear that their visit had gone undetected. Even so, there was always the unexpected to take into account. It had been a close call, especially with the police right under their feet.

Palmer reached into his pocket and pulled out the scrap of paper he had found in the art book. It was heavy and greasy to the touch, and crisscrossed with folds. He turned it between his fingers and sniffed at it, then handed it to Riley.

"What is it?" she asked. She rubbed her fingers across the glossy surface, then followed Palmer's example and sniffed at it. "Oil? Linseed or something like it."

Palmer nodded. "Waxed paper. Used by some manufacturers to wrap weapons and ammunition. Keeps out moisture and dirt during shipping and storage."

Riley's eyebrows shot up. "Weapons?"

"Either that or they've had access to something wrapped in the same type of paper. I've no idea what that might have been, but it certainly wasn't filing cabinets and desk tidies." He took back the scrap of waxed paper. "By itself, though, it's not enough." He looked at her. "Unless you've got something?"

Riley tried to hold a straight face but failed. "What?"

"You found something. In the waste bin."

Riley grinned and held out her hand. She was holding a slim piece of green metal, two inches long. "It was in the bottom of the bin in the empty office. It looked... I don't know – out of place, so I picked it up. Any ideas?"

Palmer held it up and studied it, and his face relaxed into an expression of understanding. "Yowsa. Big peanut to the lady. If I'm not mistaken, this is part of a spring mechanism from the magazine of an automatic weapon. If it is, Radnor and his friend Michael have got their fingers in a bit more than east European artwork. No wonder they're so cagey about visitors: they're moving weapons right through the capital." He looked at Riley. "Pity we don't know the name of the couriers they're using."

"We don't," agreed Riley, digging out her mobile and a notebook. "But I know a man who might."

Five minutes later, she thanked Jimmy Gough and handed Palmer a sheet from her notebook. On it was the name and address of a courier company: VTS Transit. "They use the same driver and loader each time: it's a small firm in Hayes. Jimmy says they seem to have a good relationship with Michael in particular. Jimmy never got friendly with them because they didn't speak great English. Miserable gits, he called them."

Palmer studied the details Riley had written down. He reached in his pocket and took out the note he'd made from Donald's call the previous evening. He juggled the two for a moment, then said, "Let's go visit VTS. It's a solid connection with Radnor, so it's a start. Then we'll see about the mysterious Mrs Fraser and her cool dude driver."

Szulu wasn't feeling so cool. His hands were sweating and his head pounding as he gripped a shoebox and walked along the pavement in Chiswick. He had foregone breakfast in favour of an early errand, and was feeling sick with what he tried to convince himself were merely hunger pangs, but which he knew was an acute case of nerves.

He unlocked the hire car and slid behind the wheel, taking care not to bump the shoebox, which he placed carefully on the floor next to the passenger seat. His mouth felt dry. If he was caught with what was in there, he'd go down for a very long time. But after last night's near miss at the Gavin woman's flat, and the feeling he was being watched just a little too closely by both the old woman and Ragga, he'd decided that drastic measures were called for. Which was why he'd called on a friend who ran a shoe shop, among other things. A brief transaction in the stock room, surrounded by piles of trainers, and he now had the means to protect himself against all-comers.

He shook his head, still debating the wisdom of what he'd done. Was self-protection something to be ashamed of? No way. Especially after learning from the old woman last night that Frank Palmer wasn't just some private dick, but had once been a military cop. Yet another little fact she'd forgotten to mention. Szulu didn't know much about army cops, but he figured they were trained in the use of weapons. He'd also read that they were highly rated as official bodyguards, which meant they could react to danger and kill if they had to. No wonder Palmer had been so quick to get on his arse.

He breathed deeply and wiped a hand across his face. He

was certain the old woman was losing whatever marbles she had left. She'd suddenly announced the news about Palmer as if she was imparting a hot tip on the 3.30 at Haydock. Like he couldn't have done with knowing it *before* he went anywhere near the guy's office. Or near the girl, come to that. The two of them were most probably at it, anyway, which would make Palmer act all hairy-chested, even if he wasn't some kind of ex-army super-cop.

He checked the street, then ducked down under the dashboard and flipped off the thick elastic band holding the lid of the shoebox in place. Inside was a heavy object wrapped in tissue paper advertising a brand of trainers. He peeled back the paper and touched the darkened metal beneath. It felt oddly cold, and he experienced a frisson of fear. According to his friend, who sold more than just shoes, he was looking at a Spanish .22 calibre Llama automatic pistol with a five-inch barrel. His friend had rattled on about capacity and stuff, and even showed him how to hold it steady, but Szulu hadn't taken much in. He was more concerned with worrying about if, when it came down to it, he'd have the balls to use it.

19

VTS Transit occupied the end unit in a row of small, single-storey shell structures on a commercial estate in Hayes, a few minutes from the M4 motorway and to the west of London. Overshadowed by a variety of gaudily sign-posted businesses including double-glazing fitters, panel-beaters, design workshops and printers, VTS was almost insignificant, veiled behind a busy clutter of cars, skips, trailers and tractor cabs. The air smelled of hot plastic, metal and some unidentifiable cooking aromas, and the atmosphere was one of industry and urgency.

Riley and Palmer approached a glass door marked OFFICE, set alongside a blue roller door with a hand-scrawled VTS Transit sign, as if identifying the occupants had been an afterthought. The roller was three-quarters open, revealing a small warehouse containing a jumble of pallets and boxes, and a scattering of discarded cardboard packing on a concrete floor. Along one wall stood a workbench, and beyond it, in the rear corner of the unit, was a stretch of mesh steel fencing secured with a padlocked door. Inside this cage were several heavy-looking wooden crates. A man was standing at the workbench, writing on a pad. If he was aware of their approach, he did not bother looking up, but continued with his task.

"Hi," said Palmer, ducking beneath the roller door. Riley followed, scanning the interior for signs of other staff.

The man turned and stared at them with a strange lack of curiosity. He was tall and bulky, dressed in blue overalls and heavy work boots. A patch of dark bristle covered a weak chin, and his skin had an unhealthy, doughy appearance as if he spent too much time indoors. He looked from Palmer to Riley and back and lifted his chin.

"What you want?" His voice was heavily accented.

"We're looking for a reliable courier company," said Riley, making the man drag his eyes away from Palmer. "A friend said you offered a good service." She indicated the estate outside. "We were in the area and thought we'd drop by."

"Friend? What friend?" The man turned back to his work. He wrote heavily, stabbing the pen on to the paper as if he hated his job and would rather be dissecting small animals with a chisel.

"A place in Harrow." She named the building, but it brought no obvious reaction. "He said you seemed pretty switched on and reliable."

The man shook his head. "Switched on? I not know this. We are busy. Big contract take long time. No take on new business." If the man had ever attended any kind of training course, he had plainly fallen asleep before they got to the part about customer relations.

"Not enough vans?" Palmer said, looking around. The dust of the concrete floor revealed a single set of tyre tracks. In spite of the clutter, the building did not indicate signs of a fleet of vehicles.

"Correct." The man slowly ripped the form from the pad and folded it into a plastic see-through envelope with a sticky surround. He bent and slapped the envelope on to a large cardboard package on a nearby pallet.

"You ship overseas, I see," put in Riley, indicating the form he'd just completed. "Anywhere specific?"

"All over. States of America, Europe." He shrugged.

Palmer nodded towards the caged area containing the wooden crates. "I see you've got a secure storage area, too. That's good."

The man looked at the cage. "Is for high value."

"Really?" Riley asked. "Such as?"

The man gave a hint of a smile and reached behind him to pick up a phone. "I get my colleague." He dialled a number and waited, studying them by turn, then muttered something in a language neither Riley nor Palmer understood, before slapping the phone back on its rest. "He come. You wait. Two minutes." He settled back against the workbench, arms folded across his chest, no longer interested in working.

Palmer shrugged and lifted his foot to pick at something on his shoe, while Riley bent to peer at the label on the parcel.

Three minutes later there was a grating sound at the rear of the warehouse and a man appeared. He was in his fifties, with a pale complexion and crinkly hair, dressed in dark trousers and a white shirt. Above the breast pocket was a logo and the word *SkyPrint* in flowing script.

"Can I help?" he said, with the same lifting of the chin as the man in the overalls. His accent was less noticeable, but he seemed no more welcoming than his colleague. He looked from Palmer to Riley with a frown, then at the man against the bench, who merely mumbled a few words.

Palmer repeated the story they had agreed on, then waited while the man processed the information.

"Like he said, we don't need more business at the moment," he informed them. "Who did you say recommended us?" His eyes narrowed as if he couldn't quite believe anyone had done such a thing.

"Somebody we know," Palmer replied. "It's no big deal. If you can't help, we'll find someone else." He turned towards the entrance. As he did so, another man ducked beneath the roller door and stood in the opening. Physically, he was a clone of the man in overalls, except that he was dressed in a black towelling jump suit and trainers. He also looked a lot lighter on his feet.

"Neat," said Palmer. "You guys have a unique approach to business."

The man in shirtsleeves considered Palmer's words then muttered something. The newcomer stepped aside with a sour show of reluctance.

"Get anything useful?" asked Riley, on the way back to the car. She looked over her shoulder. The three men were standing in the entrance, watching them.

"You mean apart from the shitty welcome, the heavy in the romper suit and where the man in the white shirt sprang from? Not much."

"It could be a genuine set-up."

Palmer nodded. "Yeah. At least, some of it."

"Well, well. Look at that." Riley looked pointedly in the direction of a unit they had just passed. Similar in size to VTS, it bore a large sign printed with the word *SkyPrint* and the logo they had seen on the man's shirt.

Palmer nodded. Signs out front offered express printing jobs, any value, walk in, wait, walk out. "Good cover," he said. "They turn over regular cash work, establish local credibility and the boss can keep a watchful eye on VTS, without appearing to be too involved."

"I wonder if Radnor and Michael ever come here."

"I'd bet on it. Radnor doesn't strike me as the trusting kind."

As he climbed in the car, Palmer opened his hand. He was holding a tiny scrap of heavy, greasy paper, coated in dust. He rubbed the surface to reveal a dull sheen.

"It's the same as the piece you found inside the art book in Radnor's office," said Riley.

"Funny, that. They're getting careless."

"So, what now?"

Palmer considered their options for a moment. He had not forgotten the intruder of the evening before, and was sure Riley hadn't. Was he connected with Radnor? Was he a contract 'soldier' hired to find out what Riley and Palmer were up to? If what Nobby had said about Radnor's racist inclinations was correct, it didn't seem likely. Then there was the woman who had hired the car and driver in the first place. But why the interest in Riley? "We've got two strands to look at," he concluded. "There's the Fraser woman and her driver, and there's Radnor and his little operation. Our problem is, we don't know if they're connected, and I get the feeling we're running short of time."

Riley nodded. She knew no more than Palmer about the people involved, but her instincts were telling her they were unconnected. "They feel… different in some way."

"I agree. Unfortunately, we don't have enough hands to check them both."

"Not unless we split up."

"Makes sense," Palmer agreed. "Can you handle taking a look at the driver, see where he's based?" He studied her carefully. It would mean Riley coming close again to the man with dreadlocks. Some people might not be able to deal with that. But Riley wasn't some people. He gave her the note he'd made after Donald's call with information from the DVLA. "Just nail down where he is. If you can get a look at the woman, that would help. At least we'd know what she looks like. But keep your distance until we know more."

Riley folded the note into her pocket. "What are you going to do?"

He gave her one of his annoyingly enigmatic smiles and

looked towards the VTS unit. "I'm going to hang around for a bit. I want to see what they've got in that storage area at the back of the warehouse. I'll see you back at your place."

Riley looked around at the lack of obvious cover in the area. Other than a regular flow of commercial vehicles into and out of the estate, there were few pedestrians, and passing traffic on the road running through the area was light. And it wasn't as if Palmer could keep a watch on the place from a convenient café, because there wasn't one. "They'll spot you, Palmer. And how will you get back?"

But Palmer shook his head. "Drop me up the road. I saw some waste ground behind this estate, with a couple of abandoned buildings. It'll do me nicely. I've coped with less." He smiled confidently and checked his mobile. "Don't worry – when I need to bug out, I'll call a cab."

20

Riley double-checked the address on the slip of paper Palmer had given her. It turned out to be a ratty, run-down Victorian villa on the southern edges of Isleworth. Heavy net curtains hung drunkenly at the dust-blown windows, and the remains of an old trials bike was rusting in the small front plot behind a low brick wall topped with drunken coping stones. Six cracked steps led up from the pavement to the battered front door, and a panel showing a row of bell-pushes with name-tags. The house had once been proud, and no doubt the property of a single household. But over it now hung an air of despair, with peeling paint, frost-damaged brickwork and the grey tinge of neglect.

Riley parked outside a deserted building site nearby and waited. She took out the note Palmer had given her and checked the registration and make against the cars at the kerb. None of them matched. Maybe it was parked in a secure lock-up nearby.

According to Donald's information, the assigned driver of the car was a Raymond Szulu, whose address was given as Flat 3A. She studied the building carefully, wondering which window belonged to Mr Szulu. She was tempted to take a closer look, but as Palmer had pointed out, Szulu now knew what Riley looked like. If 3A looked out on to the street, and Szulu was the cautious type, he'd have a clear view of everyone walking by. If he was brazen enough to make an entry into her house to frighten her, there was no saying how he might react if he saw her encroaching on his own turf.

She wondered if Palmer was having any joy at VTS.

After her brief encounter with Szulu, she would have preferred to have Palmer here with her, but pride had prevented her saying so. Besides, he was probably enjoying himself, skulking around the commercial estate looking for an opening. Knowing Palmer, he'd probably come away with a job driving a forklift before the day was out.

The front door to Szulu's house opened, and a woman came out, followed by two small children, both with their hair in mini-dreadlocks. Szulu's, perhaps? She watched as the trio gathered together on the top step while the woman organised a clutch of bags and told one of the children to close the front door. It banged shut but, unnoticed by the woman, didn't quite catch.

Riley waited, excitement building in her chest, as they walked away up the street. Risky or not, this might be the only opportunity she'd get to see Szulu's place at close hand. She could be out here for hours waiting for him to put in an appearance.

She got out of the car and rummaged in the boot. Among the debris and clutter was an old fleece she kept for emergencies. She pulled it on over her jacket and swept her hand roughly through her hair from back to front, then the other way. A brief look in the side window to check that she now had a suitable air of untidiness, and she set off across the street, hoping that she wasn't already in Szulu's sights.

The broken steps rocked beneath her feet as she approached the front door. She ignored the name-tags on the panel of bell-pushes. If Szulu was in, the last thing she wanted was to announce her arrival. She pushed the door open. Inside was a large lobby with a cracked tile floor in a chequerboard pattern, and a battered table holding a scattering of envelopes, free papers and junk mail. Riley flicked through the pile, but saw nothing addressed to

Szulu. In front of her was a broad staircase, the treads covered by a worn carpet. The air smelled of a cleaning product with a hint of lemon.

Two doors led off the lobby, both marked PRIVATE. She guessed these were the landlord's or a tenant-manager, if there was one. She'd check out 3A first, then come back here as a last resort. A corridor ran along one side of the staircase, with a bicycle against the wall and a pushchair just beyond it. A glass-panelled door opened on to a garden at the rear.

Riley climbed the stairs, wincing as the treads creaked loudly. If this was one of Szulu's warning signals of unexpected visitors, he'd now be on high alert and waiting for her.

She reached the first floor landing, with two doors in front of her and one at each end. Number 3A was to her right, but as she turned towards it, one of the doors facing her swung open, and an elderly black woman in a raincoat and scarf stepped out. She eyed Riley with suspicion before slamming the door behind her.

'You don't live here," the woman muttered in a Caribbean drawl, pulling herself up to her full height. "Who you looking for?"

Riley wanted to tell the woman to lower her voice in case Szulu heard and came out to investigate. But something in the woman's eyes told her she wasn't the sort to listen to any kind of advice, and probably saw herself as the house custodian. Maybe she and Mr Grobowski belonged to the same club.

"His name's Ray," she said hesitantly, pulling her fleece closely around her. "I met him… I met him in a club and he said to call by if I was in the area." She shrugged. "So I thought, why not?"

The woman looked Riley up and down with narrowed eyes and shook her head. Her expression spoke of disapproval and pity in equal measures.

"You mean Ray Szulu?"

Riley nodded. "I think that's what he said. He's got –" She gestured to her head. "– dreadlocks."

"That's the one." The woman gave a humourless smile. "What you doing calling on a man when you don't even know his name?" She gestured towards 3A and walked past Riley, stopping to add quietly: "He's out. Best you take that as a good omen and look elsewhere, girl. He's not what my mother would have called decent company, you know?" She nodded fiercely and walked down the stairs, slamming the front door firmly behind her.

Riley waited until the vibrations had ceased, then stepped over to Szulu's door and put her ear to the woodwork. There were no sounds from inside, so she decided to cut her losses. Two minutes later, she was back in her car, watching the street.

Time ticked by slowly. Then a large, black Lexus saloon drifted neatly into a slot a hundred yards away and a tall, athletic figure stepped out and surveyed the street. Riley felt her skin crawl as she recognised the familiar shape. There was no mistaking the dark swirl of braided hair around his head.

He walked along the pavement with a graceful gait and disappeared inside the house. Five minutes later, he came back out and returned to the car, before driving smoothly away from the kerb, heading north.

Riley followed, staying four vehicles behind him. Her heart was thumping at the idea that she was so close to the man without being seen, and she remembered Palmer once telling her that the excitement of the chase was what often put the follower at risk of detection. Amateur follower, Riley thought, would have been more accurate, although less kind.

The Lexus was heading west, Riley realised, towards the A30. Ahead lay the vastness of Heathrow, and beyond that, the more salubrious area of Windsor. According to Donald, this was where the woman named Fraser was staying. This could be interesting, getting the two heads together at once.

Szulu drove in a smooth, unfussy manner, using the road with evident skill. He rarely exceeded the speed limit, but took advantage of quiet stretches wherever he could. It was obvious he knew the road and the area well, a fact that made Riley take extra precautions to avoid being left adrift with no vehicles between them.

He eventually turned off the A30 and approached Windsor from the south east, through Wraysbury. When he signalled right just before a large hotel sign, Riley pulled into the kerb and watched as he drove into the front parking area and left the Lexus.

Her patience lasted ten minutes before the temptation to do something became too strong. Locking the car, she dodged across the road and entered the hotel, scanning the foyer.

The reception area was all glass and aluminium, with large ferns and yuccas dotted about to counter the almost sterile atmosphere. A waterfall trickled into a pool to one side of a staircase, and tuneless musak hummed through the air. Through an archway to her right Riley saw a dining room, and to the left a lounge. Just past the reception desk, a wall sign pointed towards the rooms and a lift.

The receptionist, a young blonde with high cheekbones and a glossy smile, was busy on the phone. There was no sign of Szulu.

Riley peered round the edge of the lounge door. There were club chairs, comfortable sofas but no people. She walked across to the dining area, empty save for an elderly waiter, slapping crumbs off tablecloths with a folded napkin. It was evidently the dead hour for the hotel trade.

"May I help you?" The receptionist had finished with the phone and looked up with a faint frown. Riley was relieved she had discarded her tatty fleece.

"I'm not sure," Riley replied. "I'm sure I saw a friend of mine come in here just now. Tall, black... with dreadlocks?"

"A friend?" The receptionist showed her teeth, and Riley realised she had probably blown it. It hadn't occurred to her that Szulu might be well known here. If he really was a freelance driver-for-hire, this might be one of his regular collection and delivery points.

"Well, not a friend, exactly," she admitted, aiming for a sister-in-need smile. "He owes me a key. He never returned it."

The receptionist made a drawn-out 'ah' of understanding and pointed behind her. "He's gone out back to the garden. His client's waiting for him. She's not feeling so good. I think she took a bit of a turn earlier." Her expression suggested that key or no key, barging in right now to settle a private spat would not be appropriate.

"No problem," said Riley easily. "I'll wait for him to come out."

The receptionist went back to her phone, and Riley wandered into the lounge. She picked a chair within sight of the foyer and the front desk, and waited until the girl was busy, then stood up and slipped past her to the stairs. If she was lucky, she might get a glimpse of the mysterious Mrs Fraser.

The upper floor was deserted, apart from a cleaner's

trolley outside one of the rooms. The sound of someone humming came from inside, and Riley moved by swiftly, heading for the rear of the building.

At the end of the corridor was a fire-escape door. She peered through the glass and found herself looking down on a stretch of lawn with a few bushes and trees. To one side stood a couple of parasols with tables and chairs.

Szulu was sitting on one chair, elbows resting on his knees. He was facing somebody, and judging by the shoes and legs, which was all Riley could see, that person was an elderly woman.

She waited for the woman to lean forward, impatient to catch a glimpse and leave. But it was soon clear that Mrs Fraser – if it was her – wasn't going to make it easy for her.

Suddenly the trolley rattled behind her. Riley gave it a few more seconds before deciding enough was enough. As she turned to leave, her phone rang.

It was John Mitcheson.

21

"You're *where?*"

"Heathrow. Landside. But don't tell anyone. Can we meet?" Mitcheson sounded undeniably breezy, and Riley could hardly take in the fact that he was just a few miles away from where she was sitting.

"Are you mad?" she demanded, momentarily forgetting where she was. "If some eagle-eyed immigration drone spots your name, you'll be arrested!"

"Well, I haven't been yet. It's risky, I know, but I'm fed up with all this subterfuge. I contacted a mate recently... he has connections with Immigration. My name isn't on any of the lists he can access, and he doesn't think there are too many others, not unless it's on one the security bods keep close to their chests."

"So what are you going to do?" Riley desperately wanted to tell him to get on the first flight out, but a large part wanted to tell him to stay, to take the chance.

"I'm leaving later this evening. My mate said if I was on a watch list, unless it was a priority, it would take at least seven hours to filter through the system. They're more interested in Al Quaeda right now than a dodgy ex-army officer."

"You're not dodgy," she protested fiercely. "That decision by the MOD was a travesty. Those men took advantage of you and the military let you take the fall."

He chuckled, making goose-bumps stand up on her neck. "God, it's great to have you on my side. Any chance of getting together – say, for a drink?"

Riley groaned. "John, your timing couldn't be worse. I'm

watching someone right now and can't just… " The idea of having Mitcheson within reach yet being unable to do anything about it was agonising. But would it be so bad to leave Szulu for a few hours? Surely Palmer wouldn't object, since he knew their circumstances. She thought about it. Dammit, Palmer wasn't her employer. "I'll pick you up." There. Decision made. If Palmer didn't like it, he could charge her with dereliction of duty or whatever the military cop jargon was.

"Now you're talking." Mitcheson chuckled again. "But forget the pick-up. I'll get the Underground to Acton Town or somewhere and grab a cab."

"That'll take *hours*."

"No, it won't. I'll hi-jack it. See you later." He rang off, leaving Riley wondering if Mitcheson's friend in Immigration had got his facts right about how long it took to spot an unwanted entry.

In the privacy of the small garden behind the hotel, Szulu looked at Lottie Grossman and felt something akin to pity. It wasn't as if she looked that great normally, but right now, she looked like shit. Pale and trembling and surrounded by pumped-up cushions, she resembled a patient in a retirement home. When she'd tried to pick up a glass of water just now, she'd almost dropped it. Whatever was ailing her hadn't worn down her nasty streak, though.

"I tell you I'm all right," she hissed, her lips barely moving. "I've felt worse than this after a good night out."

"Well, you certainly don't look all right," he muttered. "You sure that doctor knew what he was doing?"

Her fingernails scraped on the edge of the table as she leaned forward and pushed a slip of paper across to him. "He gave me a prescription for some pills. I need you to find a pharmacy for me." She nodded at a plastic bottle by her glass and added, "He left me those, just in case. Too many quacks forcing pills down our throats these days." She coughed, bringing a spasm of pain across her face. It added to the odd tilt her features had taken since he'd seen her last night, until it was like looking at a distorted reflection in a bad mirror. "I want to up the pressure on Palmer and the girl. Make them sweat."

"Yeah? You sure about that? He nearly caught me last time."

In spite of her obvious ill health, Lottie Grossman managed a sneer, her features twisting even further. "What's the matter? Scared of him, are you?" Her voice was taunting, and suddenly Szulu wanted to reach out and kick her, ill or not.

"I'm not scared of no one!" he snarled. Then he pulled himself together. Getting angry with this old witch would mean having to face the Ragga.

"Good," she cooed. "Glad to hear it. You'd better be off, then. See if you can get the girl alone. Only, this time – " She reached out and slid one of her long fingernails across the back of his hand, making him want to snatch his hand away in revulsion. "This time you can tell her…" She thought for a moment, eyes pinpoints of pure malevolence. "Tell her Lottie's back."

"Is that all?" He felt relieved that she didn't want him to do something worse. It was a sign that he needed to be done with her as soon as possible and get back to some normal work.

"It will do for now. She'll know what it means. Now go."

Szulu crossed the lawn towards the hotel, feeling Lottie Grossman's eyes drilling into his back. He wondered what kept her going. Hate, most likely. If so, it wasn't doing her a lot of good. He dismissed that and tried to figure out how best to pick up on the Gavin woman's trail and deliver the message. Maybe he'd try Palmer's office first. If they were together, it would be two birds with one stone and all that stuff. As long as he took care to stay out of Palmer's reach; the guy was way too quick for his liking. Then he remembered the .22 Llama in his car. A glimpse of the business end of that would slow the ex-military cop down. It wasn't a big gun but only a fool would be willing to take a shot they didn't have to. And Palmer most likely knew better than most what the effect of a .22 slug could be.

As he passed the front desk, he caught the receptionist looking at him. He automatically flashed a smile, but she turned away, giving him the cold shoulder.

"Hey – what's up?" he said. Damn. He thought he was getting somewhere there, too. This was turning into a bad day all round.

"You had a visitor," she told him without looking round. "You just missed her."

"Yeah? Who?" He frowned. Who the hell knew he was here? But the receptionist had already turned to answer the phone.

When he got outside, there was nobody around. Then he heard a car start up across the road from the hotel. It was a VW Golf. As it pulled away from the kerb, he saw a woman with a familiar shock of blonde hair in the driver's seat.

Szulu ran for his car.

Frank Palmer studied the rear of the VTS unit from the cover of an abandoned council road maintenance depot, pondering on the amount of foot traffic between VTS and the *SkyPrint* premises further along. Most of the time it had been the boss man with the white shirt, accompanied by faces Palmer hadn't seen before. He assumed the faces were there to lift and carry, and this was borne out when they left VTS bearing boxes and packages Palmer was too far away to identify. On two occasions the big lug in the romper suit had walked out of the rear door of VTS carrying tied bundles of paper. He had dumped these into a large metal drum on a patch of open concrete. The scorch marks on the drum suggested it was used regularly as an incinerator, and Palmer wondered what it was they were so keen on torching, rather than consigning to the dustbin.

Apart from the activity here, there was also a lot of movement at the front of the building. He could guess what was happening: the VTS birds were clearing up and getting ready to fly. They had clearly been sufficiently shaken by Palmer and Riley's visit to know they were on somebody's radar. The *SkyPrint* premises were probably squeaky clean, and would therefore pass scrutiny. Given enough time for any problems to blow over, they could set up another VTS operation somewhere else without being compromised.

The rear door to VTS opened and the man in blue overalls appeared. He was carrying a bottle. He approached the large metal drum and emptied the contents inside, tossing the bottle into the grass nearby. He reached down into the drum, and there was a muffled whump and a thin ball of smoke lifted into the air. Moments later, the atmosphere around the drum began to shimmer as heat built up and flames licked hungrily around the rim. Giving the drum a kick, the man returned to the building, slamming the door behind him.

Palmer watched the smoke billow across the open ground, and fought a powerful urge to leave his hiding place and see what he could rescue. Burning papers meant they must be worth destroying. But rushing over there might entail coming up against Romper Suit and his friend. He had attended sites in the past where documents had been torched, and he'd always been surprised by how much survived the flames. Given that the man in overalls hadn't even checked to see if the bundles thrown into the drum had been untied, he was content to take his chances and see what could be salvaged later.

He shifted his position to ease a touch of cramp and tried not to think of strong, hot coffee. He'd give it another hour. By then, they might have decided to pack up for the day. Then he'd slip across for a closer look.

Riley looked objectively at her flat. Untidy, maybe – even lived in if she was being generous – but nothing a ten-second tour wouldn't put right. It wasn't as if John would be expecting a scene from *Homes & Gardens*. Too bad if he was.

She heard a burst of classical music coming from downstairs. At least they wouldn't need violins to go with the atmosphere: Mr Grobowski was probably cooking up a huge meal for the community centre members and enjoying his favourite compatriots' musical compositions.

She plumped cushions and nudged the place into order, then put on some coffee. If John's was a flying visit, they might have enough time to go out for a meal. Then she thought about Palmer. She should call and tell him she'd bunked off. With the thought came a renewed twinge of the guilt at not sticking with Szulu and finding out more about the mysterious Mrs Fraser. But it was too late now; as her mother used to say, make your decisions by all means, but live with the consequences and get on with it.

The cat wandered in and sat licking his lips in a meaningful manner, and she decided not to make him wait. There was no saying how he'd react to Mitcheson's presence, anyway, so if he was going to slink off in a huff at having another male about the place for a couple of hours, he might as well do it on a full stomach. She spooned a generous portion of meat into his bowl and left him to it, then returned to the living room and opened her laptop.

Now they had a link between Radnor's office and Gillivray's death – no matter how tenuous it would seem to a defence lawyer – they might be able to fill in any missing pieces. Donald Brask might be able to help there. It didn't sound as if the police had made any connections between the sixth and first floors of the building yet, but the journalist in her hoped that would be the case for some time while she and Palmer carried on digging. All they had to do was forge a provable link without showing they had broken into Azimtec's offices in the process.

A knock at the door made her jump. She saved her work and closed the laptop, trying to control the smile that had been hovering since getting Mitcheson's call. As she reached out to open the door, the defensive part of Riley's brain wondered how Mitcheson had got inside without buzzing. If he'd met Mr Grobowski on the way in, surely she would have heard the elderly Pole's booming voice.

The inner warning came too late: as she tried to close the door again, Szulu burst in on her, dreadlocks swirling about his head.

This time he was carrying a gun.

22

"Who else is here? Tell me right now!" The words seemed to tumble out of his mouth in a rush as he drove her away from the door, the gun barrel level with her face. His eyes had a wild, intense look, as if he had been winding himself up into a state of readiness before coming up here. "Don't shit with me, you hear!"

Stunned by seeing the gun, Riley back-pedalled until she felt the sofa behind her legs, barely managing to prevent herself from falling. *Whatever else you do*, she told herself frantically, *stay on your feet.*

"There's no one here," she replied. "Just me. What do you want?"

Szulu reached out and grabbed her shoulder with his free hand, looking around the room and pulling her close, then swinging her in front of him like a shield. When he seemed satisfied that nobody was going to jump on him, he let her go and shoved her away. He continued to wave the pistol, though, nodding to himself and pacing about, his breath whistling between his teeth.

"You Riley Gavin, right?"

"Yes."

"Good. You listen, you hear? That's all you got to do and you won't get hurt. I got a message for you. You and the ex-cop – what's his name – Palmer? Yeah, him. Where is he, by the way?" He glanced around as if expecting Palmer to materialise from nowhere.

"He's working," said Riley, eyeing the gun. Instinct told her that if Szulu had come here to shoot her, he would have done it by now. But she wasn't about to take any chances. She looked around for a weapon – anything – but couldn't see anything even remotely useful against an armed man. Damn. So much for tidying up. Why couldn't she have the odd baseball bat lying around? She edged towards the door, which was still open from when he'd charged into the flat. She was surprised she could think so clearly, even though he was here, right in front of her, especially after the other evening. She instinctively grabbed her laptop, the repository of all her work. If she could get close enough, she could be through and downstairs. Providing he wasn't much of a shot, she might be able to get out into the street and yell for help.

"Wait!" He lunged forward, raising the gun. "What's that?"

"It's my laptop, you moron," she retorted, anger giving her words added venom. "You're not having this, gun or no gun. It cost me too much."

Szulu pulled an incredulous face. "You what? You think I've come here to steal your precious *laptop*? Where the fuck you get that idea? You think I'm some cheap crack-head?" He blew out a mouthful of air, hugely indignant. "Cheeky bitch!"

A sound came from the kitchen, and Szulu spun round, dragging the gun with him. "Who's that? Come out here!"

The cat edged past the door frame and looked at him. Instantly sensing danger, it arched its back and bared its teeth, hissing at Szulu like a high-pressure steam valve. Szulu lowered the gun to cover the perceived threat, his finger tightening involuntarily on the trigger. There was a loud click and he swore angrily and stared at the gun in dismay. "Shit!"

"No!" Horrified at the idea that he would shoot the cat – even by reflex – Riley hurled the laptop with all her strength, aiming for Szulu's face. It connected to the side of his head with a sickening smack before tumbling to the floor with a crash. Momentarily stunned, Szulu let go of the gun. It landed on the tip of the barrel, spun in the air, then hit the floor again and skittered towards Riley, ending up at her feet. Szulu, clutching his face and cursing, seemed to have temporarily forgotten the weapon, and blundered about the room, disorientated.

Fuelled by a mixture of fury and fear on behalf of the cat, which had disappeared back into the kitchen, Riley scooped up the gun in one smooth movement. Coming up to a half-crouch, she steadied her knees the way she had seen on television and cupped her right hand with her left, supporting the weight of the gun. She was surprised by how light it was, and how warm to the touch after Szulu's hand.

She lifted the gun and peered down the short barrel at Szulu's face, now turned towards her with a growing expression of horror. If she hadn't been so scared, it would have been comic. He raised one hand and shook it frantically at her, palm outward to ward off the inevitable.

"No, lady – don't do that!"

"Why not?" Riley felt a sudden release of anger. A part of her brain wanted to give way to logic and reason, and listen to the tiny echo that was Palmer's voice, telling her why shooting someone was such a bad thing, why it was easy to do yet so hard to live with. But a greater part wanted to feel the trigger move beneath the deliberate pressure of her finger, wanted to feel the recoil and see the barrel jump, and witness the man in front of her realise he had taken a step too far and with the wrong person; that there were consequences to forcing your way into someone's home and threatening them. She felt the pressure give way as the trigger moved. God, it was going to be so easy…

Then Szulu's face changed and his eyes shifted to a point just over her shoulder. A scuff of movement came from behind her and a powerful hand moved past her shoulder, clamping down on hers and gently but firmly forcing the gun away until it was pointing at the floor.

"Easy does it." It was John Mitcheson, the familiar smell of him suddenly close by, his presence enveloping her like a soft, warm blanket. She allowed him to take the gun away, and felt herself moved gently aside until he was standing in front of Szulu, the gun by his side. He looked tanned and fit, taller than Szulu by a few inches, dominating the room without trying.

"Who the fuck are you?" Szulu demanded indignantly. "Did you see that? The bitch was going to shoot me!" He pointed a trembling finger at Riley, apparently forgetting that he had been the first to pull the trigger after bursting in uninvited.

"Really?" Mitcheson looked down at the gun. "Funny. I thought I heard it misfire."

"Yeah. Piece of junk – I should get my money back!" Szulu edged backwards, eyes searching for an escape route now things had gone so badly wrong.

Mitcheson looked up and stopped him with a warning shake of his head, then worked the slide on the gun with an expert hand. The unused shell spun through the air and landed with barely a noise on the carpet. "Semi-automatics, you see," he said in a conversational tone. "They do have a tendency to jam sometimes. You just have to be quick to clear them, that's all. Especially if you're facing a live threat." He looked at Szulu as if to check that he was paying attention. "The second round usually works fine, though, if you're lucky. Like this."

He calmly pointed the gun at Szulu and shot him.

23

Palmer stepped cautiously over a patch of nettles and ducked through a gap in the wire fence to the commercial estate. He was now behind the VTS Transit unit, just a few feet away from the incinerator drum. A wisp of smoke was curling lazily into the air, which was heavy with the smell of petrol and scorched paper.

Twenty minutes had passed since the last sign of movement between the two buildings, and there had been no sounds of activity from the front. It was difficult to be certain from here, but Palmer guessed the VTS building was now deserted.

He stepped past a stack of metal storage bins and stood alongside the rear door. There were no shouts of alarm, so he tried the door. It was unlocked. He eased it open and glanced inside. Nothing. No voices, no movement, just a scattering of packaging, pallets, waste paper and clutter, and the unmistakable echo of an empty building.

He closed the door again and walked across the yard to the drum. A wave of heat was still coming from inside, but there were no flames and whatever effect the accelerant had possessed was now spent. The bottom of the drum held a shifting mass of ashes and scorched paper, with some of the print showing silver and still readable against the grey background. He picked up a length of wooden batten. Digging into the mass inside the drum, he felt something solid under the topmost layer. But as he disturbed the contents, the passage of air fanned the smouldering ashes and flames sprang up once more, feeding on the untouched paper beneath.

Palmer stepped back and kicked over the drum, spilling the contents across the concrete in a shower of burning paper, smoke and sparks. With the batten, he hooked out the largest object, a bundle of documents dumped inside by Romper Suit. Isolating the wedge of papers, he bent to peer at them. From what he could already see, there appeared to be ample evidence tying *SkyPrint* to the VTS operation. Whether it would be enough to bring it to a court case would be for others to determine.

Satisfied that the papers were in no danger of re-igniting, he picked up a discarded Tesco bag caught on the corner of a pallet and stuffed them inside it. He left the bundle in the long grass by the fence and returned to the building to investigate further.

Inside, a couple of sparrows, startled by the sound of his footsteps, swooped beneath the metal rafters and disappeared out of the door, their wing-beats loud in the silence. Palmer was grateful for their presence; it was a sign that nobody else was here.

He checked the office at the front of the building. Whoever had cleared it out had left nothing but an array of paperwork, low-value office equipment and rubbish. Even the walls were bare of evidence that anyone had worked here. As he turned to leave, he heard the rattle of a door handle, and voices at the front of the building. He glanced out of the window.

Radnor.

Palmer moved quickly. There was nowhere to hide in the office, and he prayed he had enough time to get out the back door. But even as he hurried towards the rear of the warehouse, he heard a voice from the back yard and the sound of footsteps approaching.

"The rubbish bin's fallen over. Probably kids."

Palmer swore silently. Now he was well and truly snookered. He went to the only place available, the caged area, and slipped through the door. Against one wall was a large pile of cardboard packaging, unused cardboard boxes and some broken lathes of wood. He dived to the floor and pulled the packaging over him. If they were here to move this lot, he was stuffed. Seconds later, the sound of several pairs of footsteps converged on the centre of the warehouse.

"You destroyed everything, Perric?" What Palmer took to be Radnor's voice was calm and businesslike, and came from the door to the office. "If they find a link to this place, they'll go through it with a magnifying glass. These people aren't stupid."

"There is no paperwork." Palmer recognised the voice of the man in the white shirt. He didn't sound happy.

"It's not just paper," insisted Radnor. "Packaging material, oil – even flakes of paint off the weapons and crates – they can trace it back."

"It's all done. Dino burned what papers we couldn't take. You can check the ashes out back if you want." Perric sounded resentful, as if his abilities were being questioned.

"And the boxes from the last shipment? Those laser sights are worth a fortune. We can't afford to lose them, not now."

Laser sights? Jesus, thought Palmer.

"Ready to go. We're waiting for a call from the ship's first officer to say when we can deliver without running into the docks supervisor. They should be on their way across the Med in three days."

"And the handguns?"

"They've gone already. We re-packed them as you said and got rid of the original packaging. It's in a landfill miles from here."

"What's all this?" A new voice spoke from much closer, and the wire cage rattled as somebody pushed against it. The speaker had a faint accent, but the voice was unfamiliar.

"It's nothing," said Perric. This time his voice was more respectful. "More rubbish. It won't have any traces on it. It would have taken too long to burn and there wasn't time to go to the local tip."

The scrape of shoe leather on the bare concrete floor came very close to Palmer's hiding place, and the corrugated sheet above him shifted slightly as somebody kicked at the pile of packaging. Suddenly, instead of the covering of cardboard, Palmer could see the roof of the warehouse above him, with its latticework of steel rafters and support beams. A large pigeon was looking down at him, cocking its head and shifting nervously from side to side as the men moved around.

"Are you sure about that?" The man's voice was now so close, Palmer could hear him breathing as he bent over.

The pigeon took fright and clattered from its beam in the roof space, causing the man near Palmer to swear in surprise. As the sound of wing-beats moved across the warehouse and through the rear door, somebody laughed.

"Michael, we don't have time." It was Radnor again. "Let's get out of here in case Palmer and the woman come back and bring the police with them. This place is compromised."

The packaging moved again, but this time slid back to cover Palmer's face. He hoped it hadn't left his feet in sight, and held his breath until the man named Michael had moved away. There was a clang as the cage door swung shut, and the footsteps faded into the distance towards the front of the building.

Palmer waited a full five minutes, then slid out from

his hiding place. He walked silently to the roller door and peered out through a gap in the metal slats. Radnor, Perric, and two men he couldn't see properly were standing outside, talking. One of the men had his back to the building; Palmer thought it might be the young Russian. It looked as if this was their final visit to the place before abandoning it altogether.

Palmer eased cautiously away from the door and out into the back yard. He crossed to the fence, stopping to pick up the Tesco bag with its bundle of evidence, then slipped through the gap and jogged through the deserted council depot to the road in search of a cab.

24

The sound of the shot wasn't as loud as Riley expected. A vague corner of her mind rationalised that Mr Grobowski downstairs wouldn't have heard anything, as he was too busy banging his pots and pans in the kitchen. Even so, she flinched at the shockwaves in the air.

Szulu spun away with a cry of pain, clutching his left arm. When he straightened up and took his hand away, there was a hole in the sleeve of his jacket and blood was beginning to spread through the material.

"Fuck, man – you shot me!" he whispered, as if he couldn't believe such a thing. "What you do that for?"

"Damn, that was careless," commented Mitcheson mildly. He looked at Riley and continued as if discussing the matter with a new recruit, "They don't always work after jamming like that; they usually need stripping down. Good job I was aiming at his head or I might have hit something serious."

Riley said nothing, too stunned to speak yet feeling an irrational urge to laugh. It had all happened so fast. She was mesmerised by the ease with which Mitcheson had shot her attacker, yet aware of the evident care he had taken not to kill him, in spite of his anger.

As if to demonstrate this, he grabbed Szulu by his good arm and slammed him against the wall. "Now, before I get really annoyed at you for frightening my girlfriend, what's this about?"

"John, wait." Riley stepped quickly alongside him and placed a hand on his arm. "He said he had a message for me. I want to hear what it is."

Mitcheson lifted an eyebrow. "Really? Boy, Fedex must have really changed their core business." He jammed the gun barrel beneath Szulu's chin and nudged it upwards until their eyes met. Whatever Szulu saw there made him go very still.

"Let's hear it."

"It's…yo, man, this really hurts, y'know!" Szulu sucked air through his teeth and held his wounded arm, until Mitcheson dropped the gun and pointed it menacingly against the man's good shoulder. "OK… OK. The message is… Christ, I don't understand it, but she said to tell you –"

"She?" Mitcheson echoed.

"Some woman called Fraser," Riley explained helpfully. "She hired him to drive for her. She's been hanging around, but we don't know who she is or what she wants. They already turned over Palmer's office."

"So they're not part of the other thing you told me about?"

"Radnor? It doesn't look like it."

"She said to tell you," continued Szulu, "she said you'd know what she meant. She said, 'Lottie's back'. That's all, I swear. 'Lottie's back.'" He slumped back with a sigh as Riley and Mitcheson exchanged stunned looks.

"*Lottie Grossman*?" Riley could hardly believe it. The name sent her thoughts spinning back to an assignment in Spain, when she had first met John Mitcheson. It was also the first occasion she and Palmer had worked together, and they had nearly lost their lives investigating the activities of the murderous ex-gangster's wife and her gang of mercenaries. "I thought she'd be dead by now."

"Wishful thinking," said Mitcheson. "Never bloody works when you want it to."

"Of course!" Riley said excitedly. "That explains the gardening bit in Palmer's office. The evil cow was a mad keen gardener, wasn't she?"

Mitcheson nodded. When Lottie wasn't busy plotting, she had spent most of her time in the garden, armed with something sharp. "She just liked killing things. Weeds were a ready victim. She certainly put a lot of enthusiasm into it."

Szulu looked from one to the other as if they were mad, and gestured towards the door. "Look, I hate to interrupt, but can I go now? I need a doctor."

Mitcheson looked at Riley. "You got a small towel you don't mind losing?"

Riley went into the kitchen and came back with a handful of paper towelling. Mitcheson made Szulu strip off his jacket and gave his arm a cursory examination. There was an entry wound but no exit, and he guessed the jacket and Szulu's arm muscle, and maybe a poor charge in the cartridge, had combined to reduce the round's velocity. He slapped the wadded tissue unceremoniously against the wound. "Hold that in place and don't get excited, and you might not bleed to death."

"Wha–? Hey – I need proper medical attention, not this stuff!"

"And you'll get it. First you talk. What's with the mad Lottie? She after revenge or is she trying to make another comeback?"

Szulu frowned. "Huh?"

"She used to run a gang, a few years back. Clubs, drugs, girls... that sort of stuff. You didn't know?"

"You kidding me? That old woman?" Szulu almost laughed at the idea, then clearly thought better. "I ain't surprised. She's cold. Way cold. I don't know about no comeback, though. But revenge, definitely. She said so, in fact. She hired me as a driver, see – and minder. First we went to Palmer's place. But he wasn't there. She seemed to

163

be looking for something at his place, but she never told me what. Maybe she didn't know herself. Fact is, she never told me nothing until it was almost too late. Then she told me he was some hotshot ex-army cop." Szulu looked aggrieved at the idea and shook his head. "Then she decided she wanted me to put the frights into her." He nodded at Riley, before quickly looking at Mitcheson. "But I was never going to hurt her – honest. It seemed like Grossman was building up to something... getting herself all wired up and that, but she didn't say what it was."

"Revenge?" said Riley. "Why am I not surprised?"

"She told me Palmer had caused her old man's death and spoiled some plans, and you'd helped him. It's obvious, isn't it? She was pissed and wanted payback. Said something about how she'd been waiting long enough and now was the time, before it was too late. Too late for what, she never said. Personally, I think she's nuts. But that's all I know, I promise."

"So why this?" Mitcheson waved the .22 in the air. "You're no gunman."

"It was for protection, man, what else?" Szulu glanced down at his arm and hissed quietly as a wave of pain hit him.

"But Lottie Grossman always flies mob-handed," said Mitcheson thoughtfully. "It's the only way she knows. Are you saying there's nobody else out there?"

Szulu looked from one to the other, a variety of expressions crossing his face. Then he said quietly. "Sort of."

"Sort of?"

"Wait – it's not like you think. See, I got into this problem. There's this south London guy named Ragga Pearl. He's bad news – I mean really bad. A gangsta dude with delusions. If Ragga wants to hurt someone, he don't think twice about it. Think of the worst person you ever knew, jack it up by a hundred, and you'd have the Ragga. He's a real mamba on two legs. Anyway, he thinks I disrespected him, but I didn't. See, he's got this whole thing going about respect, and is totally crazy into the bargain – I mean lethal, right?" He winced, but this time it didn't seem connected with the pain in his arm. "I also owe him some cash, which was stupid, borrowing off a freak like him, but whatever. At the time, I was desperate."

"How does this mesh with Lottie Grossman?" asked Riley impatiently.

"I'm coming to it, right? I don't know how Grossman connected with a guy like Ragga Pearl, her being old and white an' all. I mean, it shouldn't happen, even with all this multi-cultural crap they spilling out these days. You don't mix lions with zebras, right? I reckon they must know people in common, is all I can think of. Anyway, I been expecting like the roof to fall in on me for about two weeks now, what with the way Ragga is. But next thing I know is, he calls me and tells me I'm working for this white woman until he decides otherwise."

Mitcheson asked, "Doing what?"

"He says I'm to do what she says, go where she wants, stuff like that. He says she wants someone followed and needs a guy who knows the moves, you know?"

"Moves?"

"Yeah. The street. How to move around but stay out of trouble. He says he told her I was good for that, and then he tells me if it goes down well, the debt's paid off."

"Why?"

Szulu scowled. "Why? 'Cos this is the Ragga. He don't need no reasons, man. He just does stuff. It's all part of his controlling shit... so he can pull strings and make like he runs this business fuckin' empire. Doesn't mean he hasn't got an angle going, which in this case is earning money off the old woman for me being a modern-day *slave*. Only he ain't gonna tell me his reasons, is he? All I know is, I do like the woman says, and maybe I'll get out from under Ragga's thumb, which is fuckin' ace with me." He shrugged, which made him wince again. "You ask me, I reckon he knows stuff about this Grossman woman. Stuff he doesn't let on about. But that's Ragga, man. He's always looking for an advantage." He managed what could have been a smile of admiration. "First she'll know about it is when he drops a thunderbolt on her head."

"I wouldn't bet on it," muttered Mitcheson. He looked at Riley. "She's quick off the mark, I'll give her that. Her time might be long gone, but she's cottoned on fast to who the new boys in town are."

Riley shrugged. "Different style, same aims. She needed someone cheap, and Ragga sold her this mutt."

But Szulu was in full, resentful flow and appeared not to have heard the exchange. "Thing is, she never kept me in the loop about nothing. It was like everything was this big secret, and I was driving blind all the time. And there was Ragga always in the background. She even threatened to put in a bad word with him when I questioned her once; said she never put up with disloyalty, not ever. I mean, what was that about? It wasn't like I was a kid or she owned me… but she acted like she did."

"That's Lottie for you," said Riley. "Mad as a mongoose."

"Bless her," Mitcheson agreed. "So you don't know anyone called –" He looked at Riley.

"Radnor," she put in. "Or Michael – he's a Russian."

Szulu shook his head. "No, never heard of them. Far as I know, Ragga don't mix with no Russians. Like I said, no one else was involved."

"OK," said Mitcheson. "Is that it?"

Szulu nodded. "That's it, man. See, I got the gun in case the Ragga come calling, or maybe the old woman decided to do something crazy. That was all." He looked at Riley. "I'm sorry I scared you. I didn't mean no real harm, only… it kind of ran away from me." He switched his gaze to Mitcheson and stood up straighter, lifting his chin. "That's straight up, man."

Mitcheson nodded. He sensed Szulu was telling the truth, it had all poured out so freely. Now he wanted out. "Fair enough. So what were you supposed to do after delivering the message?"

Szulu shrugged. "Go meet the old witch and tell her I done the deed. Then wait for her to tell me what she wants to do next. Only, I got a feeling she might not make it."

"Why's that?"

"She's old, man. And sick. She had some sort of attack at her hotel, and it's made her even more unpredictable. You want my opinion, she's running out of juice."

"A heart attack?"

"Don't know, man. I ain't no doctor. She got some pills that seem to help, and I'm supposed to pick up some more from a pharmacy, but I can't second-guess her, you know? All I know is, I got to get away from her and Ragga, or I'm dead meat."

Mitcheson pulled him away from the wall. "Then you'd better get going, hadn't you? One thing, though." He leaned close to Szulu and stared intently at him. "You say a thing to Lottie about me and I'll know. You'd also better not come back here. You dig?"

Szulu nodded and swallowed, not liking what he saw in the other man's eyes. "Yeah, man. I dig."

They listened to Szulu stumble down the stairs and out the front door, before Riley turned to Mitcheson and leaned against him with a sigh of relief.

"Do you believe him – about him being Lottie's only man?"

Mitcheson shook his head. "I'm not sure. You know Lottie: she never employs one man where two or three will do better. But maybe she didn't have a choice. Could be she's firing on a low fuel tank. I think you'd better keep an eye out for anyone else who might be working for this Ragga Pearl. Just to be safe."

"I don't want to sound like a helpless female," she said softly, "but I'm so glad you turned up when you did." She reached round behind her and pushed the hand holding the gun away so that he could put it down. "Especially before I used that."

Mitcheson grinned and held her close. "Me, too. You'd have probably missed and made a mess of the wall."

She slapped him on the arm. "You rat. You know what I mean." She had to crane her neck to look up at him, taking in the familiar easy smile and dark hair, liking the way it curled just behind his ears. "You called me your girlfriend."

"Did I? Damn. The things I say when I'm under stress." He gestured towards the door. "Was that the bloke you were watching?"

She nodded, embarrassed that she had been followed all the way home. "I thought I'd left him at the hotel with Mrs Fraser – or Lottie, I should say – but he must have seen me leave. He arrived too soon after I got back for it to have been a coincidence. Palmer would be so disgusted -"

He put a finger on her lips to silence her, aware that there was a thin line between relief and hysteria. He made her concentrate on saying hello properly, making up for lost time until they were forced to come up for air. Then he noticed the laptop lying on the floor. "Is that yours?"

"Yes. I hadn't got anything else to chuck at him." Riley disentangled herself and picked up the machine. She switched it on and was rewarded with the usual hum of activity and the opening tunes. "Thank goodness. At least I've got some notes I can send Donald. That reminds me." She picked up her phone and dialled Donald's number, and related what had happened along with the discovery that Lottie Grossman was back on the scene.

"Do you want me to inform the police?" said Donald. "I'm pretty sure there are still warrants out for her."

"No," said Riley. "At least, not yet. It sounds like she's in a bad way, and the man she's using has been, well, dissuaded." She glanced at Mitcheson and reached out to take his hand.

"OK. Let me know if you change your mind."

"Thanks, Donald. Actually, it might be worth tapping into that database of yours and seeing if there's anything on Lottie. I think she's living abroad, but I wonder if she's got any resources here."

"I'll do it straight away." She heard a keyboard clicking. "Didn't she once have a house in Buckinghamshire?"

"Yes." Riley gave him the address and said she'd wait to hear from him, then switched off and turned to Mitcheson. "He'll ring back if he finds anything."

Mitcheson smiled and took hold of her. "Let's hope he takes his time."

"If he doesn't, I'll never forgive him. How long do you have?"

"Long enough. Just."

Behind them, the cat appeared from the kitchen and sat

watching, neat and tidy as if Szulu had never intruded. Riley sensed his presence and disengaged herself long enough to turn and say with a smile, "Top shelf tea for you tonight, my brave boy."

The cat sniffed haughtily before turning on his heels and walking away.

Szulu climbed in the car and stared through the windscreen, eyes on the house where Riley Gavin lived. Apart from the excruciating pain in his arm, he felt bruised and humiliated and wasn't sure what he was going to do about any of it. His options were limited. He knew of a former surgeon who'd been caught playing hide the stethoscope with a patient in an empty operating theatre. The man sometimes took on a bit of back-street work for ready cash and no questions asked, so maybe he'd give him a call. It would cost, but it was better than going to a hospital, where they'd report gunshot wounds the moment he walked in. Before they finished their stitching, he'd find himself pinned to the bed by an Armed Response Unit. No way would they believe he'd been shot accidentally by a drive-by, which had been his first planned explanation.

Oddly enough, though, he felt relieved. Even with the constant threat of Ragga lurking in the background, he'd decided this whole business had gone far enough. No matter what Lottie Grossman said or did, no way was he going back anywhere near Frank Palmer, Riley Gavin or the big lug who'd just put the slug in his arm without hesitation. He shivered, partly through the onset of shock, but mainly at remembering the complete absence of expression on the man's face as he'd pulled the trigger. Like he was swatting a fly.

He started the car and nudged it into gear with a grunt

of pain, then headed towards south London. He'd get his arm fixed, then go back and face the old woman. Whether he'd tell her what had happened was something he'd decide at the time. If she didn't like it, she'd have to go look for another gofer – preferably a stupid one with a death wish.

25

Donald's return call dragged Riley and Mitcheson apart, and they surfaced with reluctance. Brask had been quicker to respond than they had anticipated or hoped, but he had little in the way of solid news.

"Sorry, sweetie," he intoned smoothly. "Not a lot on the hateful Lottie, I'm afraid. Any interest she had in clubs and so forth seems to be long gone. Her house was finally put up for sale last year following the Spain fiasco, and her solicitor dealt with the proceeds. I got a name, but thereafter no joy; client confidentiality and so forth. I think we can take it that she had the money sent abroad and has been living off that ever since. The amount would have been sizeable, I expect, so she wouldn't have had a problem finding a bolt-hole somewhere pleasant. To be honest, only the police would be able to follow a money trail – if one exists. Apart from that, a woman her age would have fitted in anywhere alongside a retirement-age community of Brits in Spain, France, Portugal or elsewhere, and nobody would have suspected a thing." He paused. "I take it this is another story? Is there anything in it for us?"

"It is looking like two separate ones, actually," said Riley. "I'll get something to you on all of this as soon as I can." She put the phone down just as the buzzer sounded from downstairs. Mitcheson motioned for her to pick up the entry-phone, then went to wait at the top of the stairs.

It was Frank Palmer.

He entered the flat, eyeing Mitcheson guardedly before shaking hands and going through to the kitchen. Riley followed him and brought him up to date about Szulu's latest visit and the real name of his employer. Mitcheson hovered in the background, saying nothing. It had been a long time since he and Palmer had last spoken, and there was a hint of unease in the air between them, like two opponents meeting a long time after their last match.

"You shot him?" Palmer gave Mitcheson a wry look. "Will he live?"

"Of course." Mitcheson showed him the gun. "It's only a .22. This time tomorrow he won't even notice the wound."

Palmer grinned, knowing that was unlikely. "Serves him right. Any flak from the neighbours?"

"No," said Riley, handing him a beer from the fridge. "Mr G downstairs had the Polish Symphony Orchestra on at full bore. It would have drowned out an earthquake." She sniffed. "Palmer, what the hell is that smell? Have you been sipping meths?"

"Funny, that's what the taxi driver asked me. I told him it was a new aftershave on test. He lost interest after that."

Palmer was holding a Tesco carrier bag reeking of smoke and petrol. Using his free hand, he unravelled a roll of kitchen towel on to the kitchen work surface, then carefully slid out from the bag a collection of burned papers.

"Palmer!" Riley protested.

"Sorry. I'll clean up for you afterwards. Those folks at VTS had a big burn-up just after we left," he explained. "Somehow I don't think they were just having a little tidy. Fortunately, the bloke setting the fire wasn't the conscientious sort. I liberated the scorched remains."

They poked through the papers and found several delivery note copies showing shipments to various customers on *SkyPrint* paper, but with VTS Transit as the carriers. Other scraps were VTS documents. The same phone and fax numbers appeared on both sets of papers. There were also cardboard and packaging suppliers' advice notes for bulk deliveries to VTS, but with payment by *SkyPrint*. Most damning of all, there were several letters from both companies to suppliers, signed with the same signature and the name A. Perric.

"The man in the white shirt," said Palmer, getting a nod from Riley. He looked at Mitcheson. "They look like different companies, but the same faces and numbers fit both." He related what he had seen and heard in the warehouse, and filled Mitcheson in on the connection with Radnor and his colleague, Michael.

"Neat," said Mitcheson. "At the first sign of trouble, VTS bug out and set up somewhere else down the road, using a different name. But it's all run by this bloke Perric at *SkyPrint*?"

"Looks like it," said Palmer. "Although I doubt he's the top man. They've cleared out the secure storage area of several heavy boxes we saw when we first got there. That must have been the handguns and laser sights they were talking about. They left everything else and disappeared, but what I've got here is enough to prove they were working together."

Mitcheson nodded, then looked at his watch. "Sorry, kiddies, I've got to be going. My time could be running out." He turned to Riley. "I'm going to find a safe house where I can stay for a while. If it looks OK after a few days, and I haven't been arrested by the rubber-truncheon squad, I'll take it I'm no longer anybody's hot property."

"Why not stay here?" Riley suggested. "There's room."

"It's tempting. But if I am being watched, it would compromise you. Don't worry – I'll stay in touch. Once I get the all-clear, I'll hop back to the States and clear up a few things, then I'll be back."

"What will you do?" Palmer asked.

Mitcheson shrugged. "Same as I'm doing now: security work, that sort of thing. There's a big demand for it." He looked at Riley. "Some of it quite close to home, by the looks of things."

Palmer nodded but said nothing.

Taking it as his cue to depart, Mitcheson took Riley's arm, and the two of them left the flat and walked downstairs.

Palmer busied himself taking the Llama apart, putting each part aside for disposal later. There was no sense in holding on to it, and throwing it away intact could lead to some kid getting hold of it and ending up facing the Met's firearm squad.

He had no illusions about the shock Riley would have suffered after being confronted by Szulu's handgun. That and the news that Lottie Grossman was back. Mitcheson being here would have helped soak up part of the immediate reaction, and she at least seemed fairly relaxed, especially with the news that Mitcheson was going to be around for a while.

When she returned from downstairs, he was emptying the gun's magazine and dropping the shells to one side. "You OK?" he asked, "Or do you need another drink?"

"I'm fine, Palmer. There's no need to worry about me – I'm not a weak girlie." She tried to soften the words with a smile, but it didn't quite come off, and Palmer guessed there was still some remedial work to be done.

"Good news about Mitcheson coming back." His face was blank as he collected the gun parts and put them into the plastic bag he'd used for bringing back the burnt documents. He had always accepted Riley's relationship with the former army officer, on the basis that it was no business of his who she took up with. The only thing that concerned him was her welfare.

"Yes, it is." Riley stared at him for a moment, then shrugged. "He thought his name was no longer on the watch list and that it was worth coming in to give it a try. So far, so good. Why – don't you think it's a good idea?"

"Sure. Why not? He's done no wrong as far as I'm concerned. But he's right to be cautious."

"Christ, Palmer, don't tell me you're worried about him, too."

"Actually, I'm more concerned about the cat. Where is he?"

Riley gave a half-smile and slapped his shoulder. "Sorry. I didn't mean to be cranky. And thank you."

"What for?"

"For that pep talk you gave me – about shooting someone. It was a close call, though. I nearly did it. I think I would have if John hadn't come in at the crucial moment."

"I don't blame you. But for what it's worth, if you were still thinking about it, you probably wouldn't have gone through with it – not unless he'd come at you. That might have been different."

Riley pulled a face and hugged herself. "God, I wish I had your sense of certainty. You and John."

"Come again?"

"You'd have shot him, too, wouldn't you?"

Palmer thought about it for a second. "Actually, I'd have chosen his foot. More bones, takes longer to heal."

"He just… did it. It was so casual." Her face was a mixture of doubt and fear.

Palmer raised an eyebrow. "He was standing – what? – three feet away? Come on, he could hardly miss."

"What do you mean?"

"If Mitcheson had wanted to add another button-hole to Szulu's jacket, or just shoot the tip of his ear off, he'd have done it. It was a warning. Warnings like that to people like Szulu are better than words."

"Oh." Riley smiled then, and Palmer realised it had answered an unspoken question in her mind, now Mitcheson was no longer in the room, about whether the former soldier had been quite so cold-blooded as he'd pretended.

"About Lottie," said Riley, changing tack. "Do you really think she's *not* tied in with Radnor?"

"I doubt it. They're hardly in the same social circle. And the idea of someone with Radnor's background mixing with an old gang moll doesn't sound quite right to me."

Palmer's mobile rang. He murmured a greeting, then listened at length, signalling for Riley to get a pen and paper. She did so and he scribbled some notes before switching off the phone. As he turned back to Riley, he was looking thoughtful.

"That was Unger, the lawyer who arranged the meeting with Hemmricht. He was intrigued by what Hemmricht told us about the shooting, and did a bit of digging to see if the dead man, Wachter, had any family in the area. It seems he had a sister, Cecile. Unger tracked her down, but she didn't want to talk about the past. Said it was all too painful and she wanted to bury it and move on. Unger says that means she was probably in the *Stasi* herself, or at the very least was used by them. Former members didn't have a particularly nice time of it when they were outed, and plenty of them had to move away from where they lived to avoid reprisals."

"Did she tell him anything?"

"Only that shortly before his death, her brother admitted he was working for British Intelligence. She threatened to tell the authorities, but he insisted it wasn't spying, merely moving things around. Things of value."

"Moving things for Radnor."

"She never heard him mention any names, only that he was hoping to make a future for her as well. By then there were signs that communism was going pear-shaped, and he mentioned going to the States and starting again. She thinks he was offered papers by whoever he was working for."

"Could Radnor have done that kind of deal?"

"No idea. Depends how high he was and whether he had something truly exceptional that would have excited the Americans enough to make a swap. I don't think they'd have got too worked up about the odd work of art, though."

"So he was bluffing."

"Lying, more like. Anyway, Wachter's sister clearly chose to believe it, because she kept her mouth shut. Maybe she also saw that the old order was coming to an end and wanted the chance of a fresh start. She said her brother became very secretive and withdrawn early in 'eighty-nine, and was travelling a lot, all over eastern Germany. He would return with packages but he never told her what they were. Then one day he told her he was on the verge of completing a big deal that would ensure their future. He had to make one final trip, then he'd send for her."

Riley's eyes widened. "He was going across the wire."

"Sounds like it. But she never heard from him again. She was scooped up by the authorities shortly afterwards and spent several months in prison. All she was told while she was in custody was that her brother was a traitor and had died while trying to flee."

"Nice people. Is there any way we could get to speak to this Cecile ourselves?"

Palmer smiled. "That's the good news. Unger says she left Germany three years ago. Fancy a trip to Streatham Hill?"

26

Cecile Wachter offered tea, and asked Riley and Palmer to sit while she made it. They were in the conservatory of a neat semi-detached house, nestling in a row of identical semis on the fringe of Streatham Common, a few miles from central London. The house, like the garden, was neat and tidy, and if there were any signs or ornaments from Fraulein Wachter's past, or even that she had once abandoned her single status and married, albeit briefly, they were not in evidence. Beyond the windows, the quiet was marred only by muted traffic noise and the occasional shrill sound of children playing in nearby gardens.

"I told Herr Unger all I know," Cecile Wachter insisted, returning with mugs of tea on a tray. Her English was very precise, although her accent was still strong enough to betray her origins many miles from this very English setting. She was as neat and conservatively dressed as her surroundings, with her greying hair pinned in a bun, and rimless spectacles perched on a small nose. Her movements were economical, too, as if she wanted to merge into the background and remain unnoticed. Riley guessed she had probably been a very good *Stasi* member and wondered if anyone in the street even knew she was here.

"We're trying to find out what happened to your brother, Claus," said Riley, stirring her tea. It was pale and watery, with a faint aroma of mint. "Wouldn't you like to know, too?"

"Why?" Cecile stared at them in turn, a faint frown crossing her face. "That was all so long ago, in the past. Why should you be interested? Are you from the government?

The security services?"

"None of those," said Palmer calmly, peering into his mug. "We think the person your brother was working with was involved in art thefts from Germany and the Soviet Union. The former Soviet Union. We're trying to establish the details because we believe this man is also involved in other crimes."

"What other crimes?"

"We think he might now be bringing weapons into the country. Weapons bought from armouries and depots across the former eastern bloc."

"And you will do what with this information – put this man in prison?"

Palmer shrugged, wary of making rash promises he was in no position to keep. "I can't say. That would be the ideal solution."

Cecile nodded her head slightly. "Of course. But this man... this person who Claus worked with, he is with your British Intelligence, you know that? Claus told me. But if he is a criminal, also, how can you touch him? Where I come from, such people are beyond reach. To try to make them answer for what they have done is to invite retaliation."

"Things are sometimes different, here," said Palmer. "Not always... but there are ways."

Cecile shook her head and sighed, staring down into her mug as if she hadn't heard him. "I was such a person myself, for a while. I was never an official, not important, although I was trained in their ways of... doing things."

"Tradecraft?" said Palmer.

She nodded. "As you say, tradecraft. I don't mean I was a spy – not in espionage. But I was expected to do certain things." She looked up at them, her eyes steady. "I was a translator for many years, and worked with some important people.

People who were expected to be… exposed to the West in their work. As part of my responsibilities, I was expected to listen and to report on anything unusual – anything which was not in accordance with proper thinking. Here and now, I cannot imagine why I did such a thing. But back then, so many others were doing the same." She shrugged. "It was normal. Even your closest friends might be informing on you, and you would never know. It was the way things were. We were all part of the system. But now I have left all that behind. That is why I have come to London. I wish to forget it all and become… someone else." She waved a hand. "I don't mean a different identity, but a different person. It is not easy, however."

Palmer waited for a few heartbeats, but when she added nothing more, he said, "We need to find some proof of your brother's contact with the man he was working with. Something tangible – maybe a name. Otherwise we can't touch him. Was there anything Claus said to you, that you recall? Any details about his movements, how he contacted this man… where the man stayed? We believe he must have travelled across the border; did Claus ever say where they met?"

Cecile shook her head. "No. Nothing like that. He would not have dared, you see."

Riley leaned forward, puzzled. "What do you mean?"

But Cecile shook her head, and it was Palmer who supplied the answer, speaking softly. "Claus knew she was working with the authorities. It was too risky, even among families."

"Oh." Riley felt suddenly immensely sorry for this woman, and realised the burden she was living with. Her brother must have gone to his grave wondering if it had been his sister who had finally betrayed him.

"There is something else, is there not?" Cecile said suddenly, eyeing them both in turn. "I do not think you would be here if all he had done was steal art works and ship weapons. That would be for the authorities to deal with."

Several seconds went by, then Palmer nodded. "We think the man we are after told Claus that he would help him cross to the west. But he betrayed him."

The old woman stared at Palmer, her face undergoing a whole range of emotions she could not contain. "How? How did he betray him?"

"We don't know. But the border guards knew Claus was coming. They were ready for him. I'm very sorry." He put his hands on his knees and began to rise.

"Wait." Cecile raised her hand. She had a hint of tears in her eyes, and a look of dawning awareness on her face. She stood and motioned Palmer to stay where he was, then walked out of the conservatory. They listened to her walking upstairs, then came some muffled thumps, as if she was moving boxes, followed by her footsteps coming back down. She returned to the room with a cigar box, which she opened. Inside was a bundle of photographs, some of them pierced through with drawing pins, as if they had been hastily taken down from a wall and not looked at since. She withdrew the photos and knelt down, spreading them across the coffee table in front of her visitors.

"These are all I have from… that time," she said quietly. "A few photos of our family which I kept on a board in the kitchen. It is all I managed to bring with me." They were a collection of standard family shots, some relaxed, some obviously posed. They could have been of any family group in the world, with a range of nervous half smiles, or tilted squints against a sunny day, save for the drab clothing and surroundings which betrayed their origins. Cecile shuffled them around, then placed her finger on one of the shots and pushed it across the table.

"They came to our house one day. It was to meet a truck. Claus told me not to show myself, because it was better that way. I did as he asked. But a few days before, I had been given a small gift by a member of the Trade Ministry I had worked with. It had been difficult work with long hours, and he had been very pleased because he was being promoted. He had been given a camera by an American visitor, but he could not be seen to use it in his position, so he gave it to me. I took this photo. Claus never knew, of course. He would have been very angry with me."

The photo showed a group of three men, all in long coats and hats. The ground around them was covered in snow, and they were standing at the rear of an old army truck with a canvas screen. One of the men was elderly, with a bent back. He appeared to be pulling the screen away from the truck while the other two watched. One of these two was tall and well built, and it was obvious by his features that he was related to Cecile Wachter. The man beside him, apparently smiling at something one of the others had said, was shorter, with darker skin and a thin face. He looked younger than he did now, of course, but there was no mistaking the features.

It was Arthur Radnor.

27

Riley and Palmer drove back towards central London in silence, leaving Cecile Wachter staring at the collection of memories spread out on her coffee table. In spite of their requests and promises to take care of it, she had steadfastly refused to let them have the photo of Claus and Radnor, saying it was the last one she had of her brother and could not bear to part with it.

Palmer had relented, suggesting they bring back a portable scanner or copier so the photo wouldn't have to leave her possession. She had agreed with reluctance, but only if they didn't come back until tomorrow, as she had some translation work to complete and could not afford to miss her deadline.

Riley eventually broke the silence. "Did we do the right thing, telling her what Radnor did?"

"She already knew," Palmer replied with conviction. "She just didn't want to say it. It meant opening up all the memories."

"Maybe." Minutes later, she said, "One thing puzzles me. Bringing Wachter over would have cut Radnor's supply-line to the artwork, wouldn't it?"

"I doubt it. If Radnor was any good as an agent-runner, he'd have had a standby waiting in the background. It's how people like him operate. Never put all your eggs, and so forth. His bigger problem was Wachter, who could put him in prison if he ever got to the West."

"So he killed him."

"Cleverer than that: he allowed the border guards to do it. That way, no involvement, no links back to him. It happened all the time, so who would question it? Not the East Germans; as far as they were concerned, Wachter was a crook and a malcontent, no great loss. Radnor's men would have had time to strip the body of any incriminating evidence before we got there, and Radnor possessed the clout to cover it up as an Intelligence matter, so no questions were asked."

"Except by Reg Paris."

"Yeah. Except by Reg."

"It was still very risky, though. What if Wachter had got through somewhere else?"

"Radnor probably had limited choices. Getting an isolated farmer on the western side of the border out of the way for a couple of days was fairly easy – especially with the promise of a compensation payment. But bribing an East German border guard or trying to co-opt their local military or Intelligence hierarchy would have been impossible without blowing his cover. Radnor needed an insurance policy."

"The man with the rifle."

"Yes. If it looked like Wachter was going to make it across, his man would shoot him and they'd retrieve the body and blame the border guards. It was his way of controlling the situation."

"Or so he thought."

"Well, it worked. He had the authority to call out the nearest RMPs, to make it look like a military or Intelligence matter, and to keep a tight lid on it. The army weren't about to argue – they don't like getting snarled up in intelligence issues, anyway. They'd have treated him like germ warfare and kept him at a safe distance."

"Except for Reg."

"Reg was suspicious about it from the start. He probably made it a bit too clear what he thought and Radnor realised he'd got the wrong military cop involved. I was too junior and inexperienced, so I didn't count. But Reg was something else. In the end, Radnor must have decided he couldn't risk it, because if Reg discovered the farmer had been eased out of the way under a false pretext, he might have blown the whole thing wide open."

"So he killed Reg, too."

"I'd lay money on it. I don't know how, but he either arranged for the truck to follow him and wipe him out, or he put something in a drink along the way, timed to take hold along the motorway. Radnor probably bailed out early on some pretext, saying he would meet Reg in Frankfurt."

"Wouldn't Reg have been suspicious?"

"He hated spooks – he was probably glad to get rid of him. Anyway, on the way to making an official statement, what was there to suspect? It would all have seemed on the level, and there's no way Reg would have suspected Radnor was going to kill him. They were on the same side, for Christ's sake."

"But Radnor never counted on a woman with a camera. Is that photo going to be enough to stand up?"

"It proves Radnor knew Claus Wachter, and it puts him in East Germany. Where doesn't matter, because we know Wachter never left until the day he died. Whether Radnor has a story for knowing Wachter that would tie into his Intelligence brief, I've no idea. But if I was in Radnor's shoes, I'd say the photo Cecile took was enough to bury me."

They were silent for a few more minutes, then Riley said, "It would be helpful if we could definitely link Radnor and Michael to Gillivray's death."

Palmer shrugged. "There's the tie clip. But if the police didn't come up with something more positive, I'm not sure we will."

"The people in Gillivray's office might know something.

I could go back and give it a try."

"Why you?" Palmer didn't doubt her abilities or her courage, but was aware of the risks, especially if Radnor or Michael saw her in the building.

"Because they might open up more easily to me. And I'm not the one who braced him with the papers." She smiled artfully, knowing she had the upper hand. "And I can change my appearance so they'll never recognise me. Don't argue, Palmer – you know it makes sense."

Michael watched Riley and Palmer drive away from the house where Cecile Wachter lived, and dialled a number on his mobile.

"Yes?" Radnor answered, a hum of traffic in the background. He was out looking for other warehouse premises to replace the void left in the wake of Palmer and Riley's visit, and had tasked Michael to keep an eye on the two investigators. Michael had lost them on the way out of central London, but a chance call to Radnor, who knew of Cecile Wachter's presence in the area, had led him here.

"They've just left the Wachter woman's house," Michael reported. "They were there for twenty minutes, maybe less."

"How did they seem?"

"Neither pleased nor displeased. Perhaps she did not tell them anything." He was toying with a small set of binoculars. They had proved useless against Wachter's net curtains, and there had been too many nosy neighbours to allow him to check the rear of the house. "But something tells me they might be back."

"Really? Why?"

"Because of who they are… their body language. And I do not think they are the kind to wait for others to call. Do you?"

There was a brief silence, then Radnor said, "I agree. Wachter's no longer in the east, and I don't trust these people not to get something out of her. I should have thought of this before, when she first came over here."

Michael did not argue the point, but said, "What can she tell them? You said Wachter never spoke of your involvement, because he didn't trust her. She can hardly implicate you now."

"We don't know if he stuck to that. Claus might have given her something – some documents, maybe, to use if she had to." He paused, then asked: "Can you get in without being seen?"

"Of course."

"All right. Do it."

Michael switched off the phone and got out of the car. There was nobody in sight, and traffic was a muted sound in the distance. He walked along the pavement and turned in at the Wachter house. He rang the bell.

Cecile Wachter answered the door with a faint smile, clearly expecting to see Palmer and Riley back again. "It is not yet tomorrow –" The smile dropped from her face and the words died on her lips. She stared at Michael for several seconds, confusion giving way to a kind of recognition. She had seen men like him before, and knew what he represented. She moved quickly, driven by desperation and catching him by surprise. She tried to close the door, but only managed to slip the safety chain into place. Then she turned and hurried down the hall towards the rear of the house.

Michael stepped up close to the door and lunged forward with his shoulder. The wood was old and brittle, and the chain parted with a low crack. He strode after her, slamming the door behind him. He knew he might only have a few minutes before someone came to investigate the

188

noise, although experience told him people in most cities were remarkably keen not to get involved with the troubles of others. He caught up with her in a conservatory. She was on her knees by a coffee table, clutching a handful of faded photos and trying frantically to stuff them into a small wooden box. Even when he stood over her, she ignored him and continued with her efforts, mouth set in a stubborn line.

Michael checked the conservatory door, satisfied that she wasn't going anywhere. It was private and secluded here, with no overlooking windows. But there was a back gate just a few yards away. He nodded in satisfaction and took off his jacket, laying it across the arm of a wicker chair and taking care not to crease the sleeves.

"Going over old times?" he asked quietly in German, eyeing the photos. "How sentimental." One had fallen from her trembling hands, and he bent and retrieved it, craning his neck to study the faded image. It showed three elderly women in heavy, dark clothing, sitting outside a house and smiling nervously at the camera. The detail told him nothing, as it would tell others who might look. He flicked it away with a hiss of contempt. It clattered off the furniture with a dry sound.

"What do you want?" asked Cecile, her voice a whisper. She had given up trying to put the photos away, and was now still, not looking at him. Instead, her eyes were on the garden outside, staring through the window at the ordered shrubs and flower borders as if seeing another country a long, long way off.

28

Szulu checked his rear mirror and wondered if he was imagining things. He was sure he'd seen the same car behind him now more than once, ever since collecting Lottie Grossman from her hotel. It kept reappearing, as if the driver was unsure of his route and trying to find short-cuts, but inevitably staying on their tail. Unfortunately, with the level of traffic, keeping tabs on one specific car was practically impossible. Szulu shook his head, telling himself not to get paranoid.

"I need to get out of this place for a while," Lottie had told him when he'd called her on the way to the hotel earlier that morning. "It's stifling in here, and those tablets aren't doing me any good." Her voice had taken on a whining quality, adding to the slurring of her words after she'd been taken ill. As for the hotel, it was air-conditioned through-out. Maybe she was having hot flushes, like his gran used to get. He shuddered at the idea of this woman suffering the same ailments as any normal woman.

It had cost him a small fortune to get his arm patched up, but it was better than tangling with the cops. Fortunately, the quack had located the bullet nestling just beneath the skin, and hadn't had to dig around too much. Even so, the pain had been intense enough to have Szulu yelling like a baby.

"Fair enough," he said, relieved he wasn't expected to go out and buy an Uzi to blow anyone away. He still hadn't worked out how to break things off with the old woman without her going ballistic, but he'd have to come up with something sooner or later or he'd do something desperate.

"So what happened?" Her voice interrupted his thoughts as they cruised past Runnymede, with the river on the left. "Did you deliver the message?"

Szulu nodded, keeping his eyes on the road. He hadn't told her about being shot, or the addition to the scene of yet another psychotic military type, and hoped the bandages the quack had applied weren't obvious beneath the sleeve of his jacket. "Sure. They didn't like it. You really have history, don't you?"

He saw Lottie nodding in the back seat, her eyes half closed. "Oh, yes. We have history, all right." There was a pause, then: "You got hurt, didn't you?"

Szulu looked in the mirror, surprised she'd noticed. "A bit, yeah. Not much. A flesh wound."

"A flesh wound? Christ, who shot you – Palmer?" She cackled dryly. "He's a one, isn't he? I'm surprised to hear he's tooled up, though."

Szulu glanced in the mirror, surprised at her use of slang. He sighed and decided to tell her everything, in spite of the big guy's warning. Anyway, what could he do to him that he hadn't done already? "It wasn't Palmer. There was another bloke turned up. The Gavin woman called him John. Big, a bit posh like, but tough. Seemed to know all about guns." He explained that he'd taken the .22 with him for protection, but it had misfired when he'd been startled by the cat.

For the second time in as many minutes, the old woman laughed, but it was a sound with no element of humour. Szulu's ears burned with shame at the memory.

"You aren't cut out for this game, are you, Mr Szulu?" said Lottie perceptively, rubbing at her eyes. "Scared by a cat, eh? Dear me. Still, you were lucky he only put a shot in your arm. His name's Mitcheson. Ex-army. He worked for me, once, for a short while. Tough fella, all right; I could have done with more like him. Would've made a fortune with him alongside me."

She fell silent and stared out of the window as if recalling missed opportunities. They entered the outskirts of Egham, Szulu taking the Lexus on a random tour to avoid traffic, with no particular destination in mind. Aimless seemed the best way to go at the moment. After a mile or so, Lottie stirred again.

"Stop here, Mr Szulu. Anywhere will do."

Szulu stopped the car as ordered, and looked around. They were in a quiet street bordered by chestnut trees, the kerb on either side lined with cars. Middle class, middle income, nice lives; if they had any worries, the people who lived here, they kept them well hidden behind their neat gardens and smart house fronts. He switched off the ignition and turned to look at Lottie Grossman, wondering what she was going to do next.

"Now I've told you my secrets," he said finally, "how about yours?"

"Pardon me?" Her voice was slurred again, her lips barely moving.

"Well, you wanted out of the hotel pretty quick, it seemed to me. Why's that?"

There was a long silence, punctuated by the sound of an electric drill somewhere nearby. Then she said: "Because I want to finish this."

"Yeah? What, like go home?" He felt relieved. The sooner she was out of his hair, the better. Then he could go back to worrying about the simple things in life, like how to avoid being carved into slices by Ragga Pearl.

"No. I want you to finish it. Remember those special rates we talked about? You want to be out from under

Pearl, don't you? Only you'll have to be quick." She delved into her bag with a shaky hand and passed him a thick envelope. "That should cover it."

Szulu sighed. Deep down, he knew that whatever else he might be capable of, killing Palmer and the Gavin woman was way beyond his reach, especially now the other guy had appeared on the scene. He'd been shown his limits and realised he wasn't up to it. Strangely, he felt no sense of shame. He decided to tell her, extra money or no extra money.

"Sorry. Can't do that," he said softly. "I ain't killing no one. You were right: I'm not cut out for this. Not murder, anyway. You can go ahead and tell Ragga if you like. I'll even go there with you. You want me to drive you?"

"I don't think that would be a good idea." She sounded slightly drunk, vague, as if her mind was wandering, and Szulu wondered if she'd been taking a few crafty nips while he wasn't looking. Jeez, that's all he needed after everything else: how the hell do you get a drunk pensioner out of the back of the car? Especially one who wanted you to kill people.

"Yeah? Why not? Hey, you could ask Ragga to have his men do it. He'd kill his own mother if the price was right. I never said that, though." When she didn't reply, he continued, "Wouldn't that be better, having Ragga's men do Palmer? That way you know it gets done."

Lottie gave a snort of contempt. "You think I would trust those strutting idiots to do anything? They're street hooligans, that's all, flashing their silly gold chains and hiding behind dark glasses. Real men don't need to hide their eyes, Mr Szulu. People like Palmer and Mitcheson… they look you straight in the eye."

Szulu nodded, recognising something close to admiration

in her voice. Man, she sounded like she respected those two. That was something he hadn't expected.

"Anyway, I can't ask Pearl."

"Why not?"

"Because I went to see him two days ago, while you were busy. To talk over some stuff. While I was in his office, I noticed some papers on his desk. He seems surprisingly businesslike, for one so... uncouth. A bit careless though, with people he thinks are beyond it." She gave a slight chuckle. "We're the invisible army, us old ones, you know that? Nobody sees us until it's too late."

"So?" Something in the old woman's tone told Szulu he wasn't going to like where this was going. From rarely telling him the time of day, here she was suddenly gobbing off about some visit she'd made to Ragga Pearl's den.

"I've always had the knack of reading upside down, you know. It came in handy over the years. The paper on his desk included a list of names and bank accounts. My late husband always had a list like that, too. Piggy-banks, he called them. Bits squirreled here, bits tucked away there... makes it difficult for anyone to follow the money trail, see? Information like that, though, there's always somebody interested in buying. Always."

Szulu felt the situation rapidly slipping away from him. He couldn't believe this was happening. He'd thought all along that the old woman was crazy, but this was something else. He stared at her. "Let me get this right: you stole information about bank accounts from *Ragga Pearl*? Tell me you're joking, man! Why would you do such a thing?" He wondered if he shouldn't just kick her arse out of the car and leave her here in the middle of the street. Then drive until the car ran dry or he was out of money. It would be way better than the shit-storm she was going to bring down on their heads once the Ragga found out what she'd done. Because as sure as the man was crazy as a bed bug, there was no way he'd let her get away with it – and that included anyone around her at the time. Shit, he'd be lucky if he didn't end up floating alongside her down the Thames.

Lottie Grossman moved slightly, slumping back in her seat. It was enough to drag Szulu's mind back to the here and now. Then he noticed something wasn't right. She looked like she'd taken an over-strong hit of something. Her mouth had gone slack on one side, and her eyes were rolling towards the roof of the car. He glanced at her hands, which were now clutched tight in her lap, the brightly coloured nails digging into her palms. And one knee was trembling slightly, as if she had the fever.

"Hey – Mrs Grossman! Lottie – what's up?" He leaned over the back of the seat for a closer look, and saw a trickle of saliva worming its way down the old woman's chin. Her breathing sounded bad, too, like it was coming out of the end of a long tube, and there was a sour smell in the car. He guessed she'd had a heart attack, or maybe a stroke. Whatever, she plainly needed more help than he could give her.

He turned and flattened his forehead against the side window, the feel of the glass cool and flat against his skin. He didn't need this. What the hell was he supposed to do now? Hospital, that was the best bet. The nearest he could find. Drop her off at a casualty unit and leg it before anyone could ask questions. By the looks of it, she wouldn't be in a position to tell them anything, anyway. Then wait to see what the Ragga would do. In spite of knowing the gangster's psychotic nature, Szulu was fed up with feeling like a chicken every time he heard the man's name. No way he was going to crawl like a slug and ask for mercy. Damn if he'd do that.

He turned the key in the ignition, put the Lexus in gear, and checked his mirror, mentally planning a route to the nearest A & E. To his surprise, a large black Toyota Land Cruiser had ghosted quietly up the street behind him, and was filling his rear window with its radiator grill.

"What the –?" He turned and ducked his head a fraction and saw two large figures inside, just sitting there behind tinted glass. Szulu heard another engine and switched his eyes to the front, where a similar vehicle was reversing at speed. It stopped three feet from his bonnet, the array of brake lights flaring like fireworks. Two shapes sat inside this one, one of them horribly familiar. Shit, so they *had* been followed!

Before he could move, there was a figure at his door and another on the passenger side, peering in at him like he was a caged exhibit. Both were big, with shoulders like weightlifters and heads like cannonballs. He didn't recognise them, but he didn't have to – they were Ragga's boys. Then the door of the Land Cruiser in front opened and the Ragga himself strolled towards him, heavy body rolling, springing off his left foot like he always did and snapping his fingers to some insane inner tune. He wore trainers and a gold tracksuit, his large belly straining against the soft, silky cloth. He made a rolling motion with one fat finger, and Szulu pressed the button to lower the window.

"Szulu, my man," Ragga greeted him. He seemed to chew on the name with relish, as if they were old friends. Szulu sensed it was Ragga's way of unsettling people – especially those to whom he intended no good. The gang leader leaned over the car, filling Szulu's side window. He smelled of fried food, sweet smoke and some sickly expensive cologne that someone had probably told him was really cool this season in L A.

"Ragga." Szulu wondered how he was going to get out of this one. Damn, he should have pulled out long ago, when he first met the crazy woman in the back seat.

Ragga peered past him at Lottie Grossman, running heavy-lidded eyes over her with a peculiarly vacant expression. He exchanged a look with one of his lieutenants, then said to Szulu: "What's up with her, man? You been smackin' her around?" Ragga tittered, the pink tip of his tongue sneaking out between his lips like a schoolboy enjoying a filthy joke he wasn't supposed to have heard. "Still, we all got to get our kicks somehow, right?"

"It wasn't like that," Szulu protested. "She had some kind of attack. I was about to take her to hospital."

"You kiddin' me?" Ragga seemed genuinely surprised. He bent to study the old woman again. "Shit, Szulu, I think you're right. That's bad news, man. Before she kicked off, did she say anything about having some property of mine?"

The sudden question nearly caught Szulu by surprise, but he managed to keep a straight face. Just a bare hint that he knew what this psycho was talking about and he'd be history.

He shook his head and stared directly at the other man, allowing a little heat to creep into his voice. "Now you're fucking joshing me, right? This old bitch never even told me her real *name* until a couple of days ago. She's been dangling me like a sucker all along, not telling me nothing. Watch this guy, check out this place, take me here, drive me there, put the frights on that woman… shit, I'd learn more working for one of those monks that never speaks." He stopped speaking, mostly because Ragga had put his hand through the window and placed a pudgy finger against his cheek. It felt hot and damp and Szulu wanted to take hold of it and bite it.

"Enough, man," said Ragga softly, his voice suddenly sing-song, as if he was crooning to a child. "Don't make me lose my temper. The old woman took something from me, see. I can't be having that. Make me look soft, like I got no control. Now you sit still, nice and quiet." He muttered instructions over his shoulder and two of his men opened the rear doors and eased Lottie Grossman out of the car. They took her to the Land Cruiser at the back and placed her inside, then one of them came back and collected her handbag off the back seat. The doors closed with twin clunks.

"Now, Szulu," Ragga continued quietly, "here's what we do. The debt what you owe me? It's done. Paid, right?" Szulu nodded, too relieved to speak, and Ragga continued, "So now you're gonna get out of this car and walk away from here. You ain't gonna look back, an' you're gonna forget you ever saw this car or that woman. They never existed."

"What about the rental place? They'll remember me." Szulu couldn't give two tits for the rental place, he was so relieved at this turn of events. But pride wouldn't let him show he wasn't completely cool with it and thinking carefully, like a professional.

"Tell 'em it got boosted by some fuckin' joy-riders. It happens all the time, right? We live in a lawless world, everyone know that. Anyway, it'll turn up again soon, once we've given it the valet treatment." He tittered again, enjoying his own private joke. "Now go."

Szulu got out of the car, hardly able to believe his luck. As he did so, he was careful to slide the envelope Lottie Grossman had given him under his jacket. It was plain that Lottie wasn't going to be needing it, not where she was going. He almost felt sorry for her then, but shook it off. She'd wanted two others dead, so what right did she have to special consideration? He turned and walked past the Land Cruiser at the back, where he could see Lottie Grossman slumped in one corner, eyes closed. Neither of the men inside gave him so much as a glance.

He was fifty yards down the street when he heard all three cars move away.

He kept walking and didn't look back.

29

A new man was on duty at the front desk of the office building in Harrow. He was younger than Nobby and dressed in a grey suit, and had a tired, bored look about him, as if he really didn't want to be there.

Riley walked up to the desk with an air of confidence she didn't feel, aware that she could be under scrutiny if the police were watching for anyone showing an undue interest in the sixth floor. There was no sign of them outside, and whatever equipment the forensics team had been using had gone - but that didn't mean they weren't still around.

She checked her hair in the reflection of the glass. Clipped back as tight as she could manage, so that it made her face thinner, and minimal makeup, she was reasonably certain that neither Michael nor Radnor would recognise her if they saw her. It had only been a brief encounter before, but she didn't want to take any chances.

The man barely looked up, pushing the visitor's book and a pen across the desk for her to sign, followed by a badge. Riley signed in and picked up the badge, receiving a grunt in return and a cursory nod towards the lifts.

The same receptionist was behind the counter of Stairwell Management's offices, wearing the same hi-tech headpiece. But she seemed much less sure of herself. Her eyes showed signs of redness around the rims, and widened when she recognised Riley through the glass security door, in spite of the change Riley had made to her hair. Even so, she reached down and pressed a buzzer to spring the locks.

"You were here," she said flatly, as soon as Riley entered.

"Seeing Doug. With that bloke." Her face was stony, although Riley couldn't decide if it was out of grief, shock or suspicion. Either way, if she was going to call the police, she was taking her time.

"That's right," she admitted lightly, allowing her own eyes to widen in sympathy. "My colleague had some papers to serve on Mr Gillivray. I'm sorry, by the way, about what happened. I only just heard. Are you family?"

The woman looked startled by the question. "You what? Whatever gave you that idea?"

"Sorry. My mistake. I'm Riley, by the way."

"Vicky. Why do you ask?"

"Just interested. What do the police think about Mr Gillivray's death?"

Vicky shrugged. "No idea. They don't tell me anything. As for the rest of them… " She shook her head and looked at Riley with a small frown. "So what do you want, then? You haven't come to serve some more papers on him, have you? You can't sue the dead."

"No, it's not that. But my firm is wondering who might have killed him."

"Why?"

"Call it unfinished business. Your boss was going to be a prominent part of a big court case we were preparing. We'd already been working on it for several weeks." She shrugged. "Without him, the case probably won't happen. But before I give up on it altogether, I'd like to know who would benefit."

The girl's eyes widened. "You mean –?"

"I can't say anything more, but I'm sure you know what I'm driving at." She gave a conspiratorial smile and leaned closer. "My boss said I should drop it and put it down to experience, but I hate being beaten, you know? I know what they're thinking, of course. They think because I'm a mere *girlie*, I can't ask simple questions in case I break my nails. Chauvinist bastards."

Vicky showed a flicker of sympathy. "Tell me about it. You should try working for this lot. Only I don't see how I can help –"

"Was there anyone you can think of who didn't like him?"

"Take your pick," Vicky muttered quietly. "The little prick had more enemies than I've got shoes – and that's saying something." She pulled a face. "And don't say I shouldn't speak ill of the dead; that's the best time to do it, my dad says. That way they can't get in your face about it."

"I think your dad's right." Riley was surprised. She'd come here half expecting a volley of abuse and accusations, and had got quite the opposite reaction. Evidently the late Mr Gillivray wasn't universally popular, even among his colleagues.

"He was a slime-ball," Vicky continued calmly. "He tried it on with me every time he was in, it didn't matter who was here. Thought he was God's gift, which he wasn't. The way he talked, he was getting it on with half the women in north London. I'm not surprised someone had it in for him. It was probably someone's husband or boyfriend. Most of the time he could shout them down." She gave a sour smile. "But not this time, eh? Still, that was Doug. He was loud and he was a bully, and he didn't care who knew it. It was the way he was. He'd had more papers served on him than anyone I know, so it wasn't as if another set was going to hurt. He just liked to create, that was all, so we'd all notice what a bad little sod he was." She shrugged. "Sad, more like. Look where it got him."

"So he had a lot of enemies?"

"Hundreds, I should think. One or two of them came

in here, threatening to tear the place down. But only those who knew him. He never left much of a trail."

"So you knew what he was up to?"

"Not really. I only work this desk, I don't get taken into anyone's confidence. But it was obvious he wasn't the full shilling, by the phone calls and letters – and like I say, the visitors."

"Any serious ones?"

Vicky tilted her head. "Heavies, you mean? Yes, a couple. But he always managed to buy them off. At least, he always put in an appearance the next day, so I suppose that's what happened. He was quite a charmer when he wanted to be."

"Not this time, though," Riley suggested. "What have his colleagues said about it?"

"Not a thing." Vicky looked pained. "They shut me out of it and told me not to say a word to anyone, or I'd lose my job." She gave a half smile. "Except there's no one in today, so I don't give a toss." She looked as if the triumph, small as it was, was one to be relished.

"How about the rest of the building? Did Doug ever argue with anyone?"

"No." The shake of the head was emphatic. "He hardly spoke to anyone outside this office. It's not like he socialised much, either." She leaned back and chewed her lip. "Mind you, he went ape-shit when someone hit his car in the car park. It was the same day he died. One of the other tenants came up and told him about it. It was his pride and joy. I suppose I'd have been angry, too. I've had two prangs recently, and they cost me a bloody fortune."

Riley felt a stirring of interest. "What other tenant?"

"His name's Mike – I don't know his surname. Smart bloke... bit of an accent. Nice looking, but in a weird,

203

dangerous sort of way." She gave a shiver and smiled coyly, woman to woman. "I would, if you know what I mean?" She chuckled and tossed her head with a faint show of embarrassment at the coarseness. "At least, I would if I wasn't already engaged, anyway."

"Got you," said Riley with a smile and a roll of her eyes. "So, Mike, huh? Is he anyone I should get to know?"

Vicky looked dubious, then shrugged. "I wouldn't if I were you – he's got a dangerous look, like I said. But suit yourself. He came up and said someone had dinged an Audi, and was it one of ours. I called Doug and he came charging out to see what it was about. That was a surprise, because he didn't normally come out to casual callers. Maybe it was because his baby was hurt."

"Sounds like he was gutted."

"Yeah, well… boys and their toys, right? They had a chat right here. I didn't hang around to see what happened, though, because it was going home time."

Riley suddenly felt all her alarm bells ringing. "So you left before they did?"

"Yeah. In fact, the others had gone by then, too, and it was time for me to go, so I asked Doug to lock up. He said he would, but he was just going downstairs with Mike to look at his car, so I left. It's not like I'm paid to hang around here after hours just so they can entertain each other, is it?"

"Right. Do the police know that they were here together?"

"I suppose. I've no idea. I never said anything, if that's what you mean. You don't think…?" Her eyes widened again. "But it was only a car ding, that was all. I mean, even if he found out who did it and faced them, nobody gets *that* mad over a scrape, do they?" By her expression, she clearly thought it was out of the question, but now the idea was firmly in her mind, she began to look concerned.

"This guy Mike," said Riley, before the young woman panicked and threw a wobbly. "Which office does he work in?"

"On the first floor. Azim-something or other. I never really noticed. I mean, I never use the stairs, so why would I? You don't really think he could have done it, do you?"

Riley shook her head. "No, of course not. Why would he? It wasn't him who damaged the car. Must have been someone else." Seconds later, she was walking towards the lift, her chest thumping with excitement.

When she got back to the car, Palmer was slumped in his seat, eyes closed.

"Wakey, wakey, Boy Wonder," she said, slamming the door behind her, and stared at him until he showed some interest. He sat up and opened his eyes, then looked at her triumphant smile with a knowing expression.

"You've been bonding with that receptionist, haven't you?" he said. "Go on, tell me what you found."

"Simple," said Riley. "Have you ever seen Michael drive a car?"

"Nope."

"Minicabs, right? They arrive at the rear door. Every time."

"For both of them – Radnor and Michael." He stuck his thumbs under his collar and made like a barrister delivering a crushing argument. "Which leads me to suppose, yer 'onour, that they either don't drive, don't choose to or don't actually possess cars. Why?"

She related what the receptionist had told her about the prang in the car park, and Palmer sat up straighter, eyes alight with interest.

"Odd," he muttered at last. "If he doesn't drive, why should he be wandering around the car park? Unless he made up the prang. Clever, though: something so innocuous, nobody would give it a second thought. He must have gone up there the day after we saw them in the lift."

"Right," agreed Riley. "After speaking to Nobby, he'd have wanted to check out Gillivray's company to see what we were doing in the building. All he needed was a reason to go up and see him."

"And it had to be something that would get Gillivray out of his office without being suspicious. He'd have been on permanent alert for raids by the Inland Revenue or the police, but prangs happen every day in car parks. Michael left it until nobody else was about so he could take his time. I guess he knew what he was going to do before he went up there. Shows he's prepared to take risks, though. Either that or he's a loose cannon." He drummed his fingers on his knee. "We need to have a chat with Charlie."

"We can't forget Lottie," Riley said as she drove them south. It was a subject they had both avoided, but they couldn't entirely ignore the possibility that the old woman might still have designs on them, ill-health or not. As they knew from experience, Lottie Grossman was resourceful under pressure, and possessed a long and vengeful memory.

"Yeah, I know." Palmer stared through the window at a large truck trying to negotiate a narrow gap between two cars, with much wheezing of air brakes and millimetres to spare. "Having her around is like having a scorpion in the bottom of your bed."

"What do you think she can do? From what Szulu said, she sounds as if she's in a bad way."

"Do you want to risk it? The biggest danger with her is, she could change tack. Szulu we'd recognise – but if she sent someone else… like this Ragga or his men, we'd never see it coming. We could ask Szulu. He'd know."

"True. But he might not want to tell us."

"He will if I threaten to poke him in the arm."

Riley dug in her pocket and handed him the slip of paper with Lottie Grossman's hotel number. "Or we could ring Lottie direct."

Palmer dialled the number and waited while the receptionist checked her computer for Mrs Fraser. When she came back, the message was brief. "Sorry, sir. Mrs Fraser checked out without paying. Do you know of her whereabouts?"

Palmer hung up without answering. They had nothing else to do until they went to see Cecile Wachter tomorrow. He told Riley to head for Isleworth.

30

The house where Szulu lived looked quiet. At Palmer's suggestion, they waited a few minutes, watching the area for familiar faces. There was no sign of the car Palmer had seen, but that didn't mean Szulu was out.

When Palmer was satisfied they were unobserved, they got out and approached the front door. Riley pressed the button against 3A.

The response was instantaneous. A sash window above their heads slammed up and a voice shouted, "Yeah?". Riley went to step back, but Palmer put his hand on her arm and shook his head. They would wait for him to come down.

Eventually, footsteps pounded down the stairs and the front door was flung open, Szulu already voicing his annoyance. "…the matter, you can't hear me calling you?" He stopped dead when he recognised Riley and Palmer. He looked drawn and tired, and was dressed in jeans and a cutaway T-shirt, revealing a bandage covering his upper left arm. Whoever had fixed it had done a neat job.

"Hi. How's the arm?" said Palmer cheerfully. "Bet that smarts, doesn't it? Don't mind if we come in." He stepped forward, driving Szulu back inside until the driver was backed up against the stairway.

"Hey – what you want, man?" Szulu protested, although without any real fight. "Fuck you hassling me for?"

"So call the police." Palmer encouraged him to turn and go upstairs, and he obediently led them into a flat on the first floor. A sofa, two armchairs and several large cushions gave the impression of comfort, but the overall effect was spoiled by a scattering of clothes, CDs, empty beer bottles and fast-food cartons. A battered CD player dwarfed by a tall music rack was thumping a steady beat into the room, setting up a faint buzz from a half-empty glass containing a brownish liquid and some ice cubes on a nearby coffee table.

"Should you be drinking on top of pills?" Riley asked, flicking through his music rack. She didn't recognise more than a couple of names, but if the lurid covers were any guide, mood music it wasn't.

"Pills?" He flicked his eyes towards Palmer, who was standing by the door, then looked back at Riley. "What are you – my mother?"

"Don't tell me the doctor who fixed your arm didn't give you some pain killers."

"Yeah, of course." He shrugged as if it was no big deal, then walked over to the window and stared out, scanning the street. "So where's the other guy? He waiting to come up here and shoot me in my other arm?"

"Relax," said Riley. "He's gone."

Szulu grunted. "So what do you want?"

"Where's Lottie?" Palmer leaned back against the door and yawned.

"How the hell would I know?" Szulu picked up a slim remote and turned up the music a couple of levels, making the glass on the coffee table vibrate even more. Then he stood and stared in turn at them both, defiant.

Palmer came away from the door and walked over to the CD player. He thumbed the volume button, turning it up further until the glass began to dance across the coffee table. He picked it up just before it tipped off the edge, sniffed it then put it down again. Bourbon on ice. The beat was now pounding off the walls, and somewhere in the depths of the house, somebody shouted in protest.

Riley nudged aside a pile of clothes and sat down on the edge of the sofa. She said nothing, carefully studying her fingernails.

Szulu scowled and pressed the remote to reduce the volume, only for Palmer to reach down and put it back up. "Hey – what the fuck you playing at, man?"

"It'll drown out your screams," Palmer replied coldly. He picked up a cheap plastic pen from a sideboard and nodded at Szulu's bandaged arm. "Imagine how it will feel when I stick this in the hole and poke it about a bit. What's the bet it'll sting a bit?"

Szulu seemed to lose some colour and backed away, shaking his head. Clearly, the idea of suffering even more pain was enough to cut through his natural inclination to resist, and he held up his hands to ward Palmer off.

"Hold on… there's no need to get rough, man. I'm done with that." When he saw Palmer wasn't going to attack him, he reached down and picked up his drink and took a hefty swallow, the ice cubes rattling against the glass. This time, when he reached for the remote and turned down the music, Palmer didn't move. "She had another attack, right. We were driving out by the river – near Runnymede. She asked me to take her for a drive, see… said she was sick of the hotel. Then she told me to stop. We were in Egham by then, down a side street somewhere. It was quiet, peaceful. She offered me a wad of money to finish it with you two."

"Finish it?"

"Yeah. You know." He blinked and seemed to shrink away, plainly not wanting to say the words. "I told her straight away I wasn't up for it. Said I didn't want nothing more to do with all that. It's gone too far."

"I can't imagine Lottie taking that too calmly," said Riley. "She was a stickler for loyalty."

Szulu shrugged. "She hardly said anything. In fact…" He paused. "I suggested she get Ragga's boys to do it. Sorry, but I couldn't think of nothing else. She said she couldn't do that because she'd stolen something from Ragga's desk when she went to see him a couple of days ago."

"Oh, boy," sighed Palmer. "She never misses a trick, does she? What did she take?"

"Information. Lists of bank accounts and stuff. She reckoned it would be worth something to someone, detail like that." He shook his head. "Man, I thought I was going to piss myself. Stealing from the Ragga? You don't do that, not if you want to live. And worse was, she was going to take me down with her!"

"What then?" Riley said, sitting forward.

"Then I noticed she was looking strange… like she'd suddenly got drunk or something. There was this stuff coming out of her mouth… like spit, only thicker. It was horrible. I was about to take her to hospital, but…"

"But what?"

"Ragga Pearl turned up."

"Just like that?" Palmer looked sceptical. "I wouldn't have thought Runnymede or Egham was quite his patch. You sure you didn't call him up and tell him where you were?"

Szulu looked insulted. "Why would I do that? The way me 'n Ragga are, you think I'm crazed?"

"Because it would have got him off your back; a favour for a favour. Are you saying you didn't think about it… of maybe bugging out and leaving her?" The expression on Palmer's face was stone cold. Then he shrugged. "Not that I'd have blamed you."

"What happened?" asked Riley. "When Ragga and his men arrived?"

"They took her," said Szulu. "Right there in the middle of that street. It was cold, man. They lifted her out of the car like a baby, and put her in one of theirs. Then Ragga told me to walk away and forget I ever laid eyes on her. He said the debt was paid and we were all clear. Man, when I heard that, I did what he told me." He shrugged, and had the good grace to look sombre. "That was the last I saw of her. You'd have to ask the Ragga what happened to her next, though."

Riley nodded. "Don't worry. We intend to. And that's where you come in."

31

"You two are paddling in some very deep waters, you know that?" Charlie studied his pint then squinted at Riley and Palmer in turn. They were in a pub off St Martin's Lane, where Charlie had suggested they meet. He had done some digging around in the vast boiler house that was the security department pool of information, and agreed to share what he could.

"Adventurous, that's us," said Palmer cheerfully. "How deep is deep?"

"Well, that place in Harrow, where you might or might not have chucked some conman out of a sixth-storey window, and where you've been playing silly buggers with other persons named or unnamed? It's been red-flagged, that's how deep." He sipped his drink, pulling a face. "Try in over your heads and likely to sink."

"Red-flagged? What does that mean?" Riley knew a lot of the official jargon, culled from years of brushing up against the police. But the world of security departments was an unknown quantity to her, and there was always some new terminology waiting to be discovered.

"It means," explained Charlie, "that somebody's keeping it under surveillance. The flag is to warn other agencies to tread carefully in the area, so as not to compromise any ongoing operation." He looked at Palmer with raised eyebrows. "Am I right?"

Palmer's nod confirmed it, but he said nothing.

"I checked with a mate," Charlie continued, "but all she could tell me was that the flag was issued on a Home Office security docket. There was no department designation that she could find, but that's not unusual."

"She?" Palmer grinned happily, sensing his friend's slip of the tongue. "Well, well, you old dog. Nice, is she?"

"Behave yourself." Charlie scowled back at him, but he blushed nonetheless and concentrated on his pint.

"So it could be anyone watching the place," said Riley. "That's a pity."

"It could be anybody with the right operational clearance, from Revenue and Customs – bloody unstoppable since they teamed up, I can tell you – to MOD... and maybe one or two little Embankment ferrets we mere mortals know absolutely nothing about." Charlie went on to explain that there were various sub-branches within MI5 and MI6, neither of who were quick to disclose all of their departments to each other, let alone anyone else. These sub-branches were often created to deal with specific problems, then disbanded when no longer needed, their personnel re-assigned to normal duties.

"And you can't tell who they're watching?" queried Riley, twirling her glass on a beer-soaked mat. She didn't want to push Charlie's friendship with Palmer too far, but she sensed he needed to be guided towards disclosing any information that could help them, rather than giving it out too freely. Palmer was sitting back with his eyes on the yellowed ceiling of the bar, content to let her lead the way with the questions.

"No idea. Not listed. But if I was laying odds, I'd say it was your feller Radnor, or maybe his east European partner in crime. There's no one else in the building with the right profile, as far as I can tell." He gave Palmer a twisted smile. "At least, not since Frank tossed Gillivray out of the window. Allegedly."

Palmer rode the jibe with forbearance. "Very allegedly.

Presumably Six must know Radnor's there, though?"

"MI6?" said Riley.

"Yes. They must keep tabs on their former employees."

"If he is former." Charlie looked wary. "I can't tell that, either, so don't ask. All I know is, it appears he left MI6 several years ago and went private, but nobody knows where. He seems to have dropped out of sight before re-emerging in London. My guess is, they think – or know – he's up to something, which is why they're keeping the place under observation. He wouldn't be the first spook who hopped the reservation and went freelance. People like Radnor are hardly trained for the pipe and slippers option once their time is up. They've got too much invested in a different kind of lifestyle. It looks like he chose to go bent."

Riley frowned. "So these watchers will have recorded our visits, then?"

"Probably. Time in, time out, faces, feet, the lot. But don't panic yet; it'll take time to process all the faces. But you can be sure you'll show up sooner or later. Bad pennies." He finished off his beer and looked cheerfully at Riley. "No offence to you, of course."

"Of course."

"Purely by chance, after your call the other day while Frank, here, was taking in the delights of the German hinterland, I stumbled on some info about Radnor's little mate, Michael. If it's the same bloke, and I think it is, he's got himself a small file in one of Five's archives. His name's Mikhail Rubinov, aged thirty-eight. He was a junior officer in one of the Soviet security departments. Not KGB as was, but close enough to make him interesting. He did some work in Afghanistan – undefined, as you'd expect, although that could mean he was just some low-level junior spook – then he was assigned to a trade directorate in Berlin about five years ago. That was where he came to the notice of the watchers over there, which automatically got him a file. I think he got bored, because he jumped ship after a few months and re-surfaced in Switzerland on the open job market. He's had his fingers in various enterprises ever since – mostly bent, like currency scams."

"He might have known Radnor in East Germany, then," Riley guessed.

"Highly probable. It's a small world and shit attracts flies. Whatever, they must have formed a partnership, which is why there's a flag on the building." He looked at them in turn. "You mentioned a woman in Streatham… the dead runner's sister? There's no record of her that I could find. It doesn't mean she shouldn't be here – just that she hasn't come to anyone's attention. She could be clean. What did you get from her?"

"Not much," said Riley. "She showed us a photo of Radnor and her brother, though."

"It was taken in East Germany," Palmer put in. "It doesn't prove anything… except that they knew each other."

Charlie's eyebrows rose at the implications. "If he had some dealings with a local who was killed trying to cross the wire and never reported it, I'd say that breaks a few rules."

"How do you know he didn't report it?"

"Because Radnor's name doesn't come up in the report of the border shooting, nor on the sheets about Sergeant Paris's death afterwards. I can only guess it must have been suppressed. A bit iffy, I'd say."

"Iffy?"

"If he didn't disclose that he was actually there when – who was it – Wachter? – was shot, nor that he'd been around with Paris just prior to his death, then he was hiding something."

"Isn't that standard procedure for spies, hiding things?" said Riley.

Charlie suppressed a snort. "I know they're supposed to be the Secret Service, but not that bloody secret. They're accountable to their bosses if nobody else." He looked at Palmer. "You said something about art works. Radnor's listed as an art dealer, although I suppose that could cover anything."

"I know." Palmer handed Charlie the scrap of greased paper he'd found at the VTS premises. "He must have been bringing in works of art for years, starting when he was working in the east. But they wouldn't wrap canvases or icons in this stuff. I think they've been mixing the shipments with something a bit more interesting."

Charlie nodded, studying the piece of paper before slipping it into his breast pocket. "It would explain why he teamed up with Rubinov. The Russian would have the contacts in the east, or at the very least, know where the various arms dumps are located." He shook his head wearily. "The security over there is a joke. There are stashes of weapons everywhere, and every quartermaster with a brain is selling to the first person to come along with ready cash – dollars or euros." He paused. "I'm surprised they're risking bringing in icons and stuff, though. The Russian police have really cracked down on it. Still, it must be worth the risk."

"Who would Radnor be selling the weapons to?" said Riley.

Charlie shrugged. "Depends. If he's got the right contacts, he could be choosy and ship in stuff to order – weapons or valuables. That would jack up the price. If not, anyone with the right amount of ready cash."

"I'd bet on a specialist market," Palmer said. "Radnor's

training wouldn't let him get tied up with any old team. He'd want solid connections and selected goods."

Charlie nodded. "I'd go with that. Less risk."

"But if he's being watched," said Riley, "why are they letting him carry on?"

Charlie gave a faint smile. "Wheels within wheels. They might be hoping he'll lead them back to his suppliers, or they could just be tangled in red tape, unable to make a decision." He tapped his pocket where he'd placed the piece of paper. "This will help, though. I'll pass it on as 'information received from interested parties.'" He stared at them seriously. "But you two stay clear of the place in Harrow from now on, got it? You get in the way, and you might find a lot of violent young men in black jump-suits and goggles trampling all over your faces." He levered himself to his feet. "Now, if you'll excuse me, I've got a date."

They stood up with him, and Palmer shook his hand, aware that his friend was risking his job by having contact with them on what was a sensitive subject.

"Thanks, Charlie," he said warmly. "I appreciate your help."

"Of course you do, Frank. And my auntie's a member of the Bader Meinhof." He smiled nonetheless. "By the way, what happened with Lottie what's-her-name?"

"Grossman," said Palmer. "We're not sure, but it looks like she may have bitten off more than she could chew." He related what Szulu had told them about Ragga Pearl taking Lottie away.

"Jesus." Charlie took out a fold of paper and made a quick note, then stuffed it back in his pocket. "I'll pass that on to a mate in SOCA. He'll be pissed off that I know more than he does."

"Since when has the MOD had connections with the Serious Organised Crime Agency?" asked Riley.

"Ah, well, we're all one big happy family now, didn't you know?" said Charlie sourly. "It's called information pooling. Ever since the Sovs went belly-up and stopped pointing their nasty rockets our way, the various agencies have been scouting around for more work to keep themselves busy. And this new lot have got something to prove." He paused and eyed them both. "As a matter of interest, you don't think Radnor and this Ragga Pearl would do business, do you?"

"God forbid," breathed Riley. The prospect of the man described by Szulu in such horrific terms getting hold of some serious firepower was something she didn't like to think about.

Palmer shook his head, unable to see a valid connection. "Forget it. From what we've heard, Radnor wouldn't deal with a man like Pearl."

"It was just a thought. It's all about budgets, see? More work equals more allocation. And we can't have our common criminals going round killing each other, can we? Think of the mess on the streets." He gave Palmer a penetrating look. "How come this Szulu character was so talkative? You're both white and sworn enemies of his current employer; that hardly makes you bosom buddies."

Palmer cleared his throat heavily to forestall Riley saying anything. Mention of persuasion and gunshot wounds might lead to Mitcheson. Charlie was a friend, but he didn't want to place him in a difficult position. "He became disenchanted with his old employer." He nodded towards the note Charlie had just placed in his pocket. "Can you hold off doing anything with that information for a while?"

"Maybe," Charlie conceded. Then he studied them in

turn and his mouth dropped open. "Christ, you're never going looking for the old witch? Are you nuts?"

"Call it unfinished business," said Riley. "While Lottie's out there, we'll be looking over our shoulders all the time. She sounds seriously ill, but from what Szulu said, she's in worse danger than that if Ragga Pearl's got her."

"So? That would solve your problem, wouldn't it?"

"Maybe. But Lottie's as devious as a barrel of eels. We just want to make sure she hasn't talked Ragga Pearl into helping her."

"How are you going to find that out? These guys don't exactly see people by appointment. It's not like popping into your doctor." He gave a sigh. "Actually, with my doctor, that's bollocks – it's probably easier."

"We've got Szulu working on that right now," said Palmer. "He's currently without paid employment, so we asked him to set up a meeting."

"Asked? I'd love to hear how you did that." Charlie eyed them both, then shook his head. "On the other hand, maybe I wouldn't." He could see he wasn't going to change their minds. "OK, but don't blame me if it all goes sour and he holds you both hostage. I'll see myself out." He turned and walked away.

As the door closed behind him, Riley's mobile rang. It was Szulu. She listened for a moment, then switched off and looked at Palmer with a wary smile.

"Szulu says Ragga will see us tomorrow at noon."

32

By ten-thirty the following morning, the sun was already warm when Riley knocked on the door to Cecile Wachter's house. Palmer was carrying a small photocopier he'd borrowed from a friendly office supplier, so he could copy the precious photo of Cecile's brother and Radnor.

"You don't think she took fright, do you?" said Riley, when there was no answer.

There were no signs of life in the street; most commuters had long departed for work and their children for school. A dog paused at the gateway behind them and cocked its leg before moving on, and a radio blared somewhere nearby. Beyond that, it was a normal suburban morning.

Palmer stepped forward and bent to pick something off the step. It was a link from a gold coloured chain, about half an inch across. The two ends had been forced apart, leaving the metal raw and jagged.

"Damn – we're too late," he muttered, and put the copier on the ground. "Stay here." He pushed the door and watched it swing open, expelling a rush of warm air.

"Miss Wachter? Cecile?" His voice echoed back dully from inside, and he knew instinctively that nobody was in. Nobody alive, anyway.

He stepped inside and walked through to the living room, which was neat, uncluttered and looked rarely used. Then to the kitchen, where a saucepan full of browning potatoes stood on the hob alongside a plate of meat, curling at the edges. In the conservatory, where they had sat the day before, looking at Cecile Wachter's photographs and the proof they needed that Arthur Radnor had known her brother, Palmer stopped, feeling a sudden chill.

"Oh, no." Riley had followed him through the house ande was looking down past his shoulder; Cecile Wachter lay on the floor by the coffee table, her head on one arm as if she was asleep. Her legs were neatly arranged, and the only sign that all was not well was a dark smudge on one side of her forehead and a small trickle of dried blood from one ear.

Palmer placed his fingers against Cecile's neck. She was cold to the touch, her eyes staring sightlessly into the carpet, her glasses lying a yard away by the door to the garden, one earpiece twisted out of shape. A hank of hair had come loose from her bun and lay across one cheek.

"How long ago?" Riley asked, swallowing hard against a rush of nausea.

"Don't know. Hours, probably." Palmer straightened up and went to check the remainder of the house. He was soon back.

"No signs of a search," he said briefly. "Whoever did this knew what they were looking for. If they were looking for anything." He bent and picked up some of the photographs they had seen yesterday, which were now lying scattered on the floor. Two or three had been torn in half, others had been crumpled, a sign, perhaps of the intruder's anger. Or desperation.

"The photo," said Riley.

Palmer checked through the photos one by one. There was no sign of the shot showing Radnor and Claus Wachter, the only proof they had seen so far that the two men knew each other.

"Whoever it was," said Riley, looking round, "caught her by surprise."

Palmer nodded and studied the scene, tracking events

through from the front door to where Cecile Wachter had died. "She had the security chain on. It slowed him down slightly, but not enough to make a difference." He turned and ran through it again, but came up with the same scenario. "He must have found her with the photos."

"But why kill her? She just wanted to be left alone."

"He was tidying up. Maybe things got out of hand. She looks like she took a smack to the side of her head. She wasn't exactly robust."

"So he's got the photo. I wonder if it was Michael or Radnor."

"One of them, definitely. Who else would be interested? Christ," he swore quietly, "I've been so dumb."

"What do you mean?"

"I'm pretty sure we weren't followed here – I'd have spotted them. Which means they must have known about Cecile. When we headed in this direction, they guessed immediately where we were going."

"Do you think she was working with them? I can't believe it; she sounded pretty sincere when she said she'd left all that behind."

"She probably had," Palmer agreed. "Maybe Radnor discovered she'd come to England but took a chance on her either not talking or not knowing what his part had been in her brother's death."

"Until we showed up."

"Yes. Either they killed her because they realised she had something, or they found the photo and decided to cut their losses. Sooner or later Radnor would have reasoned that she posed a real threat to him. And now was as good a time as any to do something about her."

"Except," said Riley grimly, "she didn't know she was a threat." She sat down on the sofa and stared around the room. "That bit you said to Cecile yesterday – something about tradecraft. What did you mean?"

"The practice of spying. How to collect and sift information, how to gain contacts and get people's confidence, to wheedle out facts, to move around without being noticed. Like every trade, it has its methods -" He stopped abruptly. "Wait. Cecile might not have been a fully-trained spy, but she'd have been told how to conceal information until it was time to deliver it."

"But that photo was in a bundle of others. She hadn't hidden it because there was no need. How long was she gone upstairs while we were here? A minute?"

"You're right. There'd never been the need to hide it before. It was just a photo among a pile of others. Until yesterday." Palmer leaned over the coffee table and stirred the photos with his finger. Some still had drawing pins attached, now tarnished and bent. Others had holes showing where they had once been pinned up.

He looked back towards the front of the house.

After all these years, one photo suddenly became important. Cecile knew they wanted to copy it. Would she have had time to conceal it with Michael or Radnor hard on her heels? Make it Michael – it would have taken energy and bite to rip through the security chain, and Radnor had neither. Which meant she wouldn't have had very much time once he broke through.

"What if she managed to hide the photo," he said quietly. "Since we came here, she knew how important it was. But where?"

Riley supplied the answer for him. She knelt down as Cecile had done the previous day, and tried to imagine her in the same position when Michael had burst in on her. From the position her body was now lying in, it was possible she had resumed the same stance in trying to prevent him seeing the incriminating photo.

Yet there was nowhere close that Cecile could have reached from here. All the other items of furniture were too far away. Unless... She peered under the coffee table and gave a small whisper of triumph. When she stood up she was holding the photo, complete with one of the old drawing pins. Cecile must have put it under there when she heard someone at the front door, or moments before Michael entered the conservatory. It was the last place he had considered looking, right under his nose.

"Clever," said Palmer, with sober admiration for Cecile's quick thinking and courage.

"Do you think she knew what he was going to do to her?"

"Possibly. Where she came from, she'd have seen people like him in action before."

They cleaned any surfaces they might have touched, including the mugs they had used yesterday and the photos they had handled. Then Palmer picked up the photocopier, secured the front door and walked with Riley back to the car. Once they were clear of the area, Riley stopped at a public telephone and dialled the emergency services to tell them she'd heard a woman screaming at the Wachter home. She rang off without leaving her name.

When she got back in the car, she found Palmer looking thoughtful.

"Have you got Mitcheson's mobile number?" he said.

"Yes. Why?"

"This visit to Ragga Pearl: we need some back-up."

33

Ragga Pearl's headquarters were in one of Lewisham's quieter suburban streets lined with terraced houses not far from the main shopping area. Cars were parked nose-to-tail along both sides, and a scattering of small children were playing along the pavements, with some older people sitting or standing in front of the houses, watching the world go by. A man in a shabby khaki parka and ski hat was shuffling along the street door-to-door, a large canvas bag over his shoulder and clutching a handful of brightly-coloured mops and dusters. He wasn't getting many takers, but seemed undeterred.

At the far end of the street, a large building painted in green and cream, shaped like an old-fashioned fire-place with stepped shoulders, seemed to overshadow its neighbours and would have been spectacularly out of place had it not been in a forgotten corner overlooked by developers.

Szulu motioned for Riley to stop at the top end of the street and studied the area intensely. Tension had been radiating off him in waves since they had collected him from his flat earlier, which was the only way they could guarantee he would co-operate and accompany them. Now he licked his lips, ducking his head to scan the houses either side and breathing as heavily as if he had run a five-mile race.

Finally, as if reassured that they weren't going to be ambushed, he nodded. "Ragga's is the big green place down the end," he told Riley. "But all this round here, it's his turf. Nothing goes on here that he doesn't know about. You'd best park up here and we'll walk down, so his boys can see us coming. That way there won't be no nasty surprises waiting for us."

"Boys?" said Riley. If anything, she thought, walking down the street and giving Ragga advance warning of their arrival would only ensure a nasty surprise, but she decided to let Szulu's local knowledge dictate their moves. Besides, Palmer was sitting in the back seat, and he had so far not voiced any concerns.

"Yeah. Like those two." Szulu nodded towards two black youths lounging against a wall in front of a run-down house halfway along the street. Dressed in baggy jeans and hoodies, they could have been any pair of local teenagers, hanging out, were it not for the aura of menace surrounding them which set them apart from the other people on the street. "They're like his eyes in the neighbourhood. If they see something they don't like, he gets a warning bell."

"Are they any danger to us?"

He looked sour. "They're dangerous to anyone they don't like the look of. But they know we're coming, so they'll leave us alone if they know what's good. They're like junior soldiers; if they do a good job and don't screw up, they get to move up to a place on the inside when a vacancy happens."

"What kind of vacancy?"

"The kind when someone isn't there any more. A man gets into trouble, say, or maybe gets picked up and does time, his space needs filling, you know?"

For the first time since they had collected Szulu from his flat, Palmer seemed to take an active interest. He leaned forward from the rear seat of the Golf and stared at the building Szulu had indicated. The mop salesman they had seen earlier had crossed the street and was now working his way down towards it. "What the hell is that place?"

"It used to be a cinema. Ragga got it cheap because nobody else wanted to take the risk. He tore out the guts and made it into a pad with some offices, although the planning office don't know nothing about that." Szulu looked at the pair of them, craning round to include Palmer. "You decided who goes in with me?"

"I do," said Riley. "It'll put Ragga off his guard." She nodded down the street towards the salesman, now a couple of doors away from the old cinema, demonstrating a mop to an elderly lady. "And Mitcheson."

Szulu looked puzzled for a moment. Then his eyes grew wide as he realised who the door-to-door salesman must be. "Shit – you mean the guy who shot me? Tell me you're kidding, woman! Are you insane? They'll see him."

"I'm not kidding. And they haven't spotted him yet, have they? We discussed this earlier on. If Ragga sees Palmer, he'll smell policeman and clam up. That's if he doesn't bury us in concrete. Mitcheson's my back-up, that's all. It's what they'll expect of us. Are you saying Ragga won't have any of his crew around?"

Szulu shook his head. "Man, I don't know. I still don't know why you've got to do this. I told you, he's unpredictable. Dangerous. You realise I can't do nothing to help you once we're inside. He could have a dozen guys in there, whether your tough-guy friend's around or not." He jerked a thumb at Palmer. "What about him? What's he going to be doing?"

Palmer smiled. "I'm the cavalry. All the best cowboy films have them."

"Huh?"

"We've told you," said Riley, who had already gone over those very points several times in her own mind. Letting Mitcheson go in with her had been Palmer's suggestion, on the grounds that visible protection was what a man like Ragga would expect. Palmer was to stay on the outside with his mobile on and connected to Riley's. That way, he would hear everything that went on. If things went wrong, he'd come in after them. But he doubted Ragga would want to cause problems on his own doorstep. Riley hoped he was right. "We need to make sure about Lottie, and this is the only way of doing it. Anyway, we're no threat to Ragga."

She opened her door, anxious to get this over and done with. It had been a wild idea, but one she was sure was worth a try. Better that than constantly waiting to see if Lottie would pop up again, next time with someone unknown and a lot more deadly. "You ready?" she said to Szulu. She carried nothing in her hands, and wore a simple t-shirt and jeans, to show she wasn't wearing a recording device. She nodded to Palmer, who merely raised a hand in salute, then turned and walked along the street, Szulu alongside her, grumbling about the risks they were taking.

By the time they had gone ten paces the two young watchers down the street were tracking them, one of them talking rapidly into a mobile phone.

The children had stopped playing, too, and were watching them with open curiosity, especially Riley. Beyond them, a couple of older women called the children in, and within seconds, the street was deserted. Mitcheson was ambling up to the entrance to Ragga's place.

"Christ," breathed Riley. "It's like noon in Dodge City."

Szulu ignored her, and raised his hand as he drew level with the youths, brushing knuckles with elaborate casualness. The first youth mumbled something Riley couldn't interpret, then stood aside to let her and Szulu pass. Riley felt their eyes on her, but they said nothing, clearly briefed about her visitor status.

"He knows we're coming now," said Szulu softly. "You cool?"

"Yes."

They arrived at the front of the old cinema and joined Mitcheson. He nodded at Riley. "Need any mops, lady?"

She fought an urge to smile. "What's in the bag?" She was hoping he would tell her he was armed to the teeth.

"Cleaning stuff, mostly. But I'm hoping they don't have security scanners inside." He nodded at Szulu. "How's the arm, bud?"

But Szulu wasn't in the mood for friendly overtures. He scowled in return and led the way through a set of twin glass doors with elaborate brass handles. What had once been the ticket office foyer had been remodelled and was now a reception area like any place of business, with plain walls, discreet lighting, thick cord carpeting and a large desk behind which sat a young black woman, filing her nails. She had thick, shiny hair piled atop her head, and heavy, bright red lipstick to match her nail varnish. A sound system on the wall throbbed with a heavy hip-hop beat that seemed to vibrate through the walls and down into the floor.

"Hey, Maz," Szulu greeted the girl, his body language suddenly hip and loose, a broad smile across his face. "We're here to see the man."

Maz looked unimpressed, especially with the canvas bag over Mitcheson's shoulder, but laid down the nail file to stab a button on the communication console before her. "It's Szulu and two," she announced, before going back to her nails.

Seconds later a huge man in a pinstripe suit appeared through a door at the rear of the reception area. His shaved head glistened beneath the spotlights in the ceiling, and reflected light flickered from several large gold rings on banana-sized fingers. He nodded at Szulu and gave Mitcheson a cool once-over.

"What's in the bag, man?" He spoke in a coarse rumble.

"Cleaning materials," replied Mitcheson. "I'm multi-tasking."

The big man reached out and tugged at the side of the bag, checking the contents. All Riley could see were more dusters, scourers and hand mops. The man smirked before jerking his head back the way he had come. It was only when Mitcheson began to follow that he raised one vast hand and said, "You be still, man. She only."

"I don't think so." Mitcheson stood eye-to-eye with the man, easily as tall if somewhat outweighed by the other's bulk. In the background, Szulu was looking bug-eyed, a film of sweat building on his forehead as tension radiated out from the two other men.

The guard shrugged. "Then no way you be going in there."

"It's all right." Riley gave Mitcheson a reassuring glance. They had expected this, and had decided that a stand-off would bring them no closer to discovering what had happened to Lottie Grossman. She added, "I'll be fine. You stay here."

For a second the guard looked as if he didn't like that idea either, but he finally nodded and led Riley through the door and down a corridor to the back of the building.

They emerged into an open office area with three large desks, several filing cabinets and two leather sofas. Computer consoles sat on the desks, and the hum of technology touched the air with a gentle vibration. A slim young girl sat at one of the computers, inputting figures from a stack of paper. The screen before her was displaying an Excel spreadsheet, but she barely gave it a glance as her fingers danced across the keyboard. She was dressed in a plain black dress, black boots and silver tights, and had a pair of thick spectacles perched on the end of her nose.

A movement in a doorway to one side caught Riley's attention, and another large figure appeared. He filled the gap, hands hanging down by his sides and fingers twitching restlessly, eyes staring at Riley with little apparent curiosity. He was casually dressed in a royal blue tracksuit and white trainers, and Riley gave an involuntary shiver at the absence of warmth in his expression. He reminded her of a giant Kodiak bear she'd seen once in a wildlife reserve, and she wondered which was the more dangerous. Coming here might have been the stupidest thing she'd ever done; this man must be the infamous Ragga Pearl.

"Hey, Cindy," the man murmured softly, without taking his eyes off Riley. "You want to check the lady out for me? Cindy's my niece," he explained. "She's got a degree in economics."

The girl at the keyboard stopped what she was doing and swung her booted feet out from under the desk. She stood up and walked across the room, signalling for Riley to lift her arms. In a few brief seconds, she had completed a thorough pat-down, coming up with a small data stick and Riley's mobile. She flicked the back off the mobile and took out the battery, then returned the separate parts with a faint sneer. Riley shrugged. It had been worth a try. If anything blew apart now, Palmer would have to rely on his instincts for trouble.

"She's fine apart from this," Cindy reported, her voice mellow. She handed the data stick to Ragga before returning to her desk.

"What's this?" Ragga tapped the data stick on his thumb.

"Something you might want to see," Riley told him. "I'll

explain later."

He nodded. "OK. You want something to drink?"

"Why not? Coke, please."

The man who had escorted Riley in stepped over to one of the filing cabinets and swung back what was a false front to reveal a fridge stocked with a variety of bottled and canned drinks. He selected a plastic bottle of Coke and, with the barest glance at Riley, flicked it across the room at her. Riley caught the look and was ready. It landed with a slap in her hand and she said, "Thanks, but if you throw the glass there'll be a mess on the carpet."

For a split second there was silence, then Ragga Pearl laughed, the sound echoing in his chest, and his tongue slid out between his teeth. "You'll have to forgive Slam," he said to Riley. "He ain't got no style. In here."

She followed him into an office furnished in black leather and dark wood, with just enough subdued lighting to rescue it from looking too much like a masculine bear pit. A desk blocked off one corner, and was clear of papers save for a laptop and a phone. Slam closed the door and stood against it, watching her closely. The music faded instantly, and Riley realised the room must be soundproofed.

Ragga gestured towards a soft chair by the desk, and swung into an executive chair on the far side, where he sat and looked at her, steepled fingers to his chin.

"Szulu tells me you want to talk," he said finally, his eyes glinting and all signs of geniality suddenly gone. "Only thing is, I wasn't expecting no woman, and not with no bodyguard. That what he is, the man with the bag? Only right now he ain't sticking too close to the body, is he?" He smiled nastily, superior, and spun the laptop round on the desk. It showed a camera's eye view of the reception area, with Szulu and Mitcheson plainly visible in the foreground. Szulu looked nervous; Mitcheson was leaning against a wall, looking bored and fanning himself with a feather duster.

Riley shrugged. If this was all about chest thumping, she might as well do some of her own. "Maybe not. But he got past your boys in the street. Believe me, for him, that's close enough." As she saw the realisation that he had a dangerous opponent inside his headquarters sink home on the gang leader's face, she hoped that whatever Mitcheson had in his bag was a bit more heavyweight than dusters or dish mops.

34

Riley could have sworn the temperature in the room dropped by a couple of degrees, and hoped she hadn't pushed it too far. She'd gone over the situation with Palmer and Szulu on the way down, trying to figure out how they might gain Ragga's co-operation instead of the alternative. This was, according to Szulu, his sudden and unpredictable fury. The best they could hope for was some information about Lottie's condition and whereabouts. Without it, they would have to assume the worst... or keep looking over their shoulders for a long time to come. Szulu's advice had been to play it straight, as there was no knowing how Ragga would react. If he thought he was being manipulated, the outcome could be disastrous. And that was ignoring whether he'd got up in a bad mood or not.

"But let's think positively, shall we?" she continued calmly, twisting open the Coke and taking a sip. "I obviously didn't come here without letting anyone else know."

Ragga sneered at her. "You mean the guy in the car? Yeah, like he'll be a lot of help. He'd have to get down here first – and he ain't getting past *nobody*." He exchanged a look with Slam before settling himself deeper into his chair. If he was enjoying a sense of superiority, it was soured by knowing his defences had already proved suspect, although he wasn't about to show it.

Riley waited. This wasn't going the way they'd hoped. She had at least expected a bit more discussion before this big ape went all hairy-chested on her. But she was damned if she was going to let him see how concerned she was. "He's done it before." She used the tip of her finger to wipe condensation from the side of the bottle. "Anyway, he's the one you spotted."

Ragga's chair creaked faintly, and she felt a childish twinge of triumph as she caught the flash of a glance he threw at his colleague, before adding, "But there's really no need for aggravation here. I'm after some information that could save us both a lot of trouble. Call it business."

Ragga said nothing, his face stilled as if he'd gone into a trance.

"Lottie Grossman," Riley continued. "You probably know her as Mrs Fraser. She came to you for help and you gave her Szulu. I understand you might know where she is."

Ragga seemed to surface from wherever he'd gone, and gave her a look that was suddenly more calculating than superior. "Who says so? That man Szulu been talking out of turn?" The softness of his voice and the slowness of the delivery caused a trickle of unease to inch across Riley's shoulders, and she hoped Szulu's name hadn't been slotted back into Ragga's bad books. Szulu himself had been confident this wouldn't happen, but now she was faced with the man himself and had seen the way his mood could change in a heartbeat, she wasn't so sure.

"Not to me," she said firmly, meeting his eyes with a steady look. "We were behind you in Egham. We watched your two men transfer Lottie from Szulu's car to yours. She didn't look very well to me. Shame. All Szulu did was to arrange this meeting when my colleagues asked him to."

If Ragga was surprised, he hid it with a dismissive bark of laughter. "Right. You followed us to Egham. No way." He shook his head, but shot a mean look across at Slam, who shifted uneasily on his feet. Suddenly they were back on an even keel.

"Didn't happen, man," the big man by the door muttered.

But he didn't look quite so confident any more. "Just didn't. I'd have seen her."

"We were following Szulu, actually," Riley explained, switching tack slightly to press home her advantage and ease off from a direct confrontation. "You don't remember a black Golf?" Before either of them could answer, she forged on. "Szulu wasn't watching his back, which was how you were able to block him in so easily. OK, I admit it was only when you made your move that we realised you were in the area, but what the heck." She gave a shrug as if conceding the point, hoping the implied flattery would work. It did.

Ragga sniffed. "Yeah, well, that Szulu's no expert, is he? So why's the old woman so interesting? She owe you money?"

Riley gave him a summary of Lottie's background, during which Ragga's expression shifted from startled to plain sceptical. He shook his head when she finished speaking and drummed with his fingers on the arms of the chair, jutting his chin forward as he considered what she had told him.

"You saying that old pensioner, that ugly old *woman* was a gang boss? She ran a bunch of *men*? No way." He laughed, showing pink gums and a lot of white teeth. "You must think I'm stupid."

Over by the door, Slam sniggered in support of his boss.

"OK. Check the stick."

Ragga looked doubtful, but finally sat forward and inserted the stick into a USB port in the rear of the laptop. He looked at her over the open lid. "This ain't got a virus, has it? If it has, you going to regret it, I promise."

Riley shook her head and sipped the Coke, trying not to spill any. She'd forgotten relief could have the same weakening effects as fear, although she knew she wasn't out of the woods yet.

Moments later, she could tell that Ragga was studying a copy of the feature she had written about Lottie Grossman and her activities, tracking her gang's movements from London to Spain and back. It made startling reading, and the only sound in the room was the hum of the laptop's fan and the click of keys as Ragga scrolled down the pages. Eventually, he finished reading and closed the laptop. He looked at Riley and said, "That's pretty cool. You just can't tell with people, right? Did you know she tried to steal something from me? I couldn't believe it. Now I know how she had the balls. Man, I should have known there was something about her." He shook his head. "And she really had these squaddies working for her? What were they – SAS or something?" The idea seemed to amuse him, and Riley could guess why: Ragga Pearl might control the streets around here, but he'd never had genuine soldiers under his command. It would probably appeal to his ego-driven sense of power and status in the neighbourhood. No doubt it was something he would try to rectify sooner or later.

"Ex-Royal Marines, actually," she said. "They killed a few people before they were stopped."

"Stopped by you? But you're a journalist." He didn't need to add that she was also a woman; it was blatant in the look he gave her.

"True. But I had some help – also former soldiers. Fight fire with fire."

He nodded slowly. "Like the former military cop you hang with, right? Palmer? He the one up the street?" When Riley nodded, too surprised to speak when she realised he already had Palmer's name, he added, "Nice work." He stared at the ceiling and she wondered whether he was trying to work out what had transpired with Lottie Grossman or how to turn the present situation to his best advantage.

She decided to help him out. "After the Spain thing, we thought Lottie had gone to ground for good, or maybe died. She was mixed up with some very dangerous people over there, and crossing them was stupid. Our mistake was forgetting about her. Lottie has a long memory and can't stand being bested." She shrugged. "We just want to know where she is so we can watch our backs."

Ragga nodded. This made sense in his world. "She never said why she was interested in finding you, but I figured it wasn't to hold no tea party. She seemed pretty upset." He chuckled suddenly, his cheeks almost enveloping his eyes as he saw the humour in the situation. He nodded towards the laptop. "Now I can see why you'd want to know where she was. Sneaky old woman like that, I'd be pretty worried, too." He stopped smiling and looked at Riley. "Was it Palmer who shot Szulu, or one of your other military friends? Don't bother denying it - I heard about that."

Riley returned his look with a steady eye, hoping this wasn't all about to go wrong. "It wasn't Palmer," she replied. "It was another one. He was protecting me, that's all. Szulu was lucky to come out with a small hole in his arm."

But Ragga waved a dismissive hand and sat forward. "Shit, isn't nothing for me to worry about. Szulu carries a gun, it's his own fault if it goes off pointing the wrong way." He glanced at Slam and tapped his forefinger against his lip, the main man coming to an important decision in front of a junior employee. "OK. Here's how it is. And I'm doing this because I don't need the hassle right now, understand? I got business to attend to, and I don't need distractions."

"I understand – and I'm grateful."

"Yeah, right. The old woman, she's no longer… what shall we call it – a cause for concern."

"I see." Riley was careful not to react. Ragga spoke of Lottie Grossman's fate as if it was no more serious than a bout of 'flu.

"Now, you're thinking I killed her, right? You're wrong, lady - I didn't need to. She went and had a heart attack or something." He sat back and gestured towards his colleague. "Slam played the good Samaritan, took her to hospital. Told them he'd seen her fall over in the street and was doing his good deed for the day. What did they say to you, Slam?"

"Took her to casualty," explained Slam economically, his voice like gravel in a bucket. "They took her in. She in a bad way." He shrugged as if taking sick old ladies to hospital was the kind of thing he did on a regular basis. "I came away."

"So you see," said Ragga, "that's the end of your problem. End of mine, too. She's probably dead by now. You can check with the hospital, if you like. Ashford's the place." He stared at her. "You wondering why I'm telling you this?"

"You mean, apart from the fact that you don't want the hassle?"

He grinned. "Because I'm feeling good today, that's why. Grossman made a big down payment for my help. A kind of non-returnable deposit, seeing as I didn't know her. It was the only way I'd do business with a stranger like her. Now she's out of it, I get to keep it." He shrugged. "So I'm ahead of the game." He sat back and sighed. "Slam'll show you out."

Riley rose, feeling a sense of relief. Then Ragga pointed

a stubby finger at her, and gave her a look that froze her to the spot. "Know this, however: in case you're considering it, Riley Gavin, don't you *never* think of writing up no newspaper story about me, like you did Lottie Grossman. You do that, I'll come visiting you… and your little cat." He bared his teeth and sat back again. "And one thing I promise you, lady: neither you nor any of your soldier friends will see me coming. You hear?"

35

An hour later, Riley and Mitcheson were in the intensive care unit of Ashford Hospital, waiting for an overworked staff nurse to let them see Lottie Grossman. The ward smelled of overheated air with a tang of bleach, and had an atmosphere of intense but fragile calm, like the aftermath of a car crash moments before the victims realise what happened and begin to panic.

"If you're not family, I can't admit you," the young Australian nurse repeated, shaking her head. "I'm sorry." Each utterance ended on an up-note, as if she were asking questions. She checked her watch and muttered beneath her breath. Clearly she was approaching the end of her shift and wanted shot of these two.

"I understand that, I really do," said Riley. Having to bite back a feeling of irritation wasn't entirely a pretence; they had told the nurse they were looking for an elderly neighbour who'd wandered off. Playing the part came surprisingly easy, faced with such staunch bureaucracy. "But if she is our neighbour, we can confirm her identity, can't we? If not… well, what have you lost? Please. We're desperately worried about her." She eyed the nurse intently, hoping compassion and common sense would penetrate her rulebook armour. At least she had confirmed that an elderly woman brought in by a passing motorist carried no form of identification, and appeared to be suffering from a stroke. Unfortunately, the motorist hadn't hung around, so they couldn't even confirm where she had been picked up.

A bell pinged in the background, and a porter came skimming along the corridor with a gurney. A shrill voice cried out behind a door further along, and a nurse came bustling out, shaking her head, the front of her uniform drenched with something dark and heavy.

"Wait here." The staff nurse hurried away.

"So what exactly *did* you have in that bag?" Riley asked Mitcheson. It was the first opportunity she'd had of broaching the subject after leaving Ragga's place. After a quick consultation with Palmer to show they were all right, they let him use Riley's car to take Szulu home and grabbed a cab for Ashford Hospital. On the way, Riley had clutched Mitcheson's hand. They had said little, each wondering what they would find when they saw Lottie.

"Nothing much," he said. "A couple of flash-bangs – stun devices – hidden inside spray cans of polish." He reached into his jacket and produced the feather duster, which had an aluminium handle. "And this." He twisted the handle and discarded the feathered end, revealing a long spike with a lethal point. "I called a mate who makes security equipment. It was all he could come up with at short notice. Fortunately, Ragga's people weren't as efficient as they might have been."

Riley looked at him and wondered if anything ever fazed this man. "I was glad you were there. Szulu said Ragga was unpredictable; he was right." She told him of Ragga's final threat if she ever wrote about him.

Mitcheson nodded. "Just stay off his radar and he'll forget all about you. If he doesn't," he added, "let me know."

Before Riley could comment, the staff nurse returned. "OK, I'll let you see her. But only because we need to know who she is." She turned and led them along the corridor, her heels squeaking on the polished floor. They stopped outside a side ward, where the nurse pushed open the door and signalled for them to go inside.

"Two minutes. I'll be at the desk." She nodded and hurried away, letting the door swing shut behind her.

Riley stepped up to the bed, ignoring the cluster of tubes, wires and machinery at its head. A faint hum filled the air, and a low beeping sound came from a small monitor. She had a vague thought about how much power was being generated through all this equipment for such an evil old woman, and whether the nurse, if she knew Lottie's background, would approve.

The figure under the covers looked tiny and frail, more like a child than an adult. But the lined face was instantly familiar, the contours little changed since Riley had last seen her. Thinner, maybe, with more crepe-like sagging of the skin around the throat, but that could have been the effects of lying down coupled with the stroke. A smear of vivid lipstick was still evident at the corner of her mouth beneath the oxygen tube, and one hand lay curled like a frozen claw on the bedspread, the nails heavy with the glossy red polish that Riley remembered. There was no movement beneath the covers, and Riley thought for a moment that Lottie had already gone.

She leaned closer, aware of Mitcheson moving in on the other side, and listened. Nothing at first. Then she heard a faint hiss of breath and smelled a sourness in the air around Lottie's face. She felt nauseous and pulled away, her every instinct railing against being too close to this woman for a second longer than necessary.

In the same moment, she realised Lottie's eyes were open and looking right at her.

Riley felt the hairs stir on the back of her neck, and fought the temptation to step away from the bed and move out of the line of those twin points of cold light. Was that a lingering malevolence she saw deep inside those eyes? Or was her imagination lending the old woman an ability to express hatred even though she was this close to death? She glanced up at Mitcheson, who shook his head in surprise. He leaned over until he was looking right into Lottie's eyes.

As Riley moved back, she fancied she saw a flicker of movement in Lottie's face. But she couldn't be sure. Whatever had happened inside the old woman's head had plainly done enormous damage, either severing any recognition or memory of people she had once held in such contempt, or at least nullifying any chance of showing a reaction to their presence. So, that was that. Strange that it should all end with not even a whimper, let alone anything approaching the scream of ugly defiance they might have expected. If only her legion of old enemies could see her now. They'd probably start doing a jig around the room.

The squeak of footsteps approached along the corridor. Riley glanced at Mitcheson. "What do you think?"

He nodded. "End of the road. I can't pretend I'm sorry."

As they turned away, the hand lying on the bedspread suddenly moved. It was a brief spasm, the fingers scrunching the material into a knot, the knuckles white and tensed as if carved in marble. At the same time, a sound came from Lottie's mouth, and her eyes flickered. For a split second, Riley thought the old woman was about to sit up and spew one final burst of venom and hate at the world in general, and them in particular. But the movement was over in a second, and her hand released its grip on the covers. With that, her body seemed to relax and shrink even further, and her eyes closed just as the door opened.

The staff nurse took a second to evaluate the situation, then hit a button on the wall before shooing Riley and Mitcheson out into the corridor. As they walked away, a flurry of figures hurried past them into the room, and the door closed with a final swish.

Five minutes later, the nurse approached, shaking her head. "I'm sorry," she said. "She's gone. I'm sorry." She looked at the two of them. "Was she who you thought? Grossman, wasn't that the name?"

Riley nodded. At least they had awarded Lottie the courtesy of having her name back, rather than going unknown into whatever private hell might await her. Not that she would have thanked them for it. In the absence of an address, they had put down the house she had once owned in Buckinghamshire. The police would soon make the connection.

"Is there anyone we should notify?" the nurse continued, reaching for a clipboard and pen. "Family members? Friends?"

Mitcheson place a hand on Riley's arm. "No," he said simply, voice empty of emotion. "She wasn't the type."

36

They waited for a cab outside the main entrance. After the stifling atmosphere of the wards and the heavy aura surrounding the late Lottie Grossman, the air felt cool and fresh.

"What are you going to do now?" Mitcheson asked.

"I have to meet Palmer. There are some things to check about Radnor and his operation. What about you?" She felt guilty, knowing the question implied that whatever she was going to do did not include him. But Mitcheson appeared not to notice.

"I'm going back to the States tomorrow." He raised a hand as Riley began to protest. "It's only for a few days, maybe a week, so I can tie up some loose ends. Then I'll be back – I promise." He smiled and touched her face. "You don't think I could give up being around you for too long, do you? Life's too boring otherwise."

"All right. But stay in touch."

"I will."

They said their goodbyes, then Mitcheson saw an empty cab about to leave and pulled away reluctantly. Riley waved him off, then rang Palmer.

"Can you pick me up?" she said, and gave him the address. Suddenly, without Mitcheson by her side, she felt surprisingly vulnerable.

Palmer must have sensed something in her voice. "You OK?" he asked.

"I'm fine," she lied. "Just hurry, will you?"

Fifteen minutes later, she and Palmer were on their way to Hayes. She related the scene with Lottie Grossman, after which Palmer gave a pragmatic shrug.

"She'd have killed us, given the chance," he reminded her, steering skilfully round an indecisive learner-driver. "You shouldn't feel anything but relief." He turned and gave her a knowing smile. "But you know that."

Riley decided to call Jimmy Gough and check the current situation at the office block. He agreed to call her back. When he did so five minutes later, it was with surprising news.

"There are men in suits all over the place," he reported. "Most of them are on the first floor. Nobby says Azimtec have cleared out. Seems they might have had a tip-off."

Riley relayed the information to Palmer, who said, "Does he know where Radnor lives?"

"The cops have been asking the same thing," said Jimmy in reply. "Nobby says there's no record."

Riley thanked him for his help and switched off. "The watchers Charlie told us about jumped too late," she said to Palmer.

He nodded. "Or one of them gave Radnor the nod. He's probably still got contacts on the inside. I doubt we'll find anything at the VTS place, either, but it's all we've got."

"Do you really think Radnor's still around?"

"Possibly. If he's been bringing in arms, he'll have prepared for the eventuality of something going wrong. It's standard procedure: always have a fall-back position, even if it means going to ground and abandoning everything."

"And?"

"He'll keep his head down long enough to gather his resources, then he'll disappear. With his training, they'll never find him."

As they approached the VTS building, Palmer suddenly snapped his fingers. "Hang on. The taxi firm Radnor used.

What was the name?"

She shook her head. "I didn't notice." She rang Jimmy Gough and asked him.

"Easy," he replied cheerfully. "We always used the same firm – White Tower Cabs. They're just round the corner." He reeled off the number from memory. "Ask for Poppy – she's the owner. She owes me for all the business I put her way. If she get difficult, threaten her with a visit from the VAT people."

Riley made the call, then got out of the car to join Palmer, who was surveying the commercial estate. They were parked just along the road from VTS, behind a large canvas-covered trailer. The area was quiet, with the same mix of cars, trucks and skips as before. The space in front of VTS was deserted and strewn with litter.

The roller shutter under the VTS sign was up, revealing an empty space with just a few scraps of paper and straw packaging gusting around the inside. Sparrows flew in and out, darting up to the steel roof beams and perching on the workbench to preen, already colonising the space.

Palmer and Riley walked cautiously through the building and out the rear door to the back yard, where the drum that had held the papers Palmer had rescued was now cold and lifeless, still lying on its side. They checked the offices, but other than a mess of discarded documents and the usual array of admin paperwork, now abandoned, there was nothing useful to be found.

"*SkyPrint*?" suggested Riley.

Palmer nodded and led the way to the *SkyPrint* unit, where he pushed through the front door into a small reception area with a counter across the back wall, and a single door. In the background was the hum of machinery. Clearly it was business as usual, whatever may have happened along the road. Riley rang a bell and they waited for someone to appear.

"Can I help?" A man in a blue shirt and jeans stepped through the door behind the counter. He had thinning hair and a double chin, and was wiping his hands on a cloth.

"Is Mr Perric in?" said Riley.

The man shook his head. "Mr Perric doesn't work here any more. What can I do for you?" He looked from Riley to Palmer with a touch of impatience, and pointed to a printed sign on the wall. "We only see reps by appointment."

"Do we look like sales reps?" said Palmer. When the man said nothing, he continued, "What happened to Perric? I thought he was the boss."

"He was. But no longer. Who wants to know?"

Palmer ignored the question and gave the man a hard stare. "We're investigating certain allegations about Mr Perric. We'd like to speak to him."

"Are you the police? I want to see some ID."

"Do yourself a favour," muttered Palmer tiredly. He took out his wallet and flashed a card, and Riley recognised the Ministry of Defence logo. "I'd say you've got about an hour before this place is crawling with every kind of official suit you can imagine, so why not make it easier?"

The man looked taken aback for a moment, licking his lips and looking at them each in turn. He eventually nodded. "Perric was let go yesterday morning. His contract was terminated."

"There must have been a reason."

"He was involved in activities outside the business which the directors didn't know about. He was in violation of his contract."

"Who are the directors?" Palmer asked.

But the man folded his hands together defensively, and

merely repeated what he had said. "Like I said, he was in violation of his contract."

"Are you referring to VTS?" Palmer queried. "According to our sources, the two businesses were working in tandem. Are you saying he wasn't the overall boss?"

"All our divisions are legitimate businesses," the man replied eventually. "Perric was a manager of this one, but whatever he was doing elsewhere was contrary to our rules. That's why he was let go."

"What's your position in the company?" Riley pressed him.

But the man had clearly had enough questions, and drew himself up. "That's all I'm saying." He slapped his hands on the counter to reinforce the statement and stepped back, putting more space between them. "I don't care who you are. I am asking you to leave. Now."

Back outside, Palmer lit a cigarette and inhaled deeply. "Well, that went swimmingly," he murmured dryly. "But no more than I expected."

Riley nodded and kicked at a plastic bottle, which skittered away to bounce off a rubbish skip. "They were tipped off and got rid of the problem." She felt a burn of frustration at knowing that Perric was probably somewhere out of reach, where he couldn't be got at. Like Palmer, she knew that calling here had been a long shot, and that any vestiges of the VTS business or its people would have long gone. But sometimes even long shots pay off.

"Radnor must have ordered Perric to clear out. Blue eyes in there will be the legitimate face of the company, rolled out whenever things get sticky. He'll be as clean as the driven snow." Palmer flicked the cigarette away and watched it bounce along the ground in a shower of small sparks. "Never mind. We'll let the powers that be worry about him. In the meantime, let's go see if Radnor's up to receiving visitors."

Riley paused in unlocking her car. "It might be better to leave them to Charlie's friends. They're probably out of the country by now."

Palmer looked unusually grim. "I'll believe that when I see their names on a passenger list. Anyway, I owe Radnor for Reg Paris. And Rubinov for Cecile."

Riley gave him with a worried frown. "I never thought of you as the Great Avenger, Palmer."

Palmer grinned, his old self again. "Only when there's a full moon."

37

The address the owner of White Tower cabs had given Riley was a large detached Edwardian villa on the outskirts of Pinner. Set in an open expanse of lawn, with a few small shrubs dotted around in a haphazard fashion, the overall appearance was slightly unkempt, as if the building and the garden were in need of a friendly make-over.

The front of the property was shielded by a stretch of larch fencing and some sturdy wooden gates, but none of it prevented Riley and Palmer gaining a clear view of the house and the surrounding grounds. There were no vehicles parked out front, and no signs of movement at the windows. The gravel drive led from the gate down past the side of the house, vanishing behind the building and a heavy laurel bush.

"I thought they'd be hiding behind high walls and security fencing," said Riley, peering through a gap in the wooden panelling. "This is like a goldfish bowl."

"Hiding in plain sight," replied Palmer, nodding at the few shrubs in evidence between the house and road. "They can see anyone taking an interest and deter the local hoodies from thinking there's anything going on that might offer rich pickings." He turned his back to the fence and went to light another cigarette, then thought better of it. "What do you reckon?"

"About what?" Riley turned from peering through the fence.

"Is there anyone in?" He smiled. "I thought you might be able to tell."

She frowned. "Why on earth would I be able to do that?"

He shrugged. "Girl I went out with once, she could always tell if anyone was in a house. I thought it was a woman thing… something about atmosphere and… " He paused and gave another shrug.

"And what?"

"Curtains. She had this thing about soft furnishings. Said she could tell all you needed to know about a house by the state of the soft furnishings – especially the curtains. According to her, you could even tell what type of people lived there."

Riley gave a mild hiss of disgust. "Yeah, right. And you think I should have the same instincts? What am I – the House Doctor?"

He grinned and pulled a face. "Maybe not."

But Riley bent back to her peep-hole and studied the building for a while. She saw no evidence of occupation, but that didn't mean anything. If Radnor and Michael were inside and currently about to flee, they would hardly be telegraphing their presence to onlookers. And the absence of vehicles was nothing. They either had a car locked away somewhere, or had other means of transport, like cabs. She checked the front doorstep, but there were no telltale milk bottles to help her, full or empty.

In spite of herself, or because of what Palmer had said, she found her eyes drawn to the curtains, and wondered why there were nets at all of the windows except one; a narrow one in a room adjacent to the front door. Could it simply be a quirk of the household or was it a sign that there was no woman around to give a balanced appearance to the place? Then she noticed that at the top of the window was a curving line of pale fabric, as if the net had been tucked away to one side. Was that because someone inside wanted an unobstructed view of the front garden and gate?

"It might be a good idea to check with White Tower cabs," she suggested to Palmer, and handed him her phone. "See if they've got a booking."

"Gotcha, miss." He hit re-dial and waited. When it was answered, he asked if there were any cabs booked for Radnor that day or the next, giving the address of the house where they were standing.

Poppy replied none had been ordered, and that all their cars were fully booked.

He switched off the phone. "No booking. They must have other plans."

Riley pressed her face close to the fence. "I reckon the drive curves round the back of the house. If so, there's easily room for a car or two round there."

"Maybe. I wonder if this is the only way out." Palmer stood back from the fence and looked along the street. The larch fencing ran for fifty feet or so, then stopped at a narrow lane with a metal bollard in the centre to prevent vehicle access. Across the other side of the lane was a high wall bordering another large house.

"Give me two minutes," he said, and walked along the street, ducking into the entrance to the lane. Five minutes later, he was back. "The lane goes all the way down to another road running parallel with this one. The garden's bordered by a wooden fence like this one. I couldn't see a gate or a doorway, but the ground all around the house is wide open. There's a brick building behind the house. Could be a garage. No cars outside, though."

"I think they're still in there," said Riley, silently hoping that she was wrong.

"What makes you so sure?"

Riley managed a smile. "Because of the curtains. See how

one window is clear? It's too dark to see inside from here, but anyone standing at the back of the room would be able to see out without being spotted."

Palmer gave a quiet snort of derision at this revelation. "You're kidding me." He ducked his head to look, then grunted. "Damn. You're right."

"So it's a frontal assault, then?" Riley asked, ignoring her earlier fears about facing Radnor and Michael. She wanted to get this over with, no matter what risks they might face inside.

"Yup." Palmer walked along the fence to the gate and peered round the gatepost. "Up to the front door, see if anyone answers. You ready?"

They stepped through the gateway and walked up to the house, staying on the grass to avoid making unnecessary noise. The place had a deserted feel about it, but that might be an illusion. Even now they could be under scrutiny, their progress being tracked by the men inside.

The front door held a tarnished brass fish as a door knocker, and Palmer flipped it up and down a couple of times. The resulting booming noise seemed to echo inside the building.

"Empty?" said Riley.

"Empty front hall, maybe." Palmer gave the knocker another flip, then stepped back to survey the house. The windows stared back, blank and unhelpful. No hurried faces peering out, and no sounds of furtive movement. "Now I know what it's like to be a Jehovah's Witness," he muttered, and turned to walk round the side of the house.

As he did so, an engine started close by and a car door slammed.

Palmer glanced to their left, towards the lane bordering the property. "Bugger. There was a beat-up old Merc parked out there. I figured it belonged to someone else." He ran across the lawn towards the fence, with Riley hard on his heels.

The fence was five feet high, and Palmer looked as if he was going to run straight through it. But at the last second he swerved sideways and, placing his hands on the top, swung himself up and over, rolling his body to prepare for the landing on the other side. Riley followed, lighter and more supple, but hampered by her lack of height. She landed in time to see Palmer sprinting towards the far end of the lane. Eighty yards or so beyond him, a dark-blue Mercedes saloon was standing close by the fence, a haze of exhaust smoke puffing from the rear, its brake lights burning. The car was dirty and battered, and wore a layer of street grime as if it had been dumped there months ago. A thick bloom of dust covering the rear window obscured the inside.

Then a shadow moved at the side of the road and a man stepped out towards the car. As he reached for a door handle, he turned at the sound of Palmer's footsteps.

It was Michael.

38

Palmer slowed, realising Michael must have exited via a concealed door in one of the fencing panels. A Judas gate. That left Radnor at the wheel of the car. It looked like he and Riley had arrived just in time to interrupt their departure. Or maybe not.

Michael was dressed in a suit, white shirt and dark tie, as if he was ready for a day in the office. He was holding a black leather bag in one hand. Carry-on luggage for a sudden trip overseas, Palmer surmised.

Michael's face registered shock seeing Palmer so close, and he muttered something urgently. The driver's door opened and Radnor looked out, craning his head to see. When he saw Palmer, he grimaced, shouted at Michael, then reached out and snatched the black bag from the younger man's hand.

The car engine revved hard and the vehicle shot away with a squeal of tyres, leaving Michael standing alone at the side of the lane. He began to run after the car, screaming furiously, his words unintelligible, before realising he wasn't going to catch Radnor. He stopped and turned to face Palmer, standing squarely in the centre of the lane.

Palmer's defensive instincts went into overdrive. He had faced situations like this before, where confrontation couldn't be avoided. Yet the sweat and smoke of those army-town pubs and their drunken squaddies suddenly seemed a luxury, faced with this open space and an opponent who had already shown a propensity to kill without a second thought.

He was close enough now to see the tension in the

other man's face. The Russian's intentions were evident in his body stance as he began to turn slightly to deflect the attack, and Palmer knew this wasn't going to be easy.

At the last second, as Michael began to raise his hands, one palm open to ward off a blow, the other closed in a tight fist, Palmer swerved.

Riley, thirty yards behind, saw Michael turning to meet the threat. Beyond the two men, the Mercedes was braking hard to turn the corner, the only other movement in the lane. Riley wanted to shout to Palmer to stop, back off and leave Michael to the police. But it was too late. He was already committed.

When Michael moved, he seemed to pirouette on the ball of one foot like a ballet dancer, his body taut and controlled. It was as if he were attached by a string to some controlling force high above his head. As he turned, he leaned forward as if to reach down and pick something off the ground, but his hands remained close into his chest. Then his other foot shot out with unbelievable speed. In spite of his swerve, Palmer was unable to stop himself. There was a muffled sound of impact, and Palmer seemed to lift slightly, turning sideways with a grunt and riding on his opponent's foot. He landed on his shoulder a few feet away and rolled with the momentum. He lay there, shaking his head and trying to get up again, but seemed to lack the strength, as if the kick had knocked all the energy from his body.

"*Palmer!*" Riley shouted frantically as she saw Michael take a long, deliberate step forward. But instead of reaching down for the man on the ground, the Russian seemed to hold the pose for a fraction of a second as if taking aim, then his other leg flashed up and round, the heel momentarily poised above his shoulder but the trajectory clearly aimed at the exposed top of Palmer's head.

The leg began its downward strike. Then Palmer rolled, but instead of moving away from danger, he rolled inwards, catching his attacker by surprise. He swept his leg round like a scythe and his instep caught Michael behind his grounded ankle. The impact took the Russian's leg out from under him, and with a surprised gasp, he fell backwards, arms flailing for balance. Unable to regain his equilibrium, he crashed to the tarmac with a loud *whoof* of expelled air and tried to roll away.

But Palmer was waiting. Reaching over, he grasped one of Michael's hands and seemed to twist and bend all in one motion. There was a shrill cry of pain and a sharp crack, and Michael groaned and grabbed his broken wrist. Palmer calmly finished him off by slamming the younger man's head into the tarmac.

In the background, the Mercedes engine accelerated and faded into the distance.

"Are you all right?" Riley said, coming to stop alongside Palmer. He was dusting himself off and trying to stand upright, but didn't appear to be enjoying the experience.

He nodded and took a couple of deep breaths before replying. "Of course. Did you doubt me?" In spite of his levity, she saw a spasm cross his face and wondered how badly he was hurt. He looked towards the corner where Radnor had disappeared. "Must be great to have such close friends," he muttered.

Riley glanced down at Michael, who was past caring. His eyes were rolling and a livid bruise was beginning to blossom on his forehead where it had made contact with the ground.

"What the hell was that all about?" she demanded, rounding

on Palmer, then stopping to brush some dirt from his shoulder. There was a small tear in the fabric, and she wondered vaguely if Mr Javad's skills included clothing repairs. "You could have been killed going down like that!"

Palmer sniffed and bent to brush off his trousers. "Oh, you mean the on-the-ground bit?"

"Yes. I thought he'd finished you."

"What, you've never seen break-dancing before?" Palmer grinned and brushed his fingers through his hair. "It was close," he conceded, wincing slightly, "but he didn't get the peanut. Come on, let's get him out of the public eye." He bent to strip the laces from the unresisting Russian's shoes and used them to tie his thumbs and small fingers together, then took off the shoes and handed them to Riley. Grasping Michael beneath his arms he dragged him towards the doorway in the fence panel.

Riley followed. "What are you going to do with him? Shouldn't we go after Radnor?"

"Forget him. We'd never catch him now – even if we knew where he was going." He dragged Michael across the grass to the rear of the house and dumped him near the door of a brick garage, leaving Riley to close the fence panel and join him.

"I can't believe it," Riley grated. Now she knew Palmer was OK, she could vent her frustration on the fact that Radnor had got away at the very last minute. "We were so close."

"Never mind," Palmer said cheerfully, although he was studying Michael with a grim look. The Russian was regaining consciousness, and already staring at Palmer with a defiant air. His suit was torn and dirty and the white shirt was no longer immaculate; he was a long way from the neat figure he had previously presented. "I know somebody who can help us."

Palmer opened a side door to the garage. It revealed an

empty space with a workbench against one wall. On the wall itself was an array of tools, dusty and pitted with rust through lack of use. The air smelled dull and oily, and judging by the undisturbed cobwebs, he doubted if Radnor and Michael had ever set foot in here.

Palmer dragged Michael inside, dumping him without great care by the workbench.

Riley stood in the doorway, watching. "What are you going to do?" She looked concerned, eyes darting from the man on the floor to Palmer and back. "Shouldn't we call the police?"

"Not yet." Palmer stepped over to the workbench and cast his eyes over the tools. "I want to ask him a few questions." He reached up to where a large pair of sheet-metal cutters were held in place by two hooks, and took them down. He worked the handles until the jaws opened and closed with satisfactory smoothness. A faint squeak emanating from the unused parts was put right by a squirt of oil from an ancient can with a long spout. He took his time, and when he turned back towards Michael, the man went pale and tried to roll away.

"*Palmer!*" Riley hissed, the horror at what he was proposing to do dawning on her. Then she recognised the faint smile around his mouth, and realised something that the terrified Michael, no doubt judging Palmer's intentions by his own standards, could not know: Palmer had no such plans, and had been counting on Riley's instinctive reaction to add authenticity to the scene. "You can't…!" she added helpfully, and turned quickly away, stepping outside.

"Women," said Palmer, shaking his head, and closed the jaws of the metal cutters again with a sickening snap. "Too soft every time."

Moments later, Michael began talking.

39

"I'll see you later," said Palmer. "They won't want you there. It's best you stay out of it."

He and Riley were standing at the bottom of Trafalgar Square, looking east towards the Strand. To their right was a bookseller and a souvenir shop, with the main entrance to Charing Cross station a few yards away, next to a hotel entrance. A clutch of chattering tourists waited to cross the road on their left, barely stopping themselves from spilling out into the traffic, while a solid line of cars, bikes and buses heading west and north clogged the air with fumes.

After calling Charlie to tell him where Mikhail Rubinov could be found and, from the plane ticket in Rubinov's jacket pocket, where Arthur Radnor was heading, they had gone home to wait.

"Go see a film, visit the seaside and collect shells – anything," Charlie had advised them heavily. "Leave everything alone now. You've done enough. I'll make sure something gets done." With that he had rung off to start the process of stirring into motion the sluggish machine that operated the various arms of the law.

That had been four days ago. Since then there had been nothing in the news, no reports of sudden arrests, no passengers detained at air- or sea-ports, and no speculation about former spies or arms smuggling.

Riley had got together with Donald Brask in the hopes of working out a possible story which wouldn't upset Charlie's superiors, but her agent had advised her against taking it any further. "I know it hurts," he had said sympathetically. "But there are some enemies you don't need. Let it go. There will be other stories."

Palmer, back to his usual self, had disappeared on a job, after stopping by to check there had been no signs of Ragga Pearl's men.

Then Charlie had rung back earlier that morning, to advise them that Palmer's presence was requested at a location near Whitehall. "It's a debriefing," Charlie had added. "You've done plenty of those before. Don't worry, Frank, if they were going to arrest you, they'd have done it by now. But don't play silly buggers. These people aren't the kind to mess with."

Now here they were, with Riley alongside to see that nothing untoward happened to Palmer. She still felt she should be with him when he went in to face his inquisitors.

"They must know all about me, Palmer. You don't have to protect me, you know."

"I know. But why show up on their radar when you don't have to?" He smiled reassuringly. "They merely want to impress on me that I've signed the Official Secrets Act, so I'd better keep my mouth shut. It's the way their minds work. If I'm not out in three hours, send in the massed ranks of the Salvation Army." He turned and walked away, leaving her among the crush of people on the pavement.

The hotel foyer was shiny and polished, with a desk on one side and an array of soft chairs on the other. A large star-shape was set into the tiled floor, and a variety of pot plants conspired to give an air of freshness, light and calm. There were few people about, and little noise other than the ringing of a phone in the background.

Palmer started towards the desk but was intercepted by a young man in a plain grey suit. He knew instantly that this was no hotel employee.

"Mr Palmer?" The young man had clear skin and the

kind of tan only earned through regular exercise in the great outdoors.

"The one and only."

"You're late," said the other. He wore a subdued tie and shirt, and Palmer doubted he'd be able to remember his face after five minutes. The eyes, however, were steady and cool, a giveaway to his profession.

"Take it out of my taxes," said Palmer mildly. "Let's get on with it, shall we?"

The young man looked mildly surprised, but turned and led Palmer along a corridor and up some wide, curving stairs to a room on the first floor. On the way they passed another man, a near-clone of the first, who turned and wandered along in their wake. Palmer had every reason to suspect there were others nearby, just like them. He almost felt flattered.

"Who are you two?" he quipped. "Fortnum and Mason?"

The man he had christened Fortnum stopped outside a set of double doors. He knocked twice and opened them to reveal a large conference room with a high ceiling. Rows of chairs faced a small stage with a lectern and microphone. Two men were seated at the front, talking softly. They stopped as Palmer stepped inside. Fortnum closed the door and stationed himself in front of it, while Mason stayed outside.

"Ah, Palmer. Good of you to make it." The speaker was tall and willowy, dressed in an impeccable suit and shiny shoes. His tie knot was small and hard like a walnut, and sat with careful precision between the twin horns of his starched, white shirt collar. He had military stamped all the way through him. He gestured at the room. "Apologies for the unusual surroundings, but we thought somewhere... neutral might be more appropriate."

His companion stared at Palmer without getting up. He was holding a cup of coffee and looked as if he had just swallowed a mouthful of grouts. He was older, heavier, with the pasty skin and soft jaw-line of the serial bureaucrat, and Palmer guessed he was there as a political counterweight, to ensure this didn't become too matey between former serving men.

"So, do you two have names?" Palmer queried. He wasn't expecting anything like the truth, but it was worth a try.

The first man smiled. "Of course. I'm Shelley and this —" He indicated his companion — "is Knowles."

Palmer nodded, not believing either name, but aware it was all he was going to get.

"This… Azimtec business," Shelley continued smoothly, "has gone far enough, I think. I appreciate how you got into it, but you'll let us handle it from here on, agreed?" The query at the end was not a courtesy, but a statement of fact.

"Handle it how?" Palmer wasn't stupid. He knew he was outgunned and these people would simply jump all over his bones if he became an obstruction. But some innate sense of rebellion wasn't going to let him roll over without a show of resistance. Besides, he was genuinely interested in where this was going. Rogue elements had to be seen to be dealt with, if only internally.

"That's really none of your business." Knowles spoke for the first time, not even bothering to look at Palmer as he did so, but staring down into his coffee cup. His voice had the snap of somebody talking to a minion and expecting to be obeyed. "You are still subject to the Official Secrets Act, Palmer." He finally turned his head in what he probably thought was a threatening manner. "Or had you forgotten?"

Palmer felt himself bristle at the man's tone, even though

he had expected just this approach. Typical bureaucrat, treating everyone else like peasants. He'd met men like Knowles before, and had the soldier's special brand of contempt for those who did the talking without involving themselves in the messy bits. And Knowles struck him as definitely one who didn't do anything messy. He wasn't so sure about Shelley, however.

He did the only thing he could, which was pointedly to ignore the man. Instead, he turned back to Shelley. "I'll just say this, in case I don't get the opportunity later. I can't prove it, but I'm certain the man I know as Arthur Radnor, who once worked for the security services as an agent-runner, arranged for an east German national named Claus Wachter, with whom he had an arrangement in the shipping west of stolen artworks, to be caught and shot dead while coming across the wire from the GDR in nineteen eighty-nine. He also arranged the murder of a British Military Police sergeant that same year. Sergeant Reg Paris died on the autobahn near Frankfurt." He knew they were already aware of these facts, but he didn't think it would do any harm to repeat them. "I also believe he and his colleague, a man named Mikhail Rubinov, a former member of a Russian security department, caused the death of a small-time fraudster named Gillivray in Harrow, and murdered a woman named Cecile Wachter in Streatham. She was the sister of the man killed crossing the wire."

There was a silence in the room, during which nobody moved. A pigeon cooed and flapped its wings on a window ledge, and a muffled cackle of laughter came from somewhere above their heads. It seemed an ill-timed response to what Palmer had just outlined.

"Yes, we know what he did, and we're grateful for your assistance. And that of Miss Gavin." Shelley fixed Palmer with a glint of warning in his eye. "You know as well as I, Palmer, that there comes a point at which a private individual has to step back and leave us to deal with things. We've studied the details carefully, and come to the conclusion that it serves no purpose to let this get out into the public domain."

"You what?" Palmer didn't bother hiding his disgust. He'd been prepared for an official silence, even some stone-walling, but not this.

"I'm sorry. It won't bring back Sergeant Paris, Herr Wachter or the others. Nor will it help for the public to learn so long after the event that a member of the security services was a profiteer and a murderer." A fleeting sign of distaste crossed the man's face. "Even if I would personally prefer we strung Radnor up by his thumbs in Whitehall and let him rot."

Knowles looked appalled by this comment, but said nothing. It demonstrated to Palmer who was the senior ranker here, and he smiled openly, making Knowles flush with anger.

"That's not good enough," Palmer replied, with a coolness he didn't feel. "I'm not sure I could stomach seeing him go free, not after what he did."

The threat hung heavily between them, and Shelley looked slightly saddened and shook his head.

"Oh, for heaven's sake, this has gone far enough!" Knowles lurched from his seat, spraying droplets of coffee from his lips in the process. He glared at Palmer with hot eyes and stabbed a finger in the air. "This is not a discussion, Palmer. You're no longer in the Military Police, in case you've forgotten. You're a member of the public. We brought you here as a courtesy, not for a debate, although I opposed it from the start." He glanced at Shelley as if to apportion blame, then continued, "The matter is over, whether you like it or not. If you involve yourself any further, I will make sure the full weight of the law comes down on you. And that includes your little girlfriend, Gavin, who I'm sure would not relish a term of imprisonment. Do you understand me?"

Shelley began to turn his head, mouth open at this out-burst. But before he could speak, Palmer stepped forward, placing himself within a few inches of his companion's face. Knowles stepped sharply backwards and up-ended his cup, spilling the last of his coffee down the front of his suit.

Over by the door, Fortnum started forward, but stopped at a brief signal from Shelley.

"Don't start something you can't finish." Palmer spoke with chilling softness, so that only the man in front of him could hear. Knowles flinched and turned even paler, his mouth opening and closing in shock. He glanced sideways for support from his colleague, as if aware he had gone too far.

Shelley, however, appeared unconcerned by whatever Palmer might have said. He merely cleared his throat and placed a hand on Knowles's shoulder. "Leave us, will you, Stephen? I'd like to speak to Mr Palmer alone." His tone was less than gracious, the chill in his voice unmistakable.

Knowles looked as if he might argue, then decided against it and walked over to the door as fast as he could. Fortnum opened it and closed it firmly after him, and turned back with a hint of a smile on his face.

"Dangerous little bugger, that," commented Shelley mildly. "Fights all his battles from behind. Political appointee, unfortunately. Place is crawling with them." He rocked on his heels and gave Palmer a benign look. "I can't give you any assurances, you know that. It's not the way we work. But neither can any of this come to court."

"It should. Radnor deserves it."

"I agree, he does – and more. But it would serve no purpose, mostly because people such as our friend Mr... Knowles have created an atmosphere where the law is everything, and justice is... well, not what it used to be." His lips gave a twitch and he studied his highly polished shoes.

Palmer waited, still not sure where this was ultimately leading. He was being warned off, he knew that; but he wanted to feel there was some point in this. Some quid pro quo. Something told him he wouldn't have been brought here otherwise. Eventually, he said, "So that means?"

"Leave Arthur Radnor to us. That's all we're saying." Shelley's voice was calm and controlled, almost conversational in tone. Yet there was a hard edge to it. "Don't ask questions, don't push for answers - they won't be forthcoming. We will deal with this." He paused before continuing carefully, "I really wouldn't want to see Knowles take the kind of action he would like to."

As Palmer looked into his eyes, he realised the man was telling him something, and felt a sudden chill in his gut. It was a message and warning in one. "So you have got Radnor." He studied the other's face, but it was now carefully blank. It was answer enough; they already had Michael, he knew that from Charlie. Shelley meant what he said: it ended here.

Shelley smiled suddenly and held out his hand. "Thank you for your help," he said genially. "Please give my regards to Miss Gavin. And you might impress on her the inadvisability of writing a story on any of this."

40

Riley tensed as Frank Palmer appeared in the hotel entrance. Another figure hovered momentarily in the doorway behind him, then stepped back into the shadows and was gone.

Palmer stood for a moment on the outside, breathing in the warm air like a man who has been cooped up inside for far too long. He had his hands in his pockets, but Riley could tell he was not as relaxed as he appeared. He saw her waiting and walked across the forecourt to join her, dodging a taxi turning in off the Strand.

"What did they say?" she asked, as they walked together towards Trafalgar Square, where the usual crush of tourists was clustered around the fountains, eyeing the pigeons and taking photos in front of Nelson's Column.

Palmer didn't answer immediately, but led her across the road to the square and stopped at an ice cream cart. He bought two cones and asked the man to add two sticks of chocolate. He handed one to Riley.

"Not much," he said eventually, when they were out of earshot of the vendor. He lounged against a stretch of guardrail, watching the stream of traffic heading south towards Whitehall. "One blustered and bullied, one didn't. In the end, they did what civil servants always do: they gave nothing away."

Riley turned to him, her ice cream forgotten. "So Radnor gets away with it? That sucks." She took an angry bite of the cone, scattering flakes of chocolate and startling an elderly Japanese tourist standing nearby.

"What did you expect – a happy ending?" Palmer turned his head and looked at her with a level gaze. "Actually, he won't get away with anything. They weren't just civil servants."

"So who, then?"

"At a guess, they come from under a stone on the other side of the river – the one with tacky bits of green on the front."

"Oh." Riley finally understood. "Radnor's old firm."

"Yup." He gazed at his cone and licked around the middle. "Not the kind to mess with."

Something in the tone of his voice drew Riley's attention. When Palmer talked like this, it usually came from the darker side of his experiences, the part which recognised that pragmatism sometimes overruled what normal society might judge to be right and just. Still, for Palmer to find a suit scary was saying something. She let it ride.

Palmer finished all but the nub of his cone, dumping the rest on the pavement, where it was quickly pounced on by a watchful pigeon.

"You're not allowed to feed them," advised Riley sternly. "They're vermin, didn't you know?"

Palmer took out a handkerchief and wiped his fingers. "Give me them any day," he said softly, "compared with some."

"So what happens now?"

"Well, there won't be a trial." He put the handkerchief away. "What could they charge him with? Treason? I doubt it. Fraud? Who did he defraud – they're all gone. Theft? Proving it would be a nightmare. He'd die of old age first."

"What about murders? The man on the border, and Gillivray and Cecile Wachter?"

"Says who? The border guards pulled the trigger, not Radnor. And he'll have taken care of the men who were with him that night. As for the others, I think Rubinov will cop for them." He shook his head. "There won't be a trial, but it doesn't mean Radnor will get away with it." He gave an almost undetectable nod back towards the hotel. "They'll see to that."

He strolled away and Riley hurried to catch up with him, scattering a handful of pigeons in her wake. As they flapped away, she had visions of a dark night and blurred figures in a bleak landscape, and justice being done. Justice of a sort, anyway. Damn it, this wasn't right.

"And you're happy with that, are you?" She knew she was being unfair. It wasn't Palmer's fault that politics intruded where justice should have its say.

"Happy, no. But there are some battles you can't win. Best let it go. Get on with something else."

He was right, of course, she knew that. She shivered and wondered why it was so chilly in spite of the warm sun. She needed something else to think about. Something lighter and easier and totally mundane, to repel the shadows. Thankfully, John Mitcheson would be back soon and she could stop thinking about work for a while. That would certainly help.

"So where are we going?"

Palmer gave her a sideways look. "I don't know about you, but I'm going home for a massage and some kip. This has all been too bloody tiring for me. I'm not as young as I used to be."

Riley dug her fingers into his arm. "Ixnay, Palmer," she muttered. "You owe me a dinner, remember? The one you never turned up for? But never mind, lunch will do just as well. In fact, I haven't done lunch in ages. Or tea. The Ritz

273

for tea would be nice." She smiled brightly, determined not to let the day end on a downer. If she did, tomorrow was going to be all the more difficult. "How about The Greenhouse?"

"Can't. You have to book."

"Really?" She was surprised Palmer would know such a thing, and wondered who he'd taken there. "OK, how about somewhere a little different, then? I know – there's this brilliant little sushi place off Leicester Square. You like raw fish, don't you? It's supposed to be very good for you –"

But Palmer had already detached himself from her arm and was walking away, laughing and shaking his head.

"Palmer, wait. A girl's got to have more to look forward to than NHS scams and illegal fruit-pickers, you know." She stopped suddenly. "*Massage*? Did you say massage? Who from? Palmer… "

MORE FAST-MOVING GAVIN/PALMER ADVENTURES BY ADRIAN MAGSON

No Peace for the Wicked
ISBN: 0-9547634-2-4

Old gangsters never die – they simply get rubbed out. But who is ordering the hits? And why?

Hard-nosed female investigative reporter Riley Gavin is tasked to find out. It's an assignment that follows a bloody trail from a windswept south coast seafront to the balmy intrigues of Spain's Costa Del Crime – and sparks off a chain of murders.

Accompanied by the laconic Frank Palmer, ex-military cop turned private eye, Riley uncovers a deadly web of vendettas, double-crosses and hatred in an underworld that's at war with itself. The prize? Control of a faltering criminal empire.

But this is one story that soon gets too personal – as Riley discovers dark forces that will stop at nothing to silence her. Dodging bullets, attack dogs and psychotic thugs, she fights to unravel the threads of an evil conspiracy.

And suddenly facing a deadline takes on a whole new chilling meaning...

A real page turner... a slick, accomplished writer who can plot neatly and keep a story moving...
- Sharon Wheeler, Reviewing the Evidence website

... the excitement carries right through to the last page...
- Ron Ellis, Sherlock magazine

A hard-hitting debut...
- Mystery Lovers

No Help for the Dying

ISBN: 0-9547634-7-5

Runaway Katie Pyle died ten years ago – or so everyone thought. But her newly murdered body has just been found.

Riley Gavin has always been haunted by Katie's baffling disappearance. It was her first assignment – and her greatest failure. So when Katie turns up dead a decade later Riley has to find out what happened. Where had the girl been all those years? Why did she vanish, leaving no trace? What drove her to walk away from a loving family?

Her probing uncovers more dead runaways, and Riley realises there is more to it than drugs, or the lurking dangers of life on the streets.

Who is behind The Church of Flowing Light?

Why do they employ dark characters like Quine?

Where has a former colleague of Riley's vanished to? And why has Riley suddenly attracted the interest of two silent watchers?

With the help of Frank Palmer, Riley follows the trail down into the subways of London's street life, and up to the highest levels of society.

Gritty and fast-paced detecting of the traditional kind, with a welcome injection of realism.
- Maxim Jakubowski, The Guardian

Magson blends a dark reality with entertaining fiction to produce a dish that will please the most demanding gourmet palate of a connoisseur of crime fiction.
- Denise Pickles, Mary Martin Bookshop website

ALSO AVAILABLE FROM CRÈME DE LA CRIME
BY MAUREEN CARTER

Working Girls
ISBN: 0-9547634-0-8

Detective Sergeant Bev Morriss of West Midlands Police thought she was hardened, but schoolgirl prostitute Michelle Lucas's broken body fills her with cold fury.

This case will push her to the edge, as she struggles to infiltrate the jungle of Birmingham's vice-land. When a second victim dies, Bev knows time is running out, and she has to take the most dangerous gamble of her life – out on the streets.

Dead Old
ISBN: 0-9547634-6-7

West Midlands Police think Sophia Carrington's bizarre murder is the latest attack by teen yobs. Only Bev Morriss won't accept it.

But a glamorous new boss buries her in paperwork and insults, and even Oz, her lover, has doubts. Birmingham's feistiest detective rebels – then the killer decides Bev's family is next…

Baby Love
ISBN: 09551589-0-7

Rape, baby-snatching, murder: all in a day's work for Birmingham's finest – but when the removal men have only just left your new house, your lover's attention is elsewhere and your last case left you not too popular in the squad room, it's sure to end in tears. Bev Morriss finds herself in serious trouble when she takes her eye off the ball.

BY PENNY DEACON
TWO GENRE-BUSTING FUTURECRIME CHILLERS

A Kind of Puritan
ISBN: 0-9547634-1-6

Bodies are bad for business, but Humility, a low-tech woman in a hi-tech mid 21st century world, isn't going to let go until she knows who killed the guy everyone said was harmless.

help from the local crime boss exacts a high price. But her best friend's job is on the line, the battered barge she calls home is under threat and 'accidents' happen to her friends. She's not going to give up – even when one death leads to another, and the next could be hers!

A Thankless Child
ISBN: 0-9547634-8-3

Ruthless patriarch Morgan Vinci wants Humility to find out why a man hanged himself - before the fanfare opening of his new marina. Her mother wants her to track down a runaway niece - but how do you find one child in streets full of terrified homeless kids?

In Humility's world good wine is laced with poison, girl gangs guard their territory with knives and nightmares are terrifyingly real.

A subtle and clever thriller...
- The Daily Mail

A bracing new entry in the genre ... a fascinating new author with a hip, noir voice.
- Mystery Lovers

An amazing style coupled with an original plot. I look forward to her next.
- Natasha Boyce, Ottakar's Yeovil

... moves at a fast slick pace .. a lot of interesting, colourful, if oddball, characters... a good page-turner... very readable.
- Ann Bell, newbooksMag

IF IT BLEEDS   **BERNIE CROSTHWAITE**
Chilling murder mystery with authentic newspaper background.
ISBN: 0-9547634-3-2

A CERTAIN MALICE   **FELICITY YOUNG**
Taut and creepy debut crime novel with Australian setting.
ISBN: 0-9547634-4-0

PERSONAL PROTECTION   **TRACEY SHELLITO**
Powerful, edgy lesbian thriller set in the charged atmosphere of a lap-
dancing club.
ISBN: 0-9547634-5-9

SINS OF THE FATHER   **DAVID HARRISON**
Murder, revenge and insurance scams on the south coast.
ISBN: 0-9547634-9-1

AND COMING SOON FROM CRÈME DE LA CRIME –

BEHIND YOU!   **LINDA REGAN**
Murder and mayhem at the pantomime. Sparkling debut novel from a
professional actress.
ISBN: 09551589-2-6

*... it is good to see a publisher investing in fresh work that, although defi-
nitely contemporary in mood and content, falls four-square within the
genre's traditions...*
- Martin Edwards, author of the highly acclaimed Harry Devlin Mysteries,
writing on the Tangled Web website

Crème de la Crime… so far have not put a foot wrong.
- Sharon Wheeler, Reviewing the Evidence